HOT BITS... COLD STEEL

A Kevin Rhinehardt Mystery

D1736163

K. C. REINSTADLER

ISBN: 1539572315
ISBN 13: 9781539572312

TABLE OF CONTENTS

DEDICATION

This, the second in the Kevin Rhinehardt series, is dedicated to the memory of retired detective Edward H. Barr of the Los Angeles Police Department. Ed left us all in 2013, but his assistance in my prosecution of professional safe crackers in the early 1990s was instrumental in their conviction on multiple felonies perpetrated throughout California. This story is based, albeit loosely, on those cases. Burglary detectives, like Mr. Barr, are a dedicated breed, often fighting a never-ending battle for truth, justice, and the American way.

I'd like to thank Mr. Dave Richardson, of Richardson Safe and Vault Specialists in Santa Clarita, California, for his technical assistance during the completion of *Hot Bits...Cold Steel*. Also kudos to my faithful prepublishing editors: Jill, Molly, Carolyn, Sven, Big John and Carole, Claudia, and Robyn. Your input and support are always valuable.

This is a fictional crime story, and any resemblance to persons, living or dead, is purely coincidental.

Chapter 1
HOT BITS

"Move the car…Move it! Christ, do you want the cops to see us, you dumb-ass?"

"Sorry, Big D, I just thought…"

"Stop *thinking*, Chunk. I do the thinkin'. Just get us the hell outta here. Go over there. I keep telling ya to park out in the open. Cops look for people hidin' in the shadows. You just need to see the front and sides of the fuckin' place, got it? Can you get that into your friggin' head?"

James Gaylord started his red 1998 Honda Accord and waited for instructions from his older half brother. James was born with his umbilical cord wrapped tightly around his neck—so tightly, in fact, that his brain was deprived of much-needed oxygen just a skosh too long. Although fully functional at twenty-eight and not considered handicapped, the six-foot-three-inch-tall, 230-pound James was, as they say, a little slow. His crooked front teeth and unkempt brown hair didn't help his image. His brother had begun calling him Chunk when they were young boys: "You're just a big *Chunk*, Jimbo...get used to it!"

Dennis Fitch, on the other hand, was a steely specimen of manhood. This thirty-one-year-old, muscular, six-foot-one-inch man had spent the better part of his life staying fit. With short, jet-black hair and broad shoulders, he fancied himself quite the ladies' man. He maintained a daily routine of cardio and weight training, and he followed a paleo diet. No steroids, just good food and exercise.

He had lots of time between the ages of seventeen and twenty-one to learn this workout regimen since there wasn't much else to do at the East Mesa Juvenile Detention Center in San Diego. Developing muscle was a way of working off excess energy and essential to keeping at bay the dangerous predators who strolled the institutional hallways at night there. Fitch had continued his daily workouts after his release. It was part of his job, after all.

By the time young Dennis Fitch was sixteen years old, he was an accomplished thief. It started one sunny afternoon when he saw Mr. Johnson, the owner of the house three doors down from his mother's place, leave for work. He knew no one was at home now. Dennis had taken a shining to Cindy, Tom Johnson's seventeen-year-old daughter, but Cindy Johnson treated Dennis like he was persona non grata. "Get a life, loser!" was the last thing sweet Cindy had whispered to him the week before, and that was the last straw for young Master Fitch. When he saw Daddy Tom motor out of his driveway, Dennis swung into action.

He knew the Johnsons liked to leave their rear patio door unlocked. He'd been over there just the day before, reconnoitering while no one was home, and he'd found it so. Today, he made sure to avoid any prying eyes and slipped back stealthily through their side gate. He had a mission: get the goods on that bitch, Cindy—that too-good-for-him slut. After quietly rolling the heavy glass door open, he tiptoed through the kitchen into the hallway toward the back rooms. Rufus, the Johnsons' overweight golden retriever, stirred from his bed in the corner, managing a weak growl. Dennis knew he was a coward. He tossed a Beggin' Strip at the pooch, who laid back down in his bed with a grunt, dripping saliva as he chomped away on the treat.

Cindy was an only child, so finding her bedroom was a snap. The poster of teenage Tom Cruise in his tighty-whities in *Risky Business* above the bed and the My Little Pony dolls with their perfectly combed multicolored manes perched prominently on her dresser were sure give-aways. Yeah, this was da place!

Fitch probed her dresser for booty. *"Bingo!"* Her panty drawer. Leafing through the frilly undergarments, he chose a red-satin pair. The scent of her pubescent womanhood wafted into his nostrils as he drank in the pheromones. His young member stiffening, Dennis stuffed the panties into his pocket. He had something prime in mind for this prize! His thieving continued as he pursued his quest. He continued scoping out the rest of the bedroom. Nothing! Shit! Just girl stuff: scribbled doodles in notebooks, red frilly hearts, and puppy-dog pictures. He came up empty. There was nothing else he could use to his advantage.

But then he had a thought. *Guys hide their stuff under the mattress...I wonder?* Gently lifting the pillow-top mattress off the box spring and taking pains not to mess up the pristine bed covers, Fitch hit the jackpot! There, neatly tucked between the snow-white layers of linen, was a leather-bound book tied closed with a purdy pink ribbon. Written in perfect cursive on the front cover was "Cindy's Life."

Dennis Fitch sat on the floor next to the sweet-smelling bed and explored the pages. Cindy laid her life out for the world, or at least for young Dennis Fitch, to see. One passage jumped out and grabbed him by the testicles. "I did it with Dan'l last night in his car. He's so sweet. I think he's the one!" A red heart surrounded Dan'l's name on the page.

Oh my god, she's fucking Daniel Spencer, the jock! Holy shit! His thoughts resounded inside his teenage noggin like a ship's bell in a vacant cavern. This information didn't infuriate Fitch. No, he no longer wanted to be with her sexually, but he was going to screw her. He knew how to play this to his advantage. Carefully replacing the book under the mattress and armed with his panty prize, Dennis Fitch quietly retreated from the Johnson home. He was careful to leave no trace of his intrusion behind. He tossed another doggie treat to Ol' Rufus on the way out. "Good boy, you mangy piece of shit!"

The very next week, San Diego High was all abuzz when Old Man Markoff, the senior English lit teacher, found a love note in a small brown envelope on the classroom floor during Cindy and Dennis's class. He read out the name on the closed envelope. "Oh, look, it's for Cindy Johnson." All the teens could see that it had a red heart drawn around her first name. The class resonated in unison: "Awwww, Cindy!"

Inside, Markoff found a pair of satin panties wrapped in a piece of lined notepaper. He tried fruitlessly to palm the underwear and silently read what was written on the paper, "Hey babe, you left these in the car last night. Meet me at the same place tonight at six." The signature line read, "*Luv, Dan'l.*"

Mr. Markoff, trying to be professional, didn't relay this message to his class. He didn't have to, since June Classen, the class loudmouth, managed to spy not only the panties but the communiqué as he placed them both down on his desk. Everyone who was anyone at San Diego High knew that the only "Dan'l" in the twelfth grade was Daniel J. Spencer, the star running back on the SDHS Cavers! That, my friends, was all she wrote!

This headline news, broadcast widely by Classen, went through the school grapevine like a hot knife through butter, as did the news that Cindy Johnson and Daniel

Spencer were summoned into Principal Stodden's office soon thereafter! Dennis Fitch had reaped his reward. He hadn't stolen money from Cindy; his crime hurt her much, much more!

Soon thereafter, Fitch began his career as a prolific burglar. He'd found his niche. He was careful to stay away from his immediate neighborhood and tried limiting his capering to within his free class periods. He didn't want to leave a trail to follow; a pattern would get him caught. Within six months, he had managed to hit twelve residential homes in the suburbs of San Diego, all within walking distance of his mother's house. He always wore his school backpack and walked with a pair of headphones covering his ears. Just a regular schoolkid walking down the street. He scored almost a grand in cash, gold jewelry, a .25-caliber pistol, and several porno magazines, among many other items. Every time he walked away from a house he'd hit, he was more emboldened, more excited. Big D, as he liked to be called by his entourage, had found his true calling. Dennis Fitch was cool.

Even when he was confronted by a homeowner who had stayed home sick from work one day, he never thought of quitting. He beat feet away and was caught hiding under a parked GMC a block away by the San Diego PD. When the cops brought Dennis back home to his loving momma and they sought permission to search her son's bedroom, Brenda Gaylord told them to fuck off. As if trying to impress her offspring, she spewed a plethora of colorfully lewd epithets at the two San Diego detectives who were serving a search warrant on her home.

In their recovery of evidence against Dennis, the two cops discovered that the demure Ms. Fitch had the strangest collection of baby dolls they had ever seen. The ornate plastic infants looked like they were staring back at them! All ten of them sat in tiny cradles in one corner of the living room as if positioned there to watch whoever came by. When the investigators got close to the creepy diminutive mannequins, Momma Fitch screamed, "Keep your fucking hands off my babies, you bastards!"

Young burglar Fitch had done his best to pawn any jewelry and other easily sold items quickly after each job, but he just couldn't cut loose that .25-caliber Taurus pistol. The dicks found it hidden in his closet under one of the stolen porno mags, along with a gold heart pendant that Big D intended on using as a ploy to get laid. Dennis Fitch received a forty-eight-month sentence in the East Mesa Juvenile Detention Center as a result of this Class 1 felony, on top of the three other residential burglaries he was convicted of. Cops 1, Burglar 0. Big D left juvenile prison at the ripe age of twenty-one, buffed and armed with the resolution never to get caught again. He was determined to just get better at what he loved to do. The juvenile justice system had done its job well.

"Park over there, on the edge of the parking lot, next to Kohl's. You'll be mixed in with the other cars, and you can still see the sides and front of the Arby's...that's the kinda spot you should always pick, Chunk. The cops will just see another car in a parking lot, not some crook hidin' in the shadows. Pretend to read a magazine or something. Understand?"

"Yeah, D, I get it. I'll do better next time…promise."

Fitch slowly exited the Honda and, walking back to the trunk, retrieved a black Samsonite carry-on roller bag. He put on his worn, tight-fitting brown leather jacket, a pair of black-rimmed glasses, and an Angels baseball hat. He had 20/20 vision, so the lenses were clear. He figured he looked more like an everyday Joe by wearing them. He had decided long ago that he might raise police suspicions by shouldering his heavy black equipment backpack, strolling down the street in the late evening hours wearing his black watch cap and black leather gloves. Instead, Fitch rolled his plain airplane luggage down the block, looking like a traveler headed for a plane, bus, or taxi. He always walked by his intended mark by at least a block, to ensure that no black-and-whites were nearby with eyes on him. Tonight it was the Arby's restaurant in Costa Mesa. Having walked by the storefront and stood on the street corner for several minutes, he was reassured that the pigs were either having their Code 7 meal or that they were back at the station screwing off. He knew he'd have a second set of eyes parked next to Kohl's watching his back as well.

Strolling along and taking a side street, Dennis Fitch rolled his airline bag down the alley behind the fast-food establishment. After looking around, he crouched behind a dirty, odiferous, dipsy Dumpster to hide his next move. Unzipping the carry-on, he removed a heavy black-nylon backpack with custom-padded shoulder straps. He hoisted the twenty-five-pound sack onto his back. On came a tight-fitting pair of black lambskin gloves. He clipped a Motorola VX-261 handheld radio to his belt and placed the compact headset with a voice-operated microphone on his head. The small mic was positioned next to the corner of his mouth. Lastly, he pulled a black hooded balaclava over it all, covering his features and holding the radio headset in place. Placing the baseball cap and faux glasses in the roller bag, he pushed the carry-on under the back of the trash can, to be retrieved later upon completion of the job.

Big D turned the dial and clicked the radio on. After hearing the tone to adjust the volume, he spoke, engaging the voice-activated microphone.

"Yo, Chunk, you out there?"

"Yeah, bro, how ya doin'?"

"Just fine. How's the weather?"

"Nothing but clear sky, bro. How 'bout where you're at?"

"It's nice here. I think I'll go for a walk."

"Got you...give me a holler when you're headin' back to the area."

He was committed now; there was no going back. He always mentally prepared himself for what came next. If you prepared, you didn't get pinched. You knew what you needed for the job, and you had a plan. Fitch had spent nearly a day scouting out this Arby's on Brookhurst, and he knew the employees' and manager's habits, where the office was, and how to gain entry. The manager left at 11:30 p.m., so he waited forty-five minutes to avoid any last-minute returns because someone might have forgotten something.

Once, on a prior job, just after a place he burgled closed and he was inside the office, the manager abruptly returned to close the safe that she had forgotten to close... what a dumb bitch! The problem was that Fitch was in the process of removing the cash receipts from that very safe when the manager returned to lock it up. He thought he'd hit the jackpot—a friggin' open safe! It wasn't until he heard the front door lock click open that he realized there was no such thing as a free lunch.

Without saying a word, he opened the large folding knife he always kept and pointed it at her face as she turned the corner. Seeing the tall, dark masked marauder threatening her, she froze. He ushered her into a back storage room and whispered quietly, "Stay in here, lady, or else." The frightened manager sat in that pitch-black room until the police showed up at seven thirty the next morning, well after other employees had reported that she hadn't opened the store on time. They found her trembling, sitting in a pool of her own urine, too petrified to speak or leave the room. Big D didn't want any repeat performance of this scenario, so now he waited to make sure no one interrupted him.

Removing a twelve-inch expandable, rubber-coated treble hook from the side compartment of his backpack, he unfurled the twenty feet of three-quarter-inch black Perlon rope attached to it. The rope was knotted every twelve inches, and Big D snapped the hook to the open position and locked it. This Arby's business had ladder roof access off the back alley, so with one toss, Fitch threw the grappling hook up fifteen feet and snagged the top of the solidly locked metal sleeve. When closed and locked, that sleeve was supposed to prevent anyone from climbing up the bottom half of the ladder to the roof. It didn't stop Fitch, who easily shimmied up the rope and climbed up the remaining exposed rungs seven feet to the twenty-two-foot-high rooftop. Climbing ropes was part of his daily workout. This was a piece of cake.

"Hey, Chunk, weather check."

"Clear as a bell, bro."

Fitch then made his way to the roof-access vent. This was the trickiest part of the job. If he screwed this up, as he had a couple of times in the beginning of his career, the alarm would go off, and he would have to scramble to avoid the cops and escape prison. It was all about the risk-versus-benefit rule of thievery. In this case, Big D figured the benefit would outweigh the risk. Most vents were locked from the inside with a padlock through a hasp. The hasp was generally mounted with rivets onto the inside top of the shaft, and their nubs were visible on the outside bottom of the roof hatch. Locating these two metal rivet nubs, Dennis removed a small high-speed rechargeable drill from his backpack and inserted a three-sixteenths carbide drill bit into the chuck. He then slowly drilled into the backside of each of the rivets, destroying them.

Tapping the rivets out, the lock and hasp fell loose on the inside. Hearing the clang of the metal lock against the side of the shaft meant he was almost home free. He knew that this, in and of itself, wouldn't set off an alarm. The vent could then be opened up but not before he located the magnetic alarm sensor—if there even was an alarm. Some franchise owners didn't even bother to alarm their roof vents because all the downstairs exterior doors were protected. They generally didn't think a cat burglar would hit them from the roof. Fitch had proven many of those naive owners wrong.

He lifted the lid, ever so slightly, to see the white of the two devices: the magnet and the alarm switch. These types of contacts were cheaper for the customer and relatively easy for Fitch to overcome. When the magnet was near the switch, it closed the contact inside the switch and the alarm circuit was closed. When the magnet was pulled away, the circuit opened, and the alarm was triggered. Big D could see that the switch was glued to the hatch shaft, just below the lid, and the magnet was on the vent lid itself—an easy fix, as long as he didn't crack open the lid too far and break the magnetic field! Fitch removed a two-inch-long heavy magnet from his backpack and placed it directly next to the white switch on the hatch shaft, now just slightly in view. This powerful magnet force was more than enough to reach the switch and keep the circuit intact.

You gotta love Harbor Freight! They got a tool for everything, the crook thought. Leaving his magnet in place, he slowly opened the vent. No alarm. Voilà! He was in.

"Hey, Chunk, I'm walking."

"Gotcha."

Hoisting the heavy backpack onto his shoulders, Dennis descended the ladder to the opening in the Arby's ceiling, inside the storage room. Placing the grappling hook securely on the last rung of the ladder, he effortlessly descended the ten feet to the floor. If you'd been in one Arby's store, 99 percent of all the others followed the same floor plan. It was a franchise, after all. Taking a left down the hall from the storage room, Fitch found the door to the office right where he remembered it should be.

"Damn, they fuckin' locked it!"

Experience had taught him that fast-food store managers were lazy. They just left the office door unlocked, figuring that if they locked the safe and set the alarm, they were covered. Not so tonight. This bastard was meticulous, and the handset to the door was securely locked, too. No problem for Mr. Fitch, who reached into his satchel and retrieved a large set of Channel Loc pliers he always carried. With the jaws of the pliers firmly seated around the knob, one tight squeeze (which bent the knob destructively), and then a slow, firm turn to the right, and the lock snapped, and the door swung open. It was show time.

Dennis Fitch examined the standing safe—a Major brand model TL 30 upright, with a Sargent and Greenleaf lock. Fitch licked his lips in anticipation. This was what he loved to do. Locksmiths called this attacking a safe, and Big D was trained to do just that, thanks to Todd Starnes. Through Ol' Todd, Fitch had learned his trade well.

Retrieving a small tool resembling a large fork with two broad flat offset tines, he carefully inserted the device between the safe door and the inside edge of the number dial. A few pries later, the dial pulled away from the spindle, exposing an inner flange onto which the outside dial was allowed to spin freely when using a combination to open the safe. Although he was fairly proficient at it, Fitch had no time to try to manipulate the combination. His plan was on a strict timetable. He removed two star screws along with the flange, leaving just the short spindle exposed. Now for a little help.

From a hard pouch within his tool bag, Big D retrieved a seven-inch round paper template with a hole in the center for placement around the lock spindle. A small guide hole at exactly two hundred degrees left of the center top of the template marked the Sargent and Greenleaf sweet spot. Using a small piece of Scotch tape, once the paper was aligned exactly, the template was affixed to the door.

He pulled a heavy drill from his bag of tricks. Big D preferred using a Bosch electric two-speed hammer drill. At three thousand rotations per minute, it provided all the power he needed to do the deed. Surrounding the outside of the drill motor was a square metal bracket, screwed into the front and back of the drill. Pulling out the chrome-plated StrongArm lever rig from his satchel, along with two feet of chrome chain used with it, he was ready. Fitch inserted a five-sixteenths titanium tungsten carbide core drill bit in the drill's chuck and cranked down hard to tighten it as much as possible.

He positioned the tip of the drill bit on the sweet spot marked on the template. One quick push of the drill's trigger placed a guide mark on the safe at the right location, and the paper template was removed. This template was not easily replaced. It was a treasure map to pinpoint the booty held within. He had obtained it and all his specialized equipment through his good friend Starnes. Big D made sure to treat it like an irreplaceable *Mona Lisa*. He carefully put it away.

Dennis Fitch's daily weight training, which included grip strengthening, was crucial at this point in the safe-attack process. Using the lever rig and high-speed feature of the drill, along with the hammer function when needed, the slow penetration of the half-inch rolled carbide steel plate protecting the locking mechanism began. This took Big D several minutes, but by pushing on the StrongArm handle and methodically shortening the chain attached to the back of the drill, he inched closer to his goal, millimeter by millimeter.

Eventually, the red-hot drill bit eased through the final layer of once-cold steel! He wiped the beads of thick sweat off his forehead with his gloved hand. The drill rig was put away (just in case a quick exit was required), and he inserted a lighted speculum into the drill hole, still toasty from its birthing. This magnifying speculum allowed Fitch to see the prize just inside the door—that prize being a clear view of the three combination wheels of the Sargent and Greenleaf lock. Big D used a small blue baby's bulb syringe, inserted in the hole, to blow away the small metal shavings that now sprinkled the inside wheels like confetti littering Times Square on New Year's Eve. A few puffs later, the criminal whispered to himself, "Clean as a fuckin' whistle!"

Dennis then attached a small pair of locking needle-nose pliers to the end of the exposed spindle protruding from the safe's door. Peering carefully into the speculum, he used the pliers to turn the spindle first left, then right, and back left to line up the notches on all three brass wheels. The unlock trigger perched like Thor's hammer now, hanging just above the three aligned notches. Big D merely turned the spindle a quarter turn back right, and the hammer fell gently into the depressions with an almost imperceptible click. It was done; the maestro had completed his masterpiece! Turning the handle on the safe to the right with a clang, the heavy door creaked open.

Fitch whispered, "I got ya, bitch!"

Almost spontaneously with his jubilant declaration, the earphone under his black hood blared, "Hey, bro, hope you're done walking 'cause Daddy's nearby. He's parked across the street."

"I hear ya. Let me know if he's coming home." Fitch nervously broadcast this as he rapidly stuffed his tools back into his backpack. He pushed on the safe door, leaving it ajar.

"Where's the frigging bit? Shit!" In his haste, the safe cracker had kicked his specialty drill bit under the back of the manager's desk and out of view. Leaving tools behind was *not* a good idea, but getting arrested while inside a business he was in the process of robbing was a worse idea. Big D zipped the bag up, and shouldering it, he headed quickly into the storage room, back up the stairs to the top vent, and out onto the rooftop. He crouched silently, his hood dripping with sweat despite the cool night air.

Fifteen minutes later, a perspiring Dennis Fitch addressed his somewhat dimwitted sibling.

"Ah, Chunk, how 'bout an update? Where's Dad now?"

Five seconds passed. "Um, sorry, dude, he left almost ten minutes ago. Guess he was just pickin' his ass in the parking lot or sump'n. I got busy playing Candy Crush. Sorry, I forgot to tell ya."

Dennis Fitch was *pissed*. This wasn't the first time his shit-for-brains brother had pulled this crap on him. But, by God, it would be the last! He quickly retreated down the ladder into the Arby's and back to his handiwork. He'd left so rapidly he hadn't even had a chance to check out what was in store for him inside the metal sarcophagus.

"Jackpot!"

Stacked neatly inside the safe were bundles of fifties, twenties, tens, and ones, with the stacks of twenties being the largest. Another small box inside the safe held piles of rolled coins. There were twenty-five quarter rolls. He placed all the bills and the quarters in the bottom partition of his satchel. It now weighed well over thirty-five pounds. Fitch didn't mind the extra weight—it felt like *success*!

Rummaging through the bottom drawers of the Arby's safe, he found what he was really looking for. Cash was nice, but what he had here was worth a bundle, and all he had to do was pass them along to the right people. Before him were twenty-two Arby's payroll checks, placed in an envelope, ready for Monday's payday. Dennis Fitch had specifically planned this job for the second Sunday of the month because he knew most stores would hold onto their weekend receipts, along with the payroll checks, for deposit and distribution on the first day of the week. Big D had planned well, and he couldn't care less if some single mother couldn't pay her bills because she didn't get paid on time. Not his problem. His only problem now was getting the fuck out of there. The stealthy burglar made his way to the roof.

Chapter 2

THE NEWBIE

The light coming through my window felt toasty on my face, warming me like a mother's embrace. My brain was easing from the shadowy regions of sleep to consciousness. I felt really good; the prior night's rest had been a fabulous respite from the daily stress I was used to. Clarity was replacing the dusky fog of restful sleep. As my brain's hard drive began to spin, suddenly all the pertinent information I needed to start my day popped up on the screen of my mind's video monitor. Oh, crap! Will Phillips starts today!

My name is Kevin Rhinehardt. Most of my friends call me Rhino, and for those of you who haven't already met me, I work for the Santa Barbara Sheriff's Office. I'm one of their detectives. A month ago I finished the biggest investigation of my career, helping solve the Phantom murder case. It amounted to months of unbelievable stress and anxiety. Thanks to fabulous coworkers, a few good breaks, and some barn-burning police work on my part (I humbly add), we managed to close the case. Prison was the final address for those killers. All were indicted for the double murder of Dr. Marvin Redbone and his lover, Raul Diaz.

Greed was an insidious seductress, and it essentially ended four lives through its fatal attraction. I managed to acquire some positive press through a young reporter who worked with us along the way, Rachael Storm. Her article "Slice of Greed" for the *Los Angeles Times* earned her a Pulitzer Prize and it got SBSO—the Santa Barbara Sheriff's Office—some great community relations. So for now, I had bragging rights. The limelight never lasts long, though.

I had the privilege of working that case with one of the best around here, Ted Banner. But, as they say, all good things must come to an end, so they severed our fruitful partnership. Ted was promoted out of the criminal investigation division to patrol sergeant. He was back out on the mean streets, pushing a black-and-white while wiping the noses of young sheriff deputies. I, probably as a punishment, had been given the ominous assignment of training our newest investigator, Detective Will Phillips. Today was his very first day as my new partner! Oh, joy!

My wife of twenty-two years, Julie, rummaged around the kitchen as she fixed a sack lunch for Jimmy, our seventeen-year-old son. I strolled through, fixing my tie, and gave my boy the look—you know the kind. It's the face your dad had on when he came home to find you had backed the family car into a light pole (a personal experience). Young

James Rhinehardt knew exactly why he was on my shit list, too! The prior Friday evening, upon coming home from a long day, I answered our doorbell. Standing there with a stern look on his mug was Ed Parker. I had played poker with Ed on several occasions. He worked for the California Highway Patrol. Since he stood at my door in uniform, his CHP Mustang idling in my driveway, I figured he wasn't inviting me over for finger food and a card game.

Ed spoke up nervously. "Hi, Kev. Ya know why I'm here?"

"Should I? Clue me in, Ed."

"Has your son James spoken to you yet?" Shit, here it came! Ed gave me the news.

"I wanted you to know why I gave him a ticket. He's been driving your Chevy pickup, and twice in the last two weeks, I've pulled him over for speeding near Cabrillo High. Today, the third time, I had him on radar going eighty on Highway 246 after school. I couldn't let it go again, so I tagged him. He needs to slow down, or he's gonna hurt someone. I figured I owed you enough to let you know in person. Tell him I'll be watching him."

My face got red and toasty. I figured Ed thought I was pissed at him, so I lifted my palm and said, "Thanks, Ed. I appreciate you letting me know. Feel free to call me if you see him pulling any more shit, OK? I'll be talking to him. Thanks again."

I closed the door slowly. Ed was still standing at attention in the doorway as it shut. I guess I *was* a little pissed at him for not calling me the first time, *before* he had to write a ticket. Professional courtesy, my ass! I needed to attend to the business at hand. I had other fish to fry now, and the mackerel's name was Jimmy! My son's new BFF had a ticket book!

When a seventeen-year-old who is without gainful employment gets a traffic ticket, his *parents* usually pay the fine! I looked it up: $273! I subsequently had that little talk with Jimbo and reamed his ass. It didn't go well. He flexed his preadulthood muscle and barked back at me, "I wasn't going faster than a lot of my friends drive, and they never get pulled over! Your cop friend probably doesn't like you, so that's why I'm paying for it! This is fucked up."

"*You're paying for it*? And watch your mouth!" I was proud of myself for not ripping his head off. "Unless you've been working when I know you're out partying, you, my friend, rely on Mom and me for your money, *or am I wrong*?"

"Fine, I'll get a job this week. Just don't get pissed when my grades drop 'cause I have to work to make *you* happy."

"The way to make me happy is by pulling your head out of its warm, fuzzy place inside your ass, son, and by slowing down! I swear if this happens one more time, Jimmy, you'll be riding the bus to school. I'd love for your senior buddies to see that...so keep it up!"

My son stormed off, and then the Monday night quarterback walked into the room.

"That was uncalled for, Kevin."

"I meant it, Julie. I'm fed up with his attitude lately and the way he talks to me. He's irresponsible."

"He's seventeen, for God's sake; it's in his hormones to rebel a little."

"Then *you* better talk to him 'cause I'm done talking."

That Monday morning, along with giving Jim the look, I gave him a reminder. "If that truck's speedometer hits sixty-seven miles an hour, I'll get a call at the station."

"Yeah, right! I'll start looking for that job today. God, I can't wait to get the hell outta here!"

I smiled as Jimmy stormed away, but when I glanced at Julie on my way out the door, she was giving me her version of the look—again.

Arriving at the Santa Barbara Sheriff's main station, I strolled into the detective bureau to find everyone gathered around the secretary's desk, munching on Krispy Kreme doughnuts. I grabbed a glazed one and said, "To whom do I owe a thank you for this delicious, albeit artery-clogging, repast?" They pointed to the back of the room.

There stood a fresh-faced, newly promoted detective—William P. Phillips. A shiny seven-point detective star was affixed to the belt on his Brooks Brothers suit pants. Wearing a white, long-sleeved shirt with a stylish tie and a pinstriped dark-gray suit, he looked like a poster boy for *Detective Monthly* magazine! Will was a fit thirty-one-year-old, five-foot-eleven-inch-tall specimen and quite trim at 170 pounds. I admitted (silently to myself, of course) that he looked pretty damn good!

At forty-four years of age, I was squatty at five foot nine and 182 pounds—a balding guy with a bit of a paunch. I likened myself to Joe Friday of *Dragnet*, but my physique was more akin to Andy Sipowitz's of *NYPD Blue*. Standing next to Will in my short-sleeved, pinstriped shirt and sports coat, I paled in comparison to my newbie partner. I saw a change coming—and most likely *not* on Will's part. I had to keep up, after all! Sure, I had the experience and tenure, but experience doesn't necessarily count for shit in this business. Too many times in years past we older guys have seen the shining new stars excel around us in law enforcement. Sometimes the good-looking younger deputies, with shit for shine on their shoes and scant experience under their belts, get promoted to the level of their incompetence. You know, the Peter Principle. I'm not saying youngsters weren't talented and shouldn't get promotions. What I meant was Kevin Rhinehardt needed all the help he could get, so maybe it was time to dress better, hit the gym, and get a minoxidil prescription!

"Well, good morning, partner!" young detective Will boomed, outstretching his paw for me to obligingly shake. As I put mine out, looking at him I detected a perceptible bead of sweat beginning to form below his full hairline.

Looking directly into his eyes, I said, "Well, my friend, it's a big day for you. Are you ready to go to work?"

Looking like he hadn't expected to actually *work* today, just stand around looking good in his suit, Will said, "Well, yeah, but you're going to show me the ropes, right?"

"Sure, that's my job, isn't it?" I turned away as Phillips just stood there, that rivulet of sweat now turning into a river.

I had Will pull the chair from his desk close to mine as I waded through a pile of fifteen new case files, neatly stacked by Sally (our secretary) in my inbox. A mere fifteen new files was a light load for a weekend's activity. Sergeant Bob Roberts, our detective supervisor, always got to work early on the first day of the week because he never knew how many reports he needed to read, and he read all of them; crime reports, arrest reports, and even incidents. The detective sergeant's job required him to evaluate arrests and initial reports to see if any follow-up investigation needed to be done by his subordinates. He was expected to evaluate the arrest reports despite the fact that they might have been approved by the arresting deputy's sergeant. This proved to be interesting on occasion since the egos of the patrol bosses sometimes got in the way of Bob's constructive criticism. Once in a while, when a sergeant came in to talk to Bob and they shut the door, we figured they had one such difference of opinion on the quality of a report that was okeydokeyed through by patrol.

So as to not overwhelm my fledgling partner, now perspiring heavy because he still insisted on wearing that frigging suit coat inside the office, I gave him a couple of minor theft and assault reports to evaluate. Our job, as investigators, was to determine what follow-up was necessary on those files assigned to us—extra interviews, search warrants, and so on—in order to finish the case and close it, make an arrest, or ship it to the district attorney for prosecution. Will Phillips sat by me, eagerly taking in all my instruction. I had to admit that I sorta liked the guy.

During the investigation of the Phantom "Slice of Greed" murders, then *Deputy* Phillips developed quite a few leads while working patrol, on his own, and because he worked so hard he was temporarily assigned to help the criminal investigation division (and me) on that perplexing whodunit. He was impressive and exhibited knowledge of interviewing and investigation far beyond his years on the job. He was just so damn young! Will even managed to catch the eye of lovely Rachael Storm, the reporter who was assigned to us by Chief Walters. I could have sworn there was a spark there, but after she moved on to the *LA Times*, I hadn't seen much of her. Too bad; so sad for Mr. Phillips, since she was quite *caliente*!

After lunch, I began reviewing a few of the older cases I had inherited right after I ended testimony in the murder case. I just didn't have much time back then to deal with any new crimes, but now they wouldn't go away. I dug out two commercial-burglary case files of fast-food restaurants in Buellton (a small town in northern Santa Barbara County). The first one I read, a McDonald's restaurant, seemed to have been breached by the crook(s) through a roof vent, which wasn't alarmed. The crook cut the lock off up there and dropped down inside. It looked like he, or they, then used a big set of pliers to crank open the knob to the office door and then drilled open the safe—a very unusual, and very distinct, MO.

I had seen a couple of cases in which smaller safes had been stolen from other places and were later found beat to shit, with the doors open and cash removed. In another commercial caper, a crook actually brought a small acetylene torch to burn off the hinges—the dumb shit didn't figure on frying the paper money inside the metal box, though! We later arrested him and found charred ten-dollar bills in his freezer. Gotta love the dumb-asses. God bless 'em!

At McDonald's, the thief got $3,322 in cash and $8,562 in payroll checks that were being stored in there. He took checks? That was very unusual because cash was untraceable, but checks? Checks weren't easily altered, although not impossible to pass. We ought to be able to trace those babies if the thief cashed them. This really piqued my interest, so I perused the second burglary, this one at a nearby Burger King fast-food restaurant in the same city just a week later. The entry was by way of a Channel Loc–type pliers used to tweak open a side door. No alarm was activated since the manager apparently hadn't set it that night. Then $5,145 in cash and coins was taken from the safe. No drill job here. The door was found ajar with the booty missing. Hmm. I smelled an inside job here despite the coincidence of the other fast-food burglary just a week before. Patrol interviewed the manager who had locked up the night before, and she admitted she didn't remember setting the alarm. She swore up and down that she remembered locking up the safe, though. The finger pointing would be in her direction.

I grabbed my younger partner ('cause he's my boot) and said, "We need to go see Ron O'Hara."

Ron was the forensic bureau's sergeant and quite an interesting guy. Most CSI investigators, who spend their careers staring at the whorls, ridges, and loops of fingerprints and swabbing up blood at crime scenes, are! He also was one of the most fastidious, professional investigators I'd ever met. Will and I needed to see the evidence that had been collected in these two cases. I hoped to hell that the forensic bureau had been called out to work them, as was the department's policy on larger commercial thefts. If left to patrol...well, who knows what we'd get?

"Hey, Ron, you know Will Phillips, don't you? They scraped the bottom of the barrel, and they made him a detective."

Ron reached out and shook Will's hand (there was a lot of that going around that day). "We look forward to working with you, Will. Don't listen to Rhinehardt, though. He's usually full of shit!"

Forcing a fake smile, I said, "Will and I are looking at a couple of commercial jobs in Buellton, about a month ago. Let me check my file...yeah, a McDonald's on January third, and a Burger King on the tenth. I need to see what was collected, since the deputy only said, 'See forensic report.'"

Ron went to his office and brought up his assignment files on the PC. "OK, yeah, I gave those to Nancy. Let's go talk to her."

Nancy Robson had worked as a forensic technician for about four years at the main office, and she had a very good reputation. Standing just four feet eleven inches and probably weighing in at, oh, maybe 160 pounds, she was not your typical *CSI: Los Angeles* forensic investigator. Where were all those gorgeous chicks, anyway? I'd never found one. Most of the guys and gals who did forensic work were married to their jobs. Many were single and slightly (or not so slightly) overweight because they were forced to spend many hours stuck in crime scenes, at all hours of the day and night, and they ate a lot—I mean *a lot*—of fast food. I knew there were good-looking ID people out there—*somewhere*.

Nancy was sitting in front of her computer with a dual screen up, comparing enlarged latent prints. Did I mention that a lot of forensic folks wear eyeglasses? Nancy peered at us from over her own pair of spectacles.

"Hi, Kev, and *oh*, this must be our new Detective Phillips!"

She knew damn well who he was. Did I mention Nancy was single? She extended her hand to Will, and the bastard feigned kissing it—*puh-leeze*! The twerp loved all the attention.

I asked a question before Phillips put too much slobber on her still-outstretched knuckle. "Yeah, Nancy, right.

You have two burg cases out of Buellton. McDonald's and Burger King. I assume you did the workups on both, not patrol?"

"Sure, Kevin, right, I did 'em. Pretty interesting at McDonald's, wasn't it? They drilled the safe open. Wow! Never saw that before."

"Actually, Nancy, me neither. Can I see the flicks? What did you collect?"

"Here's the file. I need to bring up the digitals for you, but I collected the cut padlock at McDonald's off the vent, and I did a cast of the tool marks from the point of entry at Burger King and the office at McDonald's. Of course, I did some static lifts on the floors too, especially at Burger King, because they had mopped it right before closing the night before. Got some good sole impressions there—only one set coming back and forth. The McDonald's static lifts were not so good. The floor was filthy and hadn't been mopped for a few days. Everybody and their brother traipsed through that place. I dusted and got partials from the doorknobs but can't say who they belong to. There were multiple impressions from multiple sources, I think. We need to get eliminations on all the employees, I figure."

Electrostatic lifts were accomplished by placing a thin metallic sheet of material on the floor and then passing an electric current through the sheet. The dust from shoe-sole impressions left behind then became visible on the sheet and could be lifted and photographed, along with a scale to show dimensions for later comparisons to a shoe garnered from a suspect. It was like a fingerprint of the crook's shoe—not as definitive as an actual fingerprint, which the courts have ruled as direct evidence, but with an expert's testimony, a static match was pretty darn conclusive.

Nancy then brought up the digital pictures taken at the two scenes for Will and me to see. Wow! One small, clean drill hole in the door of the safe to the upper left of where the dial had been. The photos showed the dial lying on the office floor. The inside lock plate (mounted on the inside of the door) looked just fine, with no drill or pry marks. He/they must have used something to put into that hole to unlock the safe! Other pics showed some scratch marks on the safe handle. Maybe they'd had to pry it or something?

I had her do a split screen of the outside doorknob at Burger King and the office knob from McDonald's. Boy! They looked very similar. Nancy burst my bubble by saying that a pliers manufacturer uses the same die for the jaws of their pliers, over and over, until the die wears out, so thousands of pliers have the same teeth at first. Only with multiple uses do the metal jaws take on a unique bite. Just because the picture of the tool marks looked similar didn't mean they were. Only a comparison of the plastic cast of the actual unique marks made against the suspected tool itself could prove definitively that it was the same one. Then the match had to be verified by a tool-mark expert with the Department of Justice. Boy, this could get complicated!

Will flexed his new detective wings by asking Nancy if she had retrieved any evidence from the roof of the McDonald's since it was obvious the crook had gotten in from above.

"That roof was greasy, dirty, and I couldn't do a lift up there. That black tarry surface didn't show anything. I did shoot it, though. They must've had a ladder to get there… it's about twenty feet up! I only found greasy smudges on the vent and shaft…nothing usable. Funny about the Burger King—the safe was clean; no drill marks like McDonald's. Maybe someone else did that one? I pulled prints off the inside shelves and drawers and off the slick handle, though. Need those elimination prints, boys! I need to clear the managers and anyone else who goes into the safe in there."

Will and I thanked Nancy, and as we walked out of forensics, she waved to Will and yelled, "Bye-bye, detective!" *Puh-leeze!*

Once back at our desks, we talked about these cases, and I agreed to take the Burger King and assigned Will to take the lead on the McDonald's. I suspected that my caper could very well have been an inside job since the safe was obviously opened with a combination. I had a lot of interviews to do, so this one would be time-consuming.

I didn't need to give my new partner much direction. Hard to admit, but he was one sharp cookie. Before the day ended, he had sent out BOL teletypes, and a CLETS— that's a California Law-Enforcement Teletype System to you—inquiry about any similar MO crimes in the state. He had a lot of good ideas about how to work the case, as well.

I learned that Kristine Macias, the night manager at Burger King, was working, so I beat feet over to the restaurant. I spoke to her alone in the back office. The restaurant's safe sat grimly next to her as a reminder of what we were there to chat about. It took about twenty minutes of pointed interviewing, but tearfully Macias admitted she didn't remember locking the safe behind her. She'd screwed up like that before and lied because she was worried she'd get fired. I set her up for a polygraph, but I already knew she was telling the truth. She'd forgotten to set the alarm *and* to lock the safe. I figured she'd best get her unemployment paperwork in order.

The rest of the day was spent wading through the mountain of paperwork from other cases we were assigned. About 4:30 p.m., Luis Ocampo—another salty CID detective and a good friend—walked by. He'd been invaluable on the Phantom case. Today, though, he seemed a little off, and as he chatted with me I could swear I smelled something out of place at the office—stale alcohol. I think he noticed me paying a little too much attention to his breath as he spoke, too, so he made a nervous excuse and left. My gut knotted up.

Just a couple of months earlier, Luis had taken me on a "world tour" of the bars around Santa Barbara. I was stressed out back then and couldn't sleep due to some posttraumatic stress disorder, or PTSD, I was dealing with. Luis thought he would help by taking me out for some R and R. I ended up far worse off as a result of his "therapy." I came to realize then that Luis seemed to like booze just a smidge more than was healthy for him. Before the case was done, I ended up on the wagon myself. Now I realized Luis had a real problem. Before leaving for the day, I moseyed over to Detective Biff Corbett's desk to pick his brain about our mutual friend.

"Biff, I'm worried about Luis. He just came by, and well, I could be wrong, but I think I smelled booze on him."

"You're not wrong. I've smelled it more than once. Lately more than ever."

"Shit, man, what should we do...he can't throw it all away! I don't want to see him in a jam." I thought of Luis's wife. "What about Tammy?"

Biff, all six foot five inches of him, swiveled his desk chair toward me and rolled closer my way. He spoke quietly, "Look, Rhino, Tammy's been married to Luis for twenty-two years. She's gotta know what's happening with him. Let's take him to lunch tomorrow, but don't mention this to anybody, OK?"

Up to that point in the day, I'd felt pretty damn good. I care about my job and the citizens behind the cases I work, but these guys, your partners, they stand beside you in a gunfight. They'd die for you, and you for them. I had trouble sleeping that night for the first time in weeks.

Chapter 3
EL GERENTE

James Gaylord sat in his Honda, glued to the screen of his Samsung Galaxy, playing *Mortal Kombat*. Kill those bastards; off with their heads! At 2:52 a.m., the car's trunk opened and slammed shut as Dennis Fitch tossed his heavy roller bag inside. Opening the passenger door, he sat down next to his slacker partner.

The sting of Big D's leather glove slapping his face brought Jim Gaylord to full attention. A flash of anger struck Chunk hard like the glove, but then fear gripped him even harder as he spied the look on his brother's red face and those eyes, wide with rage.

"You fuckin' moron! Do you know how long I hung out on that rooftop? I almost left the job 'cause you were frigging playing your goddamn games! I ought to pull your sorry ass out of the car and kick it right here!"

Jimbo knew his shit was weak. "Man, oh man, I'm sooo sorry, Den. I was trying to act cool, like you always tell me to; I just got lost in it, man. The cop left, OK? No harm was done, bro!"

"You asshole! What would you have done if you looked up and saw some pigs dragging me into their car, huh? What would you do then, Chunk? Just to let you know, you'd be the first one I'd give up! I'd be pointing my fuckin' finger right at *you*! Listen up, tonight you worked for almost *nothing*. I'm giving you the coins from the job—that's it. No bills, just chump change for your fat ass. That'll teach you to pay attention!"

"But D!" Dennis was looking out the window now at the scenery flying by, and James Gaylord knew there was no appeal left before his brother's kangaroo court. It was a long quiet drive in the chilly Honda back to Seal Beach. Just before daylight, after the brakes squealed to a stop in the driveway of their mother's house, Dennis Fitch pulled the luggage from the trunk. He entered the upscale house silently with Chunk lumbering behind.

Pulling the roller bag behind him, he sauntered down the hallway toward his room. Stopping short of the door, he sat the heavy luggage upright and turned around toward his brother. Dennis pulled a heavy cloth bag out of the suitcase and held it out in front of Chunk. Jimbo instinctively reached out to grab it. Big D dropped it through his grasp, and it landed at his feet with a loud clunk. As Dennis walked back into his room, Jim reached down, picking up the $250 worth of quarters. He lay down in the den on the sofa, clutching the cloth bag of coins. *To sleep…perchance to dream.*

Big D was up by ten and was greeted in the kitchen by his mother. She sat at the table drinking coffee, smoking a Marlboro. Now nearly sixty pounds overweight, a wrinkled, graying Brenda Fitch sat reading her *Us Weekly* magazine. Years of nicotine and booze made for one tough lady. To put it bluntly, she looked rode hard and put away wet! Despite her stony appearance, Brenda was still a sweetheart—*to her oldest boy*.

"So what the fuck happened last night, son? When I walked by Chunk on the couch, he said, 'Is D still pissed?' Are you OK, boy? What'd that dumb shit do to you? Did anything bad happen?"

"Not much, 'cept the dipshit missed the cops driving up and parking right next to him! Never said a fucking word until they were right there, right across from the place! I sweated my ass off on the roof for almost half an hour while he sat on his ass, playing a fucking video game. He even forgot to tell me they left! It was all fucked up, Ma."

"You know your brother's slow, don't ya? I'm surprised you work with that retard at all. That boy has the brains of a fuckin' monkey. Always has. I'm just glad you're OK, Dennis. You're my good boy. So, how much ya get?"

"Well, in cash about $4,250 in bills and coins, and twenty-two checks. They oughta get another two grand, give or take. A pretty good night."

Brenda got up and shuffled along the floor in her dirty slippers to the refrigerator to get her favorite son some breakfast. Dennis Fitch had a meeting later that morning, and she wanted to send her boy off with a good meal.

Known by her maiden name of Simmons back then, Brenda had married Dick Fitch in the early eighties. She'd worked for the main US post office in San Diego as a mail carrier for almost ten years. She met him on her delivery route one afternoon. She handed him his bills, and he asked her out. Much thinner and actually cute in those days, she accepted his quick proposal of matrimony. He had a nice house and a Harley-Davidson chopper. Richard Fitch had a penchant for demon rum right from the get-go, and Brenda took advantage of his evening binges by having binges of her own—only hers were with other men instead of booze.

Almost two years into their marriage, Brenda Fitch gave birth to a baby boy; the pair named the infant Dennis. Dick never insisted on a paternity test. He probably should have. For almost a year, Brenda toed the monogamous line and played the working-mother role. She even seemed happy with Fitch—well, *almost*. Then, one afternoon back in the USPS mail room, Brenda got knocked to the floor by several falling heavy boxes. The subsequent internal investigation revealed the containers had been stacked overhead, higher than regulation, by an unknown employee.

There were no cameras in USPS work areas back then. Mrs. Fitch was sent to several doctors and claimed ongoing shoulder pain due to the work-related injury. After fourteen months of litigation, the Post Office granted her medical retirement along with lifetime medical benefits.

Just seven months after receiving her first retirement check, Brenda left Dick, claiming the magic had gone out of their marriage. Seems the magic had merely moved over onto one Bobby Gaylord. Robert Gaylord was gainfully employed, also by the USPS. It was quite coincidental that Bobby Gaylord happened to be working with Brenda back then in that very same mail room, on the very same day those boxes fell on her. He was the only witness to the incident and backed her tragic story to HR.

Brenda scored a house from Dick Fitch in the divorce, which she parlayed to a decent track home in northern San Diego County. When young Dennis was two years old, and just one year after tying the knot with Bob Gaylord, Brenda gave birth to James after a difficult pregnancy. By the time Chunk came squirting out, Brenda was already tired of her second marriage. She stuck it out for another ten years with Mr. Gaylord but finally said adios to that union as well. She received $100,000 in the divorce settlement. Robert Gaylord didn't want any part of that bitch, so he bought her out of their house and out of her claim to part of his USPS retirement.

It was good she got that money from Gaylord, too, because shortly after the ink had dried on the dissolution papers, she got a written request to contact USPS human resources. A postal inspector informed her they were suspending her retirement benefits. He cited the discovery of "obvious criminal fraud" on her part. Despite her profanity-laced objections, the evidence was clear that she had never suffered a debilitating injury. Glossy photographs of her bowling in a San Diego league and water skiing at Lake Murray, all with that same injured shoulder, were Exhibit 1. Exhibit 2 was a sworn statement from a longtime friend of hers at the post office. Shortly after claiming her injury, she admitted to the woman that she intended on taking the government for "a ride." Bob Gaylord was present during the comments and laughed about how he'd lied to HR to back her up. Poor Brenda had her pension pulled, and Robert Gaylord got suspended for a month without pay. The postal service made it clear he was lucky to still have a job.

Brenda went back to her previous alias of Fitch, and two years after her loving son Dennis was released from the San Diego juvenile detention center, she moved her crew to Seal Beach. She found a fixer-upper house on a quiet cul-de-sac. For some reason it never got fixed up, much to the delight of her close neighbors. Those quiet, safe surroundings proved to be a great base for the comings and goings of her nefarious offspring. Dennis was always good to make the mortgage payment, and Chunk was a fine errand boy. She and her bizarre collection of "reborn" dolls were quite content in those Seal Beach digs. She spent time holding those "babies" almost every day.

Later that morning, Dennis Fitch placed a familiar phone call to his business partner.

"Yo, Chuy, we need to meet. I got some more for ya."

"Big D, my man! Same place...noon."

Jesus "Chuy" Santiago hung up his cell, and looking over toward the corner of his workshop, he spied Olegario Campos beginning to light a cigarette near his workstation. "Gario, put that fucking thing out! Motherfucker, do ya want ta blow the fuckin' place up?"

As Jesus rapidly approached Campos, standing just two feet from an acetone tray, he slapped the Mexican's face, knocking the smoldering cig down to the floor. Olegario just glared at him, his hand clutching his mouth and nose in disbelief.

"This ain't the first time I caught you doing shit like this. Next time you're out, and you won't like where. You got that, *pendejo?*"

"Si, Gerente, lo siento."

Workers in Jesus Santiago's "factory" called him *Gerente* because he was the manager. Chuy ran the Santanas' credit-card-and-check operations in Orange County. The Santanas gang, or STS, was the earliest and most powerful of Orange County's Filipino gangs and currently had the illegal credit-card-and-check-washing market in Southern California. STS was one of the most violent and financially successful organized criminal organizations to ever hold territory in the OC. Partnered with the Mexican South Side Lopers, who kept ties with EME (the Mexican Mafia), the two groups laundered money through a cover business: Dragon Cleaners.

41

Owned by a Korean puppet company, the large dry-cleaning business was located in the southeast industrial district of Santa Ana. Dragon Cleaners occupied a large commercial building facing Third Street with a fenced scrap-metal business situated directly behind it. A small fleet of Dragon Cleaners vans kept many businesses in the OC equipped with clean towels, floor mats, and uniforms. Dragon contracted with several upscale hotels, too, along with Angel Stadium. Dragon Cleaners was a successful part of the Santa Ana business community. It flew well below the radar.

Chuy Santiago's operation, nicknamed the Shop, was located in a hidden room at the rear of Dragon Cleaners. This windowless fifteen-foot-deep-by-fifty-foot-wide room in the back of the expansive building was hidden from prying eyes by a tall wall of hanging dry-cleaned curtain panels. These eight-foot-tall panels, encased in their clear plastic bags, blocked all view of the back wall to the dry cleaning factory. To the casual observer, it appeared as if the rack hung against the rear wall of the building. Not so. Parting one red and one blue curtain near the center, a visitor would find a half-inch steel door secured with a sophisticated electronic combination lock.

A visitor to the illegal operation could only gain entry through the old lady, Shin Wu, who worked the front counter at Dragon. Two quick buzzes let the Shop know someone was coming back to visit. A special knock and a visual confirmation allowed entry inside—and then only by Chuy or his designee. If Wu leaned on that buzzer long and hard, it meant trouble.

There was another exit to the Shop other than the front door. Only Santiago knew about it. A four-foot-square hand-dug tunnel, covered by a piece of half-inch-thick plywood, ran from under a table inside. The tunnel extended to the scrap-metal business behind Dragon Cleaners. This escape channel came up and exited into the rusty skeleton of an old VW van. This rusty piece of VW crap sat against the back chain-link fence separating the two businesses. This last-resort exit had been dug before the clandestine operation began. It had never been used in the two years that El Gerente's operation had been under way. It was Chuy's insurance policy.

On a typical day, there were as many as ten people working inside the Shop. Two were trained to use and service the sophisticated Chinese UV card printer utilized to manufacture fake California identification cards. Santanas had paid $35,000 for this beauty. This machine was capable of duplicating the complicated images used in the latest generation of licenses and identification cards and of placing names and pictures on them. Unscrupulous computer contractors, working for the state of California, were always willing to provide stolen software for a price. The Shop always paid for the latest images.

Olegario and another of Chuy's workers "washed" stolen checks using acetone and altered them to ensure that a worthwhile dollar amount was always reached when they were passed. Santiago always had an STS or Loper lieutenant present in the Shop as well, since frequently Chuy had to leave to supervise other portions of the operation, such as distribution. His most trusted right-hand man was Joaquin "Peanut" Hernandez.

Specially trained male and female Hispanics made up the heart and soul of the check-distribution end of the Shop. They were the "runners," and every one of them was an undocumented immigrant from Mexico. If arrested, they knew very little, if anything, about the operation to tell the cops. Historically, they had suffered less severe consequences than US citizens when caught. A couple of months in the slammer, and they got a free van ride back to Mexico—coming right back after they caught up with relatives for a month or two. Back after a hand slap! All this thanks to the revolving-door immigration policy of America.

Several times a week these crews of runners were transported by the gang's vans up and down California, passing their forged checks. They identified themselves to hapless merchants with their falsified driver's licenses, matching the payee names on the washed checks. None spoke a lick of English. It was always better that way. By the time the merchants got the checks back from the bank stamped "forgery," the money had already been laundered through Dragon Cleaners, much of it sitting pretty, converted to yuan, inside a Chinese bank.

STS and Loper gang members drove the illegals around, and each runner was paid fifty dollars to pass a check. On an average day, a runner could pass four hot checks and make around $200. Not bad for wetbacks! Considering they traveled four runners to a van and daily cashed at least four checks each, ranging from $410 to $535 face value, this proved to be a profitable endeavor for El Gerente and his STS coconspirators. They targeted small mom-and-pop stores in run-down areas of cities and never hit the same business twice (at least within a two-month period). These check "drops" were all charted by Chuy and managed by his lieutenants to ensure a smooth, successful business. This was a business, after all—a *big* business. Only one of the Shop's runners made more than the others: twenty-year-old Yolanda Tafoya. This was only because she occasionally served El Gerente in other capacities.

Today, Chuy left the Shop and drove down to the Denny's parking lot on South Bristol Street. It was his usual meeting spot with Big D since Fitch was not allowed to know where the Shop was. Santiago drove a newer metallic blue Chevy Camaro. Fitch kept it low-key with a black '97 Mazda Miata. Exiting their rides to meet and greet, they fist-bumped. The two made a unique pair, Big D being big and Chuy being...well, small. At only five feet five inches, with a shaved head and lots of hidden tattoos, Chuy seemed an unlikely bedfellow for Big D. But Santiago was muscled, with multiple tats emblazoning his chest and upper arms, advertising his gang affiliation. A large black "STS" was visible on his neck, hidden just below his T-shirt line.

If a younger Santiago had realized he would one day be a shot caller in a large criminal operation, he probably would've been less willing to tattoo his flesh so it was akin to a human billboard that screamed, *"Gang member here."* Nowadays, El Gerente kept a very low profile in public. He made sure his tats stayed hidden. He waved to police cars, obeyed traffic laws, and kept his taillights in very good working order. To the average Joe, he was an ex-banger now—just another Mexican gainfully employed at Dragon Cleaners!

Jesus met Dennis Fitch eight years ago at the East Mesa Juvenile Detention Center—two kids from far different backgrounds serving time for committing far different crimes. Fitch was a middle-income thief, Santiago a barrio badass. Chuy Santiago was a Mexican member of a Filipino gang—STS. He'd stabbed a black Crips gang member on the mean streets of San Diego to make his bones at the young age of sixteen. The son of a Filipino father and a Mexican mother, he was jumped into the gang by his cousin. One evening after dinner at the detention center, two black Crips confronted Chuy in the hallway. They were in the process of bloodying him up when Fitch intervened. After that, Santiago stayed close to Big D.

Fitch got out two years before Santiago was paroled, but they stayed in touch. The relationship proved profitable for both of them. Each of them conned the juvenile justice system well. They managed to get their rap sheets sealed for good behavior. After all, what the cops didn't know couldn't hurt them.

Fitch palmed an envelope holding the Arby's restaurant payroll checks and passed it surreptitiously to Chuy as they leaned against their cars listening to the rap-crap music wafting out of the Chevy. It was placed in the Camaro without being opened, and Santiago said, "Well, *ese*, what'd you give me today?"

"Twenty-two payroll checks. I figure you owe me twenty-two hundred large."

With a wry smile spreading across his face, Chuy replied, "Twenty-two hundred? You must be dreamin', motherfucker! You know I pay eighty each for paper. You trying to fuck wit' me, *pendejo*?"

An assertive Dennis Fitch faced El Gerente and spoke up, "Look, *hermano*, I busted my hump for these, and I keep you in business. I don't give a rat's ass what you pay anyone else. I'm not anyone else. It's not fucking easy, doing what I do. I'm a professional, and if you want my product, you need to pay more for it. I want a hundred each from now on. Now, do we deal or not?"

Chuy Santiago, one hand planted deeply in the pocket of his tan chinos, pointed a steely finger in the direction of Fitch's face.

"Listen, white boy, you wouldn't have nothin' without me, *tu comprende*, *pendejo*? Without my help you wouldn't be this 'professional' dickhead you brag about! Without Señor Todd Starnes, you got nothin', *claro*?"

Big D knew Chuy had a point. It was Santiago who had introduced him to Starnes: Todd Fitzgerald Starnes, date of birth March 6, 1976. Under that name, and with a California ID card with his likeness on it to make it official, Dennis Fitch had attended classes at the California Locksmith Academy. There he learned the ins and outs of being a safe technician. All his training and all his equipment was obtained by one Todd F. Starnes. This new white-bread identity was only possible through the assistance of the Shop.

All this became necessary because Dennis Fitch had coldcocked a guy three years earlier in a bar in Costa Mesa. He beat the dude up pretty good. He belted the fellow so hard in the face that he broke his jaw and fractured the orbit of his right eye socket—all that 'cause the dude cock-blocked him with a chick at the bar. Despite the not-so-fastidious work of his dumb-ass public defender, the real Dennis Fitch copped to misdemeanor assault with injury and received two years on probation as a result. His juvenile rap sheet had long since been expunged, but this new charge prevented our aspiring burglar from finishing the training under his true name. They preapproved ol' Todd, though!

Todd Starnes managed to get most of the way through the locksmith training programs, despite the fact that he had to pull out of classes shy of certification. The fucking school wanted to run Fitch's prints before graduation— and his fingertips would have betrayed his true identity.

Big D had learned all he needed to know to get the job done by then. He didn't need no fuckin' certificate!

He laid it out for Chuy. "Yeah, Starnes saved my ass, but you and I...we always got each other's back, right? So why try to fuck me on this, *amigo*? I jus' wanna keep doin' business with you, but I know of a guy in LA willin' to pay a hundred...I might just hafta drive a little farther to make my money. It's only business, *mi amigo*. How 'bout it?"

A wry smile replaced the scowl on Santiago's face, and he responded, "Well, Dennis, I guess, but don't think you can up the price on me again, motherfucker, 'cause you only doin' business with me, understand? I made you; I can take you out of business...*comprende*, Señor Starnes?"

Big D didn't quite understand what his tattooed associate had said, but he figured he wasn't paying him a compliment. Dennis got what he had come for. Sitting down in Chuy's Camaro, the Mexican opened the center console and, pushing aside a nine-millimeter Smith and Wesson pistol, he picked up a thick wad of bills. He counted out twenty-two Franklins and handed them to Fitch.

The tall white boy exited the Camaro and, turning to El Gerente, whispered, "We'll talk some more. I'm working up an even bigger job soon."

Chuy gave him a thumbs-up. "*Que bueno! Esta listo, amigo.*"

Fitch chirped tires leaving the parking lot. Jesus Santiago frowned and drove out slowly, making a three-second stop at the sign. He signaled properly before making his left turn onto the street.

Chapter 4
JUST A HICCUP

I walked into the Santa Barbara detective bureau and, looking around, realized that Louie Ocampo wasn't anywhere around. His recent pattern of tardiness was obvious to all his coworkers, and I wondered what Sergeant Roberts might have to say about it. Today was the day Biff and I intended on confronting him about his downward spiral with booze. In a way I felt good, since I hoped he would've done the same for me, had I been screwing up by the numbers. Best to nip it in the bud with a friend rather than have it bite him in the ass later on!

I met up with Detective Will, who (as always) looked fresh and well dressed. *Make me look bad once again, eh, partner?* He was pissing me off. I needed to talk to that boy—buy him a short-sleeved shirt, drip some gravy on his tie, do something to ugly him up!

"Hey, Rhino, I got some very interesting information on those safe burglary cases. Let's grab a cup and talk."

"Sure, Willy, let me grab a doughnut first." I walked over to the coffee machine and was devastated to find the nearby table devoid of any sugary treats. Guess the dew was off the lily and newbie Phillips felt secure enough not to have to bribe his coworkers into liking him today. Damn!

Meeting Phillips at his desk, hauling my cup of black joe, he seemed more excited than usual. "Boy, I think we're part of a much bigger thing here with these burglaries."

"How so, Shamus? Did Ronald McDonald or the Hamburglar hit Burger King in retaliation?"

"No, smart-ass! What if I told you these guys did almost two dozen similar jobs, up and down California, and one place hit was right next door—in Santa Barbara!"

"What?" Quickly forgetting that my junior partner had just called me an ass, I asked, "Are these all *safe jobs*? Is the entry MO similar, and has anyone identified a suspect yet?" I fired off a dozen questions, with some revealing answers coming in response from my fresh-faced colleague.

"I checked the MOs. Very similar, with minor differences but only because the guy had to make entry differently sometimes. All the safes were drilled in basically the same way. He always takes the cash and any checks left inside. They've linked this guy to twenty-two jobs, as far north as San Jose and south to the California border, all over the last eight months. They hit a Denny's in Santa Barbara city a month and a half ago the same way. The other agencies think the dudes are connected to a lot of bogus check cashing, too, all over the place. The checks mostly came from these same fast-food jobs and are passed by Mexicans, probably illegals. This is really big, Kevin… they're asking us to be part of a task force that's just been formed!"

"Task force?" I replied in disbelief. "And no one saw anything suspicious? I can't believe this fucker pulls off all these jobs, and we got shit for witnesses! He must be friggin' Batman!"

"Oh, yeah, I forgot to tell ya—one lady *did* see the suspect. She's a night manager, and she ran into him at midnight as he was in the middle of a job at her restaurant. She could only describe the perp as tall, athletic, and being either an African American or white guy. She was so shook up, she couldn't even describe his clothing much, only recalling he had on some kind of black mask, wore gloves, and had a knife. The one investigator from Los Angeles I talked with said that afterward the lady was a nutcase— she's still seein' a shrink over it!"

"Sounds like she gave a description of someone we already figured out probably did it. A big, strong dude… and wow, he was dressed in dark clothes. Duh. Hell, you're telling me she couldn't even give us a race, black or white? Man! So who's heading up this task force anyway—which department?"

Looking at his burgeoning case file filled with teletype responses, Will said, "Orange County SO, since they've a lot of the cases, and many of the checks were passed there and in LA. All food places, McDonald's and Burger King, like ours. An Arby's, Olive Garden, Denny's—if they sell greasy food out of the joint, seems like they hit 'em. The guy's smart, too. Most of the time he figures out their paydays and rips the payroll checks before they're handed out. He scores a bundle."

Will and I met with Bob Roberts, who agreed that Phillips could take the lead on our two safe cases, with my superlative supervision, of course (I threw in the "superlative" descriptor). The sergeant seemed distracted as we spoke. After leaving Roberts's office, Will said he'd be in contact with the Orange County sheriff to determine when and where their task force would meet. I was intrigued by this new information but knew I was up to my ass in alligators with my own caseload, and my upcoming chat with Luis weighed heavy on my mind. I was relieved Will would be primary on these cases, but I would never have told him so. He was doing well so far; dotting all the i's and crossing his t's. It was my job to make sure he continued doing so.

About eleven that morning, I sat down with Biff. Corbett and I went way back, having worked patrol together for a while and now in the criminal investigations division. Biff, whose actual first name was Buford, was one of the largest guys on the department. You never, *ever* called the man Buford, lest he rip your head off and crap down the hole! Because he was six feet five inches tall and 235 pounds, we figured they had to make him a detective because he couldn't fit in our teensy-weensy patrol cars, with all those rifles and gadgets crammed inside them! I'm just kidding. He was great at what he did—a damn good investigator! He and Luis Ocampo proved invaluable in the Phantom murder case, and we were all tight compadres. Biff and I figured something bad was happening with our friend, and it nagged at us both. At noon, we found out just how bad. Sergeant Roberts paged all of South County CID to respond to the bureau's meeting room for a meeting.

"Last night, about eight thirty, Ocampo was driving his unmarked on the way home and was involved in a non-injury accident. Luis is fine, but he nailed a parked car. He was off duty, and the city of Santa Barbara investigated the crash. Bottom line, they arrested Luis for DUI. He was cited and released to me at about three this morning. I've been up all night talking with staff about what's gonna happen with him."

We all sank deeper in our respective chairs. I shot worried looks at Biff. Roberts wasn't done. "Luis has been placed on administrative leave and won't be working until the sheriff reviews the arrest report and our own admin review's been done. You're welcome to call him, but you're ordered *not* to discuss this incident with him, or you'll become a witness and can be interviewed. Am I clear on that point? And, in case you are unclear on this issue, it is against department policy to do personal business in a department vehicle, and drinking alcoholic beverages while you're working is prohibited. Drinking after work, while driving a county car, is also a no-no. I was told to clarify that little detail with all of you, just in case anyone didn't understand. Any questions about that? I didn't think so. By the way, they'll probably be speaking to some of us about this before it wraps up."

As we shuffled out, heads down, Roberts grabbed me by my lonesome in the hallway. "Kevin, the LT said he wants to talk to you in particular since your little drink fest with Luis back during the Phantom case is common knowledge. I just wanted to give ya a heads-up. Keep your shirt white." This reference to my staying out of trouble bugged the hell outta me!

During the Phantom murder case, I was experiencing a bit of stress due to internal and external pressure to solve those murders quickly. My angst prompted Louie to take me out to blow off some steam. We were *not* working, and we were *not* in a department car. I was taken home by Ted Banner, my partner at the time. Luis parked his AMC Pacer early on during the "tour," and I knew he took a cab home—that was my understanding, at least.

I got pretty wasted. Luis took great joy later in describing to everyone how I'd barfed all over a dude in one of the places. Yeah, it was *real funny*. No big deal at the time, but it was obvious to many that Luis loved his juice, and I had no urge to compound his situation by having to describe it once again to anyone—least of all to an admin cheese eater bent on nailing him to the wall!

———

Meanwhile, in Seal Beach, the malefactors responsible for the pending establishment of a law enforcement task force were busy planning more cases for the police to solve. The matriarch was complaining that her son James had backed up the toilet in their happy home, once again.

"Goddamn it, Chunk! Haven't I told ya, over and over, flush right after you take a dump...don't wait till ya pile ten pounds of crap paper on top of them turds! They don't go down the shitter then. I gotta call the fuckin' sewer truck to suck the tank again, I guess. Damn you, Chunk! You're always costing me! Your brother never causes me no problems like that."

The septic company responded expeditiously due to the "overflowing" of frantic, expletive-laced calls by Mother Fitch. They knew her from prior problems with her septic tank there, and the drivers all drew straws to see who'd be the one to come out. The lucky technician determined the real cause of Chunk's potty explosion: tree roots. The only solution was about three grand worth of repairs to the plastic tank and the connecting sewer lines. Of course, after showering the workers with ranting curses, Brenda went directly to her cash cow for the funding.

"Dennis, darlin', Mommy needs some money to fix the fuckin' mess Chunk made. I need about ten grand pretty quick. I can pay the bill for now, but can you get me the cash by next month...I put a roof over your heads and cook for you. Least you can do is pay me back for all I do around here. Help Mommy out, please?"

Brenda conveniently padded the sewer repair estimate because she figured she was owed as much by her offspring. Big D had been negotiating recently with the owner of a twenty-one-foot Sea Ray powerboat, which included twin Mercury ninety-horsepower engines. It was a beauty! It had everything he wanted: a fly bridge and a cabin that slept four. The owner wanted just fifteen grand for it—a real steal! He'd managed to stash a bit of his ill-gotten proceeds by keeping the Shop in stolen checks for months. Dennis had saved almost thirty grand by now. He gave Chunk only 10 percent of his take on jobs, along with the quarters he found, so his take-home usually amounted to around seven or eight grand a pop (including the stolen check sales to Chuy). If his mother made him pay her ten thousand bucks now, buying that Sea Ray might be a stretch. Boy, he wanted that fucking boat bad!

"OK, Mom, but I have to figure out another job, a big one, before I can get it to ya, OK?"

"Thanks, my baby...just get me the dough in about three weeks. I gave you two life, *remember*!"

Dennis Fitch had already been thinking about his next job, one he had been told would be worth well over the seven or eight grand he was used to pulling in. Word was he might score as much as three times that if he timed it right. He had a mole in the place, someone who could give him a heads-up on the payroll schedule there, a onetime acquaintance: Stevie Rampling.

Rampling was employed by the state of California as a custodial technician, working at the California Department of Motor Vehicles office on Normal Street in San Diego. Dennis connected with Steve in a chance meeting at the Orange County Probation office six months earlier. Fitch was on summary probation and met with his PO only once. Fortune would have it that on that very day he sat next to his snitch. The DMV didn't really care that Rampling was on misdemeanor probation for a DUI. Hell, he never even told them. Over a beer that afternoon, Rampling told Big D where he worked, and Fitch knew he had his mole.

That DMV office was a licensing hub for San Diego, and Stevie owed him since Big D had scored Steve's high school girlfriend a fake Cal ID card through Chuy and the Shop. She was just seventeen and *hot*. Rampling complained he couldn't go clubbing with her. After hooking her up with her license to drink, Dennis dropped a dime on the janitor and reminded him of his debt.

Fitch trusted his newfound friend enough to ask him to do a couple of things: find out when payday there was and get him the name and model number of the office safe. Rampling bragged that he cleaned the manager's office every week, so that would be a cinch. Rampling wasn't stupid, though, and told Fitch that he figured Dennis would owe him back, should something happen with the tidbits of information he provided. Fitch promised to reward him if the information was ever used.

One week later, Rampling came through. He'd discovered that payday was the last Friday of every month, always on schedule. Employees came into the DMV to pick their checks up. Stevie had managed to see the big five-foot-high safe in the office (which was always locked, even during business hours). It was an Amsec model TL 30 safe. This was like music to Big D's ears! Todd Starnes's training taught him that although this safe was armored more than most, with a one-and-a-half-inch-thick steel door, it had the same S&G locking mechanism as most of the others he had dealt with. It would take longer to breach, but the time and muscle would be worth it.

Rampling estimated that, all told, this DMV office employed about forty employees, give or take a few. He also mentioned that all DMV offices take personal checks. Dennis had visions of thousands of dollars in cash and untold numbers of paper gold he could score on this one job alone. His Sea Ray yacht was a sure thing now!

On February 26, the Wednesday preceding the last Friday of the month, Dennis and James checked into the Motel 6 on Pacific Highway in San Diego. Dennis sat in the waiting room of the DMV office for more than two hours the next day, drinking it all in. He spied the location of the office and figured out where it was in relation to the back room, where Rampling told him he saw a roof access vent. Then, Big D watched all the people writing their checks, handing over lots and lots of cold, hard cash to the tellers. He smothered an erection.

After sitting down with his slow-witted brother and going over every small detail of the upcoming job, Big D told Chunk they'd have a prejob celebration. He took him to the Olive Garden on Carmel Mountain Road beforehand. They couldn't help but giggle throughout the meal since four months before he'd drilled open the safe in the back office there. Dennis told Jimbo it wasn't every day that the Garden actually paid for two meals—with interest!

There was no need to wait too late to begin the job. Dennis decided to break with tradition and start the job earlier than usual. Just after 8:00 p.m., Jimbo Gaylord nudged his Honda into the back of the Harbor Freight parking lot, almost directly across the street from the DMV office.

"Stay off the fucking video games, Chunk. Are we clear on that?"

"As a bell, bro. Remember to let me know you started walking and when you're comin' home, OK?"

"Got it, my brother...wish me luck."

Giving Chunk a thumbs-up, Big D, costumed in his disguise as a traveler, pulled his black Samsonite roller bag out of the parking lot and down the block across from his ultimate destination. As he approached the alley behind the DMV, the final remnants of sunlight deserted the sky. Darkness was this criminal's friend, and Dennis embraced it as he tossed the grappling hook up twenty feet to the rooftop.

This vent had a slide-bolt closure on it. Hmm. It had rivets on both the shaft and the vent...no problem. Both were drilled and knocked out.

As he cracked the lid open, ever so slightly, his small flashlight reflected off the brilliant white of the small alarm contacts protecting the place. Fitch thought to himself, "Fuckin' cheap California! Could've kept me out with an infrared."

The magnet disabled the sensor in place, and the cat burglar descended the ladder, dropping onto the floor of the file room right where Steve Rampart said he would be. Listening for the distinctive high-pitched whine of a tripped alarm, Big D heard only wonderful silence. He knew he was home free—no motion sensors.

Carefully looking around for dark ceiling domes or other security camera mounts, he spied neither. "Shit, the state is really cheap!" Continuing to scan for other motion detectors or cameras, Fitch crossed that wing of the building and found the office where Steve said it was. It was secured with a deadbolt lock.

Removing a mechanical lock-pick gun from his backpack, with a few squeezes of the trigger and a slight manipulation here and there, he turned the gun to the right and disengaged the bolt—the door swung open. The Amsec safe loomed large before him. It was one big motherfucker! It was designed to defeat 90 percent of all traditional attacks, but the state of California didn't know they were dealing with Todd Starnes, certified (almost) to crack these beauties by the Safe and Vault Technicians Association! Big D got right to work.

———

At 8:08 p.m., preparing to place a forkful of mashed potatoes in her mouth, Jeannie Metcalf paused. "Crap, I did it again!" Her husband looked up with a quizzical look as she confessed her sin.

"Dave, I gotta remember to set the damn alarm down there! This'll be the third time in a month, and Frank is getting pissed at me. Should I call him again or just go down there myself? I don't know; he's only three blocks away, and it'll take me thirty minutes. What should I do?"

"Look, Jean, just call him. He's marking time anyway, so an hour of OT for fifteen minutes of work isn't bad. Ring him."

Pulling her cell from her purse, the new DMV manager placed a call to one of her assistant managers, Frank Gilroy. "Hi, Frank, it's Jeannie. I know it's lame, but I did it again—forgot to set the damn alarm. I'll understand if you can't do it, but if you can, would you be a saint and go down there and take care of it for me? I'll owe ya big time!"

Frank Gilroy was in his twenty-second year as a California state employee. It was his second career, having spent twenty hard years in the US military. At sixty-four, it was no secret that Frank was retiring at the end of that year. He lived alone with his wife of forty-six years and his tabby cat, Herman.

"Jean, Jean, Jean…I know you're new to management, but hell, girl, you need to pay more attention! One of these nights, it may bite you in the butt," he said, chuckling. "I'm done with dinner and just sittin' around watching *Conan*. Yeah, boss, I'll head down there for you."

"Thanks, Frank. I owe you lunch."

———

Dennis Fitch had managed to place the template over the spot the dial used to be and had just begun drilling the thick steel plate protecting the inside mechanism. This safe had nearly an inch more of hardened steel to forge through with his drill. Less than half an inch in, his tungsten carbide bit snapped in two, causing Big D to lurch forward and damn near smack his forehead on the safe with the momentum. Picking up the broken piece of bit, he placed both pieces back into his bag and retrieved another.

Starting to drill again, he began pushing hard and steady on the chrome lever bar with his left arm. The vibration and burn inside his bicep caused a deep rivulet of sweat to run down the inside of his balaclava mask. He periodically had to stop his progress to wipe the stinging sweat from his eyes. Fitch was content. He had only about a quarter inch to go when the front lights of the DMV snapped on with a noticeable hum.

The previously confident crook spoke quietly into the microphone: "Fuck."

Chunk, alert and dutifully monitoring on the other end, broadcast, "Something wrong, bro?"

Dennis Fitch, now frightened, whispered, "Shut up. Someone's here."

Frank Gilroy heard a high-pitch whining sound after unlocking the door as he walked toward the light switches on the waiting room wall. Just after flipping on the switch, it went away. "Huh, maybe a printer was left on? Gotta check that."

Gilroy walked quickly toward the service area and into the hallway leading to the printer room, where the alarm pad was located. Frank was heading right toward the manager's office, where the office safe was located. As he began to pass the four-foot-high window to Jeannie's office, he stopped abruptly. There, against the safe door sat a high-speed drill with some kind of chrome bar attached to it. A drill bit stuck out of the safe, embedded firmly in a hole penetrating the door! "What the fuck!"

Almost concurrently with his whispered declaration, a large man in dark clothing, wearing a full face mask jumped up from within the doorway to Frank's left and punched him hard in the face. Frank staggered back but didn't fall.

Frank John Gilroy had spent his military career as an army ranger. Sixty-four years young, Frank was still muscled and fit. He regularly jogged and did cardio and weight training at the senior center. Frank was not a pansy. He quickly reacted to Big D's blow by regaining his footing. Gilroy nailed the crook with a roundhouse punch of his own. It caused Fitch to fall hard, flat on his back.

Now, fighting for his freedom, Fitch snapped to his feet, tackling Frank Gilroy, causing the pair to fall to the hallway floor. Blows were being freely exchanged as they rolled back and forth between the walls. At one point Gilroy got an arm-bar hold on the younger Fitch's neck, but a swift elbow to Gilroy's diaphragm ended that, and the pair rose to their feet simultaneously. A winded but determined Frank attempted another right cross to the safe burglar's jaw, but as he did so, a desperate Fitch hit him fast with a linebacker rush.

As Fitch was driving Mr. Gilroy rapidly backward, the back of Frank's skull was driven into the unmoving steel edge of the doorframe to the printer room. As the synapses of his brain faded, one by one, the last vision the army ranger had was of the black-masked face of his murderer.

"Brother, Dennis, what's happening? Answer up! Come back, come back!"

James Gaylord had heard the grunts and banging of the exchanged blows on the Motorola's speaker from the beginning of the struggle. He'd been calling his brother repeatedly, but this was the first time Big D could catch his breath and hear the frantic calls resonating from his accomplice. All the tough guy could manage to say was, "I gotta come home, *now!*"

Looking down at the floor where Frank Gilroy lay, a widening pool of thick dark-red fluid was oozing from behind his skull like dirty Quaker State flowing out of a hot oil pan. Fitch knew immediately that he'd graduated from master thief to murderer.

Scrambling in the office, he began throwing tools into his backpack. "It's stuck; it's fucking stuck!" Thoughts screamed through his racing mind as Fitch tried desperately to dislodge the drill bit, now firmly lodged in the steel door. As the crook struggled feebly to extract it, the tip broke off. The business end was embedded an inch inside the rapidly cooling steel of the door.

"Fuck it!" Big D's only thought was of escape now. A quick glance around, and he sped out of the office toward the file room. He made a point of not glancing at the man or the expanding red pool on the floor. In a flash, he was up the ladder, out the vent, and running back to where the hook was hanging on the parapet edge of the roof. Dennis slid down the rope so rapidly it singed his gloved hands. A quick jerk upward on the perlon, and the grapple fell to the asphalt, narrowly missing the burglar's skull. Retrieving the roller bag and donning his hat and fake glasses, he almost ran down the block while dressing. Dragging the roller bag quickly behind him, the wheels were off the ground more than they touched it.

After throwing the carry-on into the trunk, Dennis jumped inside the Honda. "DRIVE, just fuckin' drive, Chunk!" Big D sat there, rocking back and forth in the passenger seat, repeating, "Fuck no, fuck no. Goddamn, *no!*"

James Gaylord might have been slow, but he wasn't stupid. Although he glanced frequently at his brother, sitting silently now with his face covered by his hands, he dared not ask what had happened. There would be time for that later, with Mother.

After pulling into the driveway on Rhapsody Drive, Fitch, now exhausted, walked directly to his bedroom. Chunk entered last and was met at the door by Brenda.

"Where did Dennis go? What's the matter with you two?"

"I dunno, Mom, but something bad happened. D didn't tell me."

Walking to the door of her elder son's bedroom, she knocked.

"Dennis, *honey*, come out and talk to Momma. *Talk to me, son.*"

Exiting the door, Brenda saw his wet, red eyes, and taking Big D by the arm, she ushered him into the living room. They sat, knee to knee, on the couch. James Gaylord stood, half hidden in the kitchen doorway, with an ear cocked toward the room, eavesdropping.

"Mom…I fucked up. I don't know what to do. *I…I killed a guy tonight.*"

Chunk, now visibly shaking, turned and slowly walked away. His superhero was no more.

"Dennis, oh, Dennis, *how?* How did it happen? Did he try and hurt you? Oh, God, was it a cop?"

"No, not a cop. Some guy came in during the job, and…well, *he hit me first*. I had to do something. I fought back, and he hit his head on the door. It killed him, I think. I'm fucked!"

"Baby, baby, calm down, and listen to me. You're saying he started the fight. You didn't have a choice. You had to defend yourself, right? You'll get over this an' move on. Take a few weeks off; just relax a little. The heat'll die down, and the cops will get tired of looking for whoever did it."

"No, Mom, *I'm done*. I gotta leave, get the hell outta here. They'll find me. I know it."

"Son, you need to stay right here. This is just a hiccup. Listen to your momma. Stick it out. If you leave it'll look like you're runnin' from something, tryin' to cover up."

"Bullshit, I gotta go!"

"Son, if they show up, I don't know how long your brother and I can cover for you. You know how they are… I might have to give you up or lose the house. They could even take my dolls. No, you can't leave me!"

Dennis Fitch sat quietly as his mother stroked his sweat-soaked hair. After minutes of thick silence, he merely said, "OK, Ma."

Brenda Fitch rose slowly and shuffled toward the hallway. She paused before rounding the corner, turning back toward her son as she lit a cigarette. She took a long drag.

"Honey, I know it's a bad time and all...but do you think you could get me that three thousand to pay for the sewer fix?"

Raising his head from his hands, Dennis Fitch merely stared back in disbelief.

Chapter 5

THE DRILLER

Monday morning, just after nine, I got a call from Lieutenant Casey. Ron was one of those "shining star" promotees I mentioned earlier. Almost ten years my junior and already a lieutenant, he'd never worked criminal investigations. He was promoted out of narcotics, and after a year there they stuck him in CID for "career development." In our business that meant they wanted to raise him to the next pay grade as soon as the system would allow. I knew what Casey was calling about.

After inviting me into one of our interview rooms, he started it off. "Hi, Kevin, I need to talk to you about Detective Ocampo. I take it you know what happened last week?"

"I think everyone knows what happened last week, Lieutenant. I just don't know how this involves me."

"Kevin, you aren't the focus of the investigation, but I believe you're a witness, so, as you know, I must advise you of General Order 77-1, and I'll be recording our conversation."

Here it comes, the "you lie, you die" order! GO 77-1 says, in a nutshell, that I was being ordered to answer all his questions, and if I didn't do so, truthfully, I could be fired! Yeah, that little tidbit of information always makes a cop feel at ease! Not that I would lie, but the pits of my dress shirt started to moisten nonetheless.

"OK, Detective Rhinehardt, what do you know about the drinking habits of Luis Ocampo?"

"His drinking *habits*? I have no idea what you mean by the question. I've only had drinks a few times with Luis and always after work. Other than that, I have no idea what his habits are."

"It's no secret that a couple of months ago you two went on a binge. It's all over the detective bureau. Tell me about that."

"Binge, huh! Well, if you actually spoke to people in the bureau, you'd know that it was during the Phantom case, and I was under a lot of stress. Luis saw I wasn't doing so well and suggested we go out, *after work*, for a few beers. That's it."

"Did you get drunk? Did he get drunk?"

"We got happy, yes, but I was taken home by a very sober Ted Banner, and Luis took a cab home."

Shuffling his paperwork around, he looked at me and asked, "Have you ever consumed alcohol at work, detective?"

"*Hell no!* What reason do you have to ask me that question anyway?"

"I'm just doing my job. Do you know if Luis has been drinking at work?"

I was dreading this one…if I lie, I die. "I would have to say I believed he might have, one day last week…"

I went on to tell that cheese eater (cop slang for a rat) about the day I had smelled stale alcohol on Ocampo's breath. I felt like Judas Iscariot as I relayed the story. I made sure Casey knew that it was just a couple of days before his accident—one time—and that I believed his drinking must just have reached a crescendo for some reason I wasn't aware of. I made sure he knew of all the occasions Luis had been professional, all the times he'd assisted me with absolutely no hint of him having had a drink… about all the good work my friend had done.

By the bored look on Casey's face, he didn't give a shit about good work, only about getting his dirt. Our little chat lasted about thirty minutes. I walked out of the room soaking wet and pissed. For some reason I've felt that same way after speaking with the brass recently—not a good recipe for success!

At four thirty that same afternoon, I got a call from my son Jimmy's friend, traffic officer Ed Parker. My face turned crimson as he related that about an hour earlier he had witnessed Jimmy, in my truck, burning rubber out of the parking lot at the high school. He wrote him up for exhibition of speed. "I just wanted you to know." *Fuck you very much, Ed!* My mood couldn't have been any worse as I entered the door at home that evening, but my Julie managed to change all that.

"Tommy called! He's now in Paktia Province with the First Battalion. They're on some operation there named Anaconda. He's doing fine, and he sounded great. He wanted to wait to make the call, to get to speak to you, but they only get the SAT phone at certain times, and that was his. He wanted me to kiss you and give you all his love." She rushed up for a hug and a wet kiss.

My son Tom, now twenty-one, enlisted in the army just six months after 9/11. I must admit that his doing so scared the crap out of me, but it also swelled my chest with immeasurable pride along with the concern. I'm convinced that had I experienced an attack on my country, at his age and situation, I would be right there on the front lines as well. I chose to enlist in a different kind of war, right here at home.

"He said he missed my cookies! I'm sending another care package. Anything you want me to put in it?"

"I'll get a couple of movies for him...I know he'd like *Men in Black*, and maybe that new sci-fi movie with Mel Gibson...ah, what's it called?"

"Yeah, *Signs*. It's scary, I hear. About aliens, I think."

"Yeah, I know it's out on DVD. Maybe we can watch it first and then send it to him?"

Wagging a scolding finger my way, she retorted, "No way. We send it *unopened*, you cheap bastard!"

We sat chatting at the table, and I kissed her. God, I love that woman! All the crap I had put her through, and she still looked good for me at five o'clock! My mood was calm. I felt relaxed…until the front door opened and Jimmy came in! Him throwing his coat on the couch and my seeing it roll off onto the floor of the den was all that was needed to bring back the dark mood I'd had after my call from the CHP.

"Jim, get in here." He walked into the room with the look of a newborn baby on his face—all innocence.

"Is there something you want to tell Mom and me? Anything interesting happen after school today?"

"That asshole called and told you, didn't he?"

The top blew off my thermometer. "That *asshole*? You, my little friend, are the asshole. How the fu—" I caught myself before I used the *F* word. "How do you get off calling Ed by that name when all he did is call you out for burning rubber at the high school? Sorry, Julie, I forgot to tell you about this new ticket. I got wrapped up in hearing about our *other son*—you know, the one who loves us. Jim, this is it—give me your keys; you're done!"

Throwing the keys at my chest, my seventeen-year-old turned to storm off down the hallway but not before dropping this little gem on us.

"Tommy, Tommy—all you care about is Tommy! I'm here in hell while he's off being the hero somewhere! Just leave me alone. I'll get a ride to school from now on, and after graduation you won't hafta worry about me anymore. I'm getting the fuck outta here!"

Without thinking, I replied, "Don't let the door hit you in the ass on the way out!" The sound of his actual bedroom door slamming behind him send a shockwave through my senses. My head felt like it would explode.

It was silent and frosty around the dinner table that night. I regretted what I'd said but was too cowardly to speak up to make it right. I hoped that pride was the only thing standing in the way of an apology from my son, as well. Later, as I washed up for bed, I heard Julie sobbing into her pillow. Her fears had been realized: both our sons were separated from our family—Tom by his service, Jim by his attitude.

I couldn't take it; I grabbed a beer and sat alone in the lonely blackness of our living room. What had happened to my relationship with Jimmy? His rebellion and my lack of compassion and stubbornness were like an impenetrable wall that separated us. I missed and worried about Tom. My soldier always got me, but then I always had fun with Jimmy…finally, emotions prevailed, and my own tears flowed like rain upon the arm of the sofa.

Sleep was an evasive commodity that night, and I left early for work to get out of my personal war zone. Will Phillips and Bob Roberts approached my desk at 8:00 a.m. We needed to drive to the Orange County Sheriff's Department for an impromptu meeting of the burglary task force. They wanted Will and me there by 1:00 p.m.—we had to step on it.

We arrived with a scant fifteen minutes to spare, and that taco I stuffed down my gullet was acting like it wanted to see daylight again.

"Gentlemen, guys, ladies, please, take your seats...we need to get this rolling; we've got a lot to cover. My name is Lieutenant Sam Gilstrap, and I'm with Orange County sheriff. I've been put in charge of this task force, but in reality each of you will be working with a supervisor in the individual areas you will be assigned to investigate. Sorry to have y'all come on such short notice, but our crooks upped the ante four days ago when our driller killed a man at the San Diego DMV office during a job.

"Preliminarily it appears that the assistant manager...umm...a Mr. Gilroy, fought with our suspect and at some point died of a cerebral hematoma when his skull struck a door during the scuffle. The victim put up a helluva good fight...it was tragic he lost it. Mr. Gilroy could have saved all of us this damn get-together.

"Hitting a DMV employee is new territory for this guy since he normally sticks with fast-food places. At this point I want to turn the briefing over to Sergeant Chuck Stiles with the sheriff's office, who's in charge of the burglary end of things."

The sergeant shuffled to the lectern. "Good morning, everybody. We appreciate all of you making it here on such short notice. Every one of us has a stake in catching this asshole, 'cause he's hit places in every one of our cities and counties. So far we've tracked twenty-three burglaries of restaurants from San Diego and Orange to Santa Clara counties, all with similar MOs. Because of his unique trademark, we believe all these burgs have been done by the same person or persons.

"The Driller, as we're now calling him, knows his shit. He's good at defeating alarm systems, and he's a damn second-story man to boot! That's right, in several of the capers we've found scrape marks on exterior ladders and the edges of roofs, which make us believe he's using a hook—some type of grappling device—to climb up there. He likes vent entries but isn't afraid to breach doors or whatever stands in his way of getting to the offices where the safes are. He drills the safe and takes paper money, quarters, and always looks for checks: personal and payroll. The Driller must have a connection to another criminal syndicate, as well, because those checks are being passed, up and down California, by several other individuals. We'll talk about that end of things in a minute.

"He knows what he's doing, and none of us investigators have ever run across anyone doing it the same way. That's why our next speaker's here. I'd like to introduce Mr. Bill Edwards. I've come to know Bill very well recently. He's a retired LAPD burglary detective. He's one of us, and he's a recognized expert on safe and lock attacks. He's here to let us know what we're up against."

William Edwards, a burly, brusque gentleman of about sixty-five years, slowly rose from his chair and sauntered over to the lectern in the sheriff briefing room. His combed-back gray hair and neatly trimmed beard accentuated the modest yet distinguished suit he wore. His presence filled the room. Every investigator sat on the edge of his or her seat, poised to learn from his experience.

"Well, boys and girls, you can tell your grandkids that you helped catch the premier safe cracker working in America today...and rest assured, folks, we *will* catch him!" Edwards had everyone's attention by now.

"Just so that you know, crooks actually *did* crack safes, just like this...twenty years ago when I worked for LA. Back then, our criminals had style. Hell, nowadays they usually just *rip* a safe open, beat the crap out of it, and sometimes torch it. No finesse—just get in any way they can. They got no style. Not so with this Driller. This fellow takes pride in his work, but he's gotten sloppy.

"This DMV wasn't above his skill set. The lock was the same; the safe was just bigger, thicker. He just had to drill a little farther...he would have gotten away with this one, too, but the manager forgot to set the fuckin' alarm! The Driller should have checked and known that. Big mistake for him and our deceased victim. That poor guy came in to set the alarm, and it cost him his life. Hell, they told me the man was a vet and was just a few months out of retirement. What a shame. Our crook didn't stab him or shoot him. Our vic died in a fistfight. If I had to take a guess, I'd say our Driller isn't a killer at heart. I think our DMV man gave him a good fight, and the Driller was losing. I think our crook's scared now, so we've got to work fast. Now, write notes and take pictures, too, 'cause I'm going to give you all a show-and-tell on how he does it..."

Bill Edwards knew his stuff, showing us lever bars, drills, and the template our man was using to defeat the S and G locks. We got a class in safe cracking 101! He reiterated that this guy has received some training, either firsthand or by an accomplice who is a certified lock and safe man. All the equipment the perp carries was laid on a table in front of us, and quite frankly I couldn't believe the weight of it all! I mused earlier with Will that the guy must be the Batman—now I believed it! Mr. Edwards gave everyone his personal telephone number and told us all he would make himself available for any of us at any time.

During the break the twenty-some of us investigators became more acquainted. Many of the police departments, up and down the south and central coast, were represented. Lots of good guys and gals *but* lots of big egos to go with the badges. Seems many felt they should be heading the endeavor, running the show. We heard some real bitch biting! My protégé, young Will, drank it all in. We later discussed how this egomania plays out negatively during an investigation. Will had no ego (yet), so he was above the game at this point. I knew that Will would be the one primarily dealing with these others, so my ego (big as it is) didn't factor in. Probably a good thing.

We were mustered back up for the final speaker. Sergeant Randy "Moose" Moore stood before us in his Los Angeles sheriff polo shirt, emblazoned with "Sheriff" on the back, and "Gang Detail" on the front. Standing just my height, he had absolutely no neck, and his ripped biceps easily measured eight inches across! How did this dude have time to be a cop? He had to spend hours in the gym every day! His shaved head and the bulldog tattoo on his right outer forearm rounded out his image. He spoke without the prompting of notes.

"I represent the segment of the investigation handling all the paper being passed as a result of this dipshit's capers. Most of all of his checks are being passed by others, probably involved in a southland criminal organization. He's probably their biggest supplier. These dickwads are passing personal checks, stolen in mail thefts, in SoCal, too. That's how we know he's not the one in charge here, on the check side. The same wetbacks—oh, sorry—'undocumented immigrants'—are dropping washed paper from San Diego as far north as Sacramento County. They've passed about eighty grand worth so far. We got grainy photos of several of them as well as a pretty decent pic of one female Hispanic who had balls enough to pass paper at a small savings and loan in San Luis Obispo for over seven hundred bucks. We know they always carry California ID cards in the same names as those on the checks. The names sometimes correspond to the actual people the original stolen check is made out to, and sometimes the names and the checks are completely fictitious. The cards are so good, even the bank took one as legitimate ID. They must have a sophisticated setup to crank out these cards and must be using a primo program to duplicate the California DMV logos and so on. No doubt about it, folks: we need to find these fuckers.

"You may ask why my unit and other gang details will be involved in this task force. It's because we've reliable info that a criminal street gang—perhaps the OC Lopers—are involved in the bad-check end. It may even be Santanas—STS—since they hang with them. We get rumors from rival gang members about them, but so far we've come up empty for any firsthand info from any of the members themselves. Those bastards are wily. Whenever we surveil them, they make us. They must figure we have a bird in the air, too, 'cause when they figure it out, they always either drive to their homes or merely run back to their clubhouse...we need to know where this operation is being rat holed! Even when we bust 'em, they play stupid. Guess they figure doing a few months, even years, in the can isn't worth their lives or their family's safety. So far we got shit for good info, and we're pissed!"

Before we adjourned, all of us were assigned to work a different part of the investigation. Will and I would help out on the safe-burglary end of things. Everyone agreed to indoctrinate their respective patrol counterparts so that we could have eyes on the streets and lots and lots of FIs (field interviews) to provide us leads to follow. We were reminded that our Driller was no longer just a romantic character, a beloved crook like Robert Wagner played in *To Catch a Thief*—we were hunting a killer.

Chapter 6
"YA GOTTA PRODUCE."

For days following the murder of Frank Gilroy, the Driller, now a killer, kept to his room. Brenda served catered meals to her favorite boy. She accommodated his mood because her son finally handed her $10,000 to shut her the fuck up.

James Gaylord moped around Brenda Fitch's home like a troll hiding under a moldy bridge. Chunk was uncharacteristically angry at his brother, who'd fallen off the pedestal he normally occupied. More than once, the lumbering sibling had stood at Dennis's door, wanting to knock. He had no nerve to lose, so he always walked away. Today, the guy he used to worship came out and went to the kitchen for a Coke. Chunk seized his chance.

"Brother, we need to talk. I got sumptin' to say."

"Not in the mood, Chunk…catch me later."

"No, it's now. You fuckin' killed a guy! How could you do that, Dennis? You did it and didn't even apologize to me. Never said why! I'm screwed, too, ya know. They'll lock me up for what *you* did. Don't you care 'bout me at all?"

Forced out of his gray mood like a rubber band was snapping him on his arm, Dennis Fitch went on the offensive. "You're pissed at *me*? What a goddamn joke! Didn't you happen ta see that guy friggin' drive into the parking lot? Didn't you think to let me know he was coming? You fucking idiot! He caught me off guard. I could've maybe gotten out before I had to fight him. I could've avoided the entire fucking thing...*but no*. You were probably playing with yourself or something, weren't you?"

"Brother, I looked up an' saw it was just a normal car pulling in. I figured he was just parkin' there to make a call or somethin'. It wasn't a cop, so I didn't think it was a danger to you. The car was parked weird, so I never saw him get out of it...I'm sorry, D, but I wasn't the one who killed the dude—it was *you*! Now we're both fucked, man!"

Dennis Fitch grabbed his larger brother by the front of his shirt and threw a heavy fist into his face, causing Chunk to stumble back and fall against the kitchen counter. Instead of cowering, as was his first instinct, James Gaylord picked up a nearby plate and hurled it directly at Big D. It struck him hard in the chest and knocked the wind out of him. Perhaps because of this, or perhaps because the struggle resurrected images of the DMV fight, Dennis Fitch ceased his angry response. Dropping his clenched fist to his side, he bowed his head and began sobbing loudly.

"I'm sorry, Chunk. I'm sorry. I never wanted to kill that guy. I hit him first; he was only protecting himself. I never wanted anyone to get hurt. Please, please, believe me. I don't know what to do anymore, man. I'm done."

Having been emotionally stifled by both Dennis and his mother for so long, Chunk Gaylord just stood there, mute. He could see that Big D was suffering, but although inside he felt he should react, he just didn't care anymore. Thinking to himself, the lunky brother mused, *He wants me to feel sorry for him. FUCK HIM! He gives me nothin' for all the driving, for all the watchin' I do. Thanks for nothing, for the fuckin' quarters, brother! No, I gotta walk away. Just walk.* And that's what James Gaylord did; he just turned and walked out of the house.

Hearing the commotion from outside, Brenda Fitch waddled back inside to find her sobbing elder son. "What's going on now, Dennis? Did you and Chunk fight or somethin'?"

"Nah, Ma, don't worry. No one's hurt."

"What about this mess here? I suppose you want me to clean it up, don't ya?"

Drying his eyes, Dennis continued, "Mom, I don't know what to do. I can't go back to doin' safe jobs; I just know they'll catch me now. I have some money set aside, but it won't last long. Maybe it's best if I just get outta California, go somewhere alone, and start new. I could probably go back to it, maybe in Arizona or even

Colorado! Hell, at least I can get decent dope there," he said, chuckling.

"Look, baby, I already told ya, the heat on you'll cool down soon enough. Once a body gets cold, those damn cops will just move on to the next killin'. If you stay away from those burger joints, an' don't get caught out at night for a while, you'll be just fine. My daddy always told his kids, 'You just can't mooch off your kin; ya gotta produce. You hafta contribute.' Same here. You just need to find something else you're good at...you're a smart boy; just figure it out!"

Dennis Fitch made a call two days later. "Yo, Chuy. We need to talk, so meet me at the place at six tonight."

Right on time the pair sat in Chuy's Camaro, listening to some kind of weird Mexican rap CD the gangster had blaring over his Bose speaker system. Chuy didn't waste any time.

"Waz up, homie? I see you got into some shit down in Diego. *Lo siento*, Big D. Guess I ain't getting no checks no time soon, right, *ese*?"

"Yeah, I gotta lay low. Don't know for how long, either, so what can I do that'll kick me down some cash? I can't live for long on what I got stashed. I gotta help support my mom, and you don't wanna know how much of a bitch she can be! Help an amigo out."

El Gerente let out a slow laugh...looking around, he gave Dennis an interesting proposal.

"Ever use a skimmer...you know, for credit cards?"

"You mean like at the market when I buy shit?"

"No, shithead, the sneaky kind. You can steal a dude's information using one. Wait, I'll show ya..."

Getting out of the car and strolling to the back, Jesus Santiago lifted the trunk lid. Under the mat, beneath the spare tire, he retrieved a locked plastic box. Taking two of the small devices from within, he neatly tucked the container back under the tire in the stash spot and returned to the waiting Fitch.

He handed the Driller a small black plastic object, about one-third the size of a pack of cigarettes. "Put the fuckin' thing in the palm of your hand...do it. See, when it's there, no one can see it. You can slide a card through, and nobody's the wiser. Motherfuckin' thing holds about a thousand card numbers in its memory. You gotta love fuckin' China! Ya just hook it up to a PC with a USB and download the numbers. I got lots of people willing to pay for those fuckin' numbers, too, amigo. Now, only question is, *you* gotta figure out how to use it, but I'll buy the numbers from you. Want in, *ese*?"

Fitch examined the small device, his brain processing it all. "Yeah, Chuy, can I have these two, and maybe more later, but I'll start with two. Give me a couple o' weeks to figure out what I wanna do with 'em, but I think I may come up with a way to use them. How much you paying for numbers I get?"

El Gerente stroked his goatee. "Hmm, you're a good dude. I'll pay you fifty bucks a number."

"A hundred…c'mon, Chuy, you got the money."

"OK, eighty—no more, or I take the fuckin' things back!"

"Deal!"

After a high-five, Dennis Fitch traveled back to Seal Beach to plan his next move. He had lots of planning ahead of him, too, since this new caper didn't involve drill bits and brute strength! He was glad that it wouldn't involve Chunk. After their last encounter, he had no desire to include the retard in his plans. Big D felt that man's blood laid squarely on his brother's hands. This rationalization allowed him to make plans, to produce once again.

Two days later, twenty-six-year-old Sarah Wilson, assistant manager for Carl's Jr. on Newport Boulevard in Costa Mesa, walked to her car after closing. As she approached her car, she saw a small white envelope stuck under the driver's-side windshield wiper. Opening it, she found a typewritten note:

> *You don't know me, but I know you. I have a business proposal for you that could help you raise that little girl of yours. It's easy money. If you aren't interested, thanks, and you won't hear from me again. But if you want to make some money, just leave this empty envelope on your windshield tomorrow, and I'll be back in touch.*

It was signed "*A Friend.*"

Dennis Fitch had spent the better part of a day in and out of the Carl's Jr. in question. He could see Sarah was the night assistant manager, and her name and picture were proudly displayed on the wall as being part of the store's management crew. The night before he placed the note on her car, he had seen her walk to her VW in the parking lot. The next afternoon, before typing his business proposal out, he managed to see some elementary-school papers with the name Tammy Wilson written on the top, strewn about the station wagon's backseat. Two plus two equals *bingo*. He banked on Sarah being a single mother, but either way, a low-paid fast-food manager could always use some extra green.

The next afternoon at 5:00 p.m., Big D found the empty white envelope tucked under the wiper, and he knew he had a fish on the line. The next night another envelope, sealed shut with tape, sat in the same spot for young Sarah to retrieve. She read it with trembling hands:

Sarah, you've made the right decision. Look on top of the right rear tire. You will find another bigger envelope with a small black device in it. Take it and place it in the center of your left palm. See how small it is and how it's hiding in there! That's where you'll hold it to use it. I know that you work the register a lot at night…keep doing that. When a customer hands you a credit card to swipe at your register, take it quickly behind the screen. Don't look nervous. Quickly pass the magnetic strip on the card first through the slot on the black box in your palm, just like you do on a normal scanner, and then quickly lift and scan it a second time as usual through your terminal. Then hand the card right back to the customer. Make sure you always put your back to the video camera that is pointed toward the register. What your boss doesn't see can't hurt you!

No one will use the number from the credit card for at least two weeks, so the person and the cops won't be able to figure out where the number was taken from. Now the best part! For every number you scan into your little black box in the two weeks we will work together...you get $20! You scan a hundred, you get $2,000 cash. More numbers, you get even more. I know you usually scan at least thirty cards a shift, so imagine how much money you can get for your family in two weeks! Christmas presents, a new car—it's all yours!

Now, if you don't want to do this, just leave the box on the back tire tomorrow when you come to work, and you will never hear from me again. If you make the unfortunate decision to tell your boss or the cops about this, your family will hear from me. If you keep the box, I expect it left on the same tire two weeks from tomorrow, or you'll hear from me again. When I check it and see how many numbers you have, I will pay you the very next day.
—*Your Friend*

The young Ms. Wilson was excited but very frightened. Her boss had fired a girl for taking cash from the till a month ago, so he sure as hell would fire her for doing this! She could even get busted! But this did look like easy money because she could see how easily she could pull it off. At night they usually worked understaffed, so she worked at the counter all alone. The others were scrambling to put together orders and never came up there much. Wow, $2,000 or more! She made only $8.75 an hour now. She began rationalizing it immediately in her mind. *It's just one time. They won't know I did it. The credit-card company will pay the customer back, and they couldn't care less about a few bucks anyway—after all, they're gazillionaires!*

The next afternoon at 4:50 p.m., Fitch was watching with a set of binoculars from across the street as Sara Wilson's car drove into the Carl's Jr. parking lot. She got out, glanced back and forth, and walked straight into the restaurant while tightly clutching her purse. She went nowhere near the back tire. The hook was set. All he had to do was wait two weeks to see how big a mackerel he'd landed!

However, after the young woman walked away with his skimmer, the normally confident Big D started to worry. The seed of doubt, that fear of arrest, all hovered in his cerebrum like the Goodyear blimp floating over the Super Bowl. He had thoughts of never coming back to the Carl's Jr., just walking away. Shit, he'd pay Chuy for the damn skimmer—no harm, no foul.

Then he remembered how much pressure Mommy Dearest was putting on him to produce for the Fitch clan. His love/hate relationship with the family's matriarch made him feel conflicted. Then, what about Chunk? As pissed as Dennis was at his brother, he knew he had to take some responsibility for his support as well. He'd been his brother's sole employer for almost a year. *Shit. What am I gonna do?*

Two weeks after leaving the skimmer on Sarah Wilson's back tire, he was in his spot across the street from the restaurant when he saw her drive her worn Volkswagen station wagon into the lot. She didn't hesitate. Walking to the right rear of her car she placed a small package on the right rear tire. Big D had already come up with a plan.

About an hour earlier, Dennis Fitch cruised a nearby strip mall. He knew what he was looking for, and it didn't take him long to find it. *It* was a fifteen-year-old boy— long-haired, dressed in tattered jeans, and riding a skateboard up and down a sidewalk, passing "No Skateboards Allowed" signs and signaling his disregard for the rules. *Yeah, he's my guy!*

Once the delinquent stopped for a smoke, Fitch made his play.

"Hey there, you wanna make some money?"

"Fuck you, man. I ain't into that kinda shit!"

"No, man, I don't mean any kind of sex crap...I'm not into that either. I'm talking about you making a hundred bucks for just walking over there and picking up some-thing for me. That's it."

"Look, man, the narcs are heavy as shit around here, and I ain't gonna get busted for pickin' up your dope!"

"I swear it isn't dope; it's just a small thing in a bag. Nobody's watchin'. I just can't be seen picking it up; that's all."

"You swear that's it…lemme see the money."

Fitch displayed a Ben Franklin and snapped it in front of the kid. The delinquent's eyes widened.

"So what do ya want me to do?"

Ten minutes later the young delivery boy skated through the Carl's Jr. and up to the ugly VW. As though he did it every day, he walked by and quickly scooped up the package. He threw the board down and was off in less than fifteen seconds. *Easy money, dude.*

Back at the strip mall, the bag was quickly exchanged for the bill, and the young entrepreneur mouthed, "Hey, man, anytime you need something, I'm here for you, man. Want my cell number?"

As Big D walked to his Miata, looking over his shoul-der, he replied, "Nah, dude, we're cool."

Fitch met two hours later with his gangbanger cocon-spirator, who conveniently brought a laptop containing special Chinese software. When the USB plug connected the skimmer to the PC, the program opened and…

"Holy shit, my man! You got a hundred an' twenty-three in here—man, you did good!"

Rather uncharacteristically, Chuy Santiago seemed eager to peel off a lot of hundred-dollar bills and one fifty. Fitch's eyes widened as the wad grew bigger and bigger. Counting quietly, the Driller found that the Mexican's count was right: $9,850. Chuy even rounded up the payment by ten bucks! *Thanks, amigo!*

Once the cash was in Dennis's hot palm, the Driller told Chuy, "And I'm going to need two more skimmers right away. I think I can get you at least two to three hundred numbers every two weeks from now on."

Looking wide-eyed at the Driller, El Gerente laughed and said, "*Si, mon.* You one bad motherfucker!"

Santiago didn't bother to tell Fitch that he already had overseas buyers for all the hot credit card numbers he provided. He kicked Big D down eighty bucks a pop, and his European partners paid STS two hundred a number. Not much overhead for a 140 percent profit! It's all business, you know! It was a no-brainer for El Gerente, since STS had none of the risk and took in the majority of the profit.

Those numbers could garner the recipients upward of five hundred thousand in stolen goods and services. The credit card companies, not the customer, normally paid the loss, so who cared, right? Unfortunately, customers and merchants using the credit card services really did pay since their fees went up along with the company's losses due to credit card thefts. The APR a company charged the customer depended on their profit *and* their loss. The gazillionaires want to stay that way.

Dennis Fitch traveled straight home after his meeting with Santiago. He found James Gaylord on the back porch playing a video game.

"Chunk, I been thinking."

"Yeah, 'bout what?"

"Well, I know you didn't mean to mess with me at the DMV. It wasn't your fault what happened. Do you want to help me on some other jobs?"

Chunk Gaylord seemed to have grown a few more brain cells because he was now suspicious of his brother's motives. "Why do you need my help NOW? I don't work for chump change no more, Dennis. Maybe I don' wanna work for you no more."

Dennis Fitch wasn't prepared for his brother to grow a pair of balls and question his offer. Big D realized that the only person taking a risk during his new credit-card-skimming scam was the one placing the notes and placing and picking up the skimmers. It was actually the only time an actual person was visible. Dennis had decided to use his dumb brother as this front person. If he ever saw Chunk get picked up, he could have time to make his escape. Might as well keep it in the family, and considering he was now ready to put the credit card plan into full operation, he needed regular help and didn't want to trust teenage skaters to do his dirty work and not dime him off to the police.

"Look, I'll pay you a thousand bucks a month if you help me. All you do is put some notes on cars and pick things up. Nothing else, Chunk! No driving, no late nights, and it will only take about an hour a couple times a week...not bad money for not a lot of work, right, brother?"

James Gaylord wanted the elder Fitch to sweat a little despite the fact that he already knew he'd do it. "Let me think about it."

Big D said, "You only got an hour; the job starts *today*."

At eight o'clock that evening, under the cover of darkness, a slouching, shuffling Chunk Gaylord walked the long way from the mall across the street and into the corner of the Carl's Jr. lot. The elder Fitch had held Chunk back since he kept seeing Sarah Wilson walk to the window to check on her car. James placed a gray envelope containing $2,460 on the top of the right rear tire and quickly walked away. Right as rain, thirty minutes later Sarah Wilson went to her car and nonchalantly walked to the trunk side. She retrieved the envelope and looking around, ducked down to open it. Afterward she quickly stashed it inside the car and jogged back into the business. Fitch thought he saw her skip a couple of times along the way! Everyone left happy.

Dennis Fitch's new full-time job was to scout fast-food places from San Diego to Los Angeles counties. He liked LA, despite the fact the drive was farther, since Los Angeles County had so many burger and burrito places! He'd do his homework, look for assistant managers under thirty, and try to figure out something about them for a hook. He'd concoct notes similar to that left for Ms.

Wilson. Of course his dimwitted brother was the messenger, and for a change, Chunk seemed to do his job well. Got pretty slick at it, too! Every time, Big D scouted the surroundings for prying eyes and the telltale signs of undercover cops—pastel-colored cars with stubby antennas, guys with short beards, occupied cars with two people inside, just sitting and watching—and he'd drive off if he spotted anyone remotely resembling the profile. Fitch was just paranoid, though, because he chose his participants well, and the cops never had a clue. Big D, at the end of the first month, had three skimmers in place, with a plan for the fourth. He was in his element—he was producing.

That first month, Dennis Fitch, through El Gerente, earned a whopping $19,450. He paid out $4,860 of that to his "participants" and another thousand to his brother. Chunk, living up to his handle, had no fucking idea how much cash his disingenuous sibling was making. Chunk took his grand, without questioning his brother—for the time being.

Chapter 7
GOYAKOD

"I don't understand it, Kev. The guy just stopped. He was doing at least one job a week, now *nada*? It's been almost three weeks now! He's disappeared off the radar."

The question from my newbie partner seemed almost nonsensical to me. Hmm, he kills a guy, almost gets caught. Gee, I wonder why he's laying low?

"He's gone underground, William. He probably took off. He beat feet, took a powder, is on the lam...do I need to draw you a friggin' picture, partner?"

"I just got excited about working this case, and I guess I'm frustrated. Got to admit it, Rhino, I'm having trouble concentrating on my other cases."

I hadn't been paying close enough attention to my young friend. I'd been immersed in my own caseload. I was working an attempted-murder case involving a father suspected of shooting his own son and had hot leads on a string of residential burglaries. Despite my own caseload,

I should have seen that my trainee was struggling. After all, that was my job. My head just hadn't been in the game lately, with worries about my friend Luis and dealing with a rebellious offspring at home. Excuses are like assholes, though—everyone has one, and they all stink!

"Gosh, Willy, let's sit down and figure this out...Dad will hold your hand!"

Phillips gave me the look and sarcastically replied, "Gee, thanks, *Papa!*"

Each morning a detective gets a stack of new case reports dropped in his inbox. It's the worst on Mondays. It's his or her job to wade through that paper and figure out what, if anything, needs to be done to clear them out. Will had about fifteen reports he hadn't even looked at! Not a good practice to get into. I once worked with a guy, Brian Nesbit, who was assigned to work burglary cases. Thank God I was not his field-training officer because Nesbit lasted only six months.

Seems he was just sticking the mundane paperwork in his bottom desk drawer—you know, the cases that didn't excite him. The sarge kept asking him what was happening with them, and Ol' Nes just kept okeydokeying him! Well, Bob Roberts took care of the problem in short order. Nesbit was back pushing a black-and-white in just six months. Without fanfare, Brian's detective position was being flown again. He should've gotten off his fat ass and taken care of business!

Cases aren't solved by sitting on your butt, talking on the telephone, or surfing the Internet—they're solved by burning shoe leather! We call it GOYAKOD (Get Off Your Ass and Knock On Doors). Nesbit never left his desk. His shoes were like new. I didn't want Will having to wear his old Sam Brown gun belt again until he wanted to!

I rolled my chair next to his workstation. "OK, let's see what you got, Lil Willy!"

We read the reports together—mostly burglaries with no obvious leads. I laid my pearls of wisdom on him on how to run a caseload.

"Separate your cases; I have a 'leads' box and a 'shit cases' box. Perhaps use the words 'no leads' instead of 'shit'—only a suggestion. You work the ones you see have leads, and you put the shit cases on the back burner.

"Call the victims up; see if they suspect anyone. Many times victims themselves know whodunit. Do they have teenage kids? Have they or their children hosted a party recently, or were there any new people over in their houses that might have scoped out their valuable stuff? Have they changed gardeners or housekeepers recently? If the victim can't help, go canvass the neighbors to see if anyone saw anything. Go over the forensics reports…were there any prints found? Look at the pictures. Is there any parolee or probationers, with a drug or theft history, living nearby? You may be surprised at what stands out.

"Be creative; think outside the box. Once you shake the trees a bit and nothing falls out, don't fuck around—suspend the case. Move on if you can't work it right away. You can always reopen it. You need to access each case independently, but don't waste time on dead enders… if you don't close them out, they haunt you like a missed house payment. Sometimes forever; just ask Brian Nesbit!"

My partner spent a few hours reviewing and prioritizing his caseload. I could see that he understood the routine. Phillips then went out in the field to burn up some of that shoe leather, so I began writing a search warrant on my 664/187 (attempted murder) case. I was in a fairly good mood, until I spied Ron Casey. The new CID lieutenant was walking through the bureau, chitchatting with unwitting personnel, with that fake, shit-eating grin plastered all over his face.

Did I hate this guy because he worked Luis's IA or just because I figured he was a dickhead? One might never know. Casey had made his rounds in here for about two weeks, picking out guys and gals to "interview" about Ocampo. Word was the internal affairs case was done and in the sheriff's hands.

Our lieutenant slithered into Bob Roberts's office and closed the door. We could see in through the louvered blinds, and at one point I saw Sarge look down for more than a few seconds. I figured he didn't like what he was hearing. After about fifteen minutes, Casey left the office. Roberts closed the door behind the lieutenant and shut his blinds. I waited twenty minutes, and then knocked on his door.

"Come on in."

"Bob, I saw Casey in here. We hear the IA's done. Can you tell me what's goin' on?"

"Well, Rhino, I'm not supposed to say, but it's going to be announced this afternoon. Luis is getting a one-month suspension and demoted back to patrol."

Despite this bad news, I was relieved.

"Well, Bob, I suppose that's better than what could have happened. I don't know what Luis and Tammy would have done if they canned him. God, he hasn't worked patrol for years…do they even make an XXL-size gun belt?" Our laughter broke the dark mood in the room.

"Damn, Casey wanted him gone. And I don't mean just from the bureau."

I could feel my face heat up. "What? Are you telling me he wanted Billingsly to fire Luis?"

"Yeah, he told me that outright. It was his recommendation. He even implied I should have paid more attention to him—nipped the drinking in the bud. He figured I should have found and addressed his problem myself. And you know, maybe I was in denial, maybe he's right. I got a whiff of booze off him one day myself. He wasn't acting drunk, so I just put the thought away. I let Luis down, I guess."

"Bob, we all let him down. Remember, no one twisted his arm; he screwed that up all on his own. I am just so thankful he won't be leaving us!"

Just like Bob had predicted, a memo came out from the Sheriff two hours later:

To All Sheriff Personnel:
    Effective immediately, Detective Luis Ocampo is reinstated to his permanent status of Sheriff

Deputy. Deputy Ocampo is reassigned to the South Coast Patrol Division effective 5/1/2002 and should contact his division commander for assignment.
Todd Billingsly, Sheriff/Coroner

Then we got the rest of the story through the normally accurate sheriff's grapevine. Luis was suspended for thirty days and had to report to Operations Chief Deputy Walters on a regular basis. The chief had been assigned by the Sheriff to be Ocampo's probation officer. I had gotten to know Chief Sam Walters quite well during the Phantom case. He oversaw patrol and investigations, and, to put it mildly, he could be a real prick. He had been all over me during that case, like stink on shit! His ranting had almost given me an ulcer.

Walters put the pressure on all of us. He wanted me off the case and berated us every chance he got. The only saving grace was that we heard the Sheriff chewed his ass over a little mishap we had during one of the arrests. I'd rather not talk about it. Just check out the *LA Times* article; it makes for interesting reading.

I knew the Sheriff's decision in the IA would hit Luis hard. I planned to go visit him soon to commiserate, but now wasn't the time. An open wound like this needed time to heal.

About 4:30 p.m. Detective Phillips came back from an afternoon of pressing shoe leather to pavement. He'd developed a few leads. I found out that the boy could actually work on one case and think about another at the same time. Wow, quite a desirable investigative trait! I've known cops who couldn't talk and chew gum at the same time. Will wasn't one of them. I surmised I'd taught him well (taking credit where none was due).

Will came to me with an idea for follow-up on his Driller cases. He told me he intended on calling Bill Edwards, the safe expert. Will wondered if Edwards might turn him on to a contact with the Safe and Vault Technicians Association to explore who might have received safe training in the last twelve months. Since the Driller obviously knew his stuff, maybe Will could get a lead to identify the crook through the people who might have trained him. It was a long shot but worth the effort. Wearing a stunned expression on my face, I sarcastically encouraged my protégé.

"Holy crap—*Will Phillips has a brain*! Actually, it's a good idea, partner. Let me know if I can help. My boy, I think you've got the hang of this detective thing!"

———

"Edwards Safe-and-Lock, how may I direct your call?"

"This is Detective Phillips from Santa Barbara Sheriff; can I speak to Mr. Edwards? Tell him it's about the case he's helping us on."

After being placed on a quick hold, Will recognized the deep throaty drawl as the call was picked up. "Hello, Bill Edwards here."

"Hi, Mr. Edwards, it's Will Phillips from Santa Barbara SO; do you remember me?"

"You're the new guy, right?"

"Well, not *so* new, but yes, that's me."

"How can I help you, lad? Have you broken the case yet?"

Will detected a chuckle on the other end.

"No, sir, but I hope you can help me do just that. I'd like to try to find out how many safe technicians have been schooled in the last twelve months within California. I figure this guy probably had some recent training. You said he must've, so if I can contact these companies I might just figure out who trained our Driller."

"Well, I'll tell you that a certified locksmith must be licensed with the Bureau of Security and Investigative Services. But, you know, when they do that, they run a criminal history on all the applicants, detective. Our Driller must not have had a prior criminal history, or he somehow scammed the Live Scan background-check process. That's doubtful. However, BSIS certifies only those who actually apply for their final license. I know many people that have received training and either didn't do well, didn't finish, or for whatever reason dropped out before they were licensed. Those folks normally can't buy equipment, though, without a BSIS card. Maybe you need to check on those folks. It might be a start, don't you think?"

Edwards provided Phillips with a total of four lock and safe training academies statewide. Over the next week,

Will diligently contacted each school. Every company kept files on their trainees, along with file photos taken for identification purposes—bingo! Problem was, between the four schools there were forty-two dropouts over the last year! Forty-two potential suspects, spread all over California. I suggested that Will contact BSIS and find out if any of these forty-two had gone on to get licensed with them—after all, if they bothered starting a training curriculum, maybe they finished the course with someone else.

My hunch paid off, and Phillips was able to whittle down his list to thirty-one. Of that number, sixteen claimed a residential address south of San Francisco. Since our Driller had concentrated his crimes within that geographical area, my partner decided to start making contact with those sixteen. Will had other cases to work, too, so this follow-up would take some time and effort. Talk and chew gum, partner; talk and chew!

Three days after the Ocampo memo came out, I knocked on Luis's door. Tammy answered. "Hi, Kev, he's in the back watching TV. I suppose you wanna talk about what's been going on? He's pretty down, just to let ya know. We're managing."

Tammy Ocampo led me back to Luis, who was still in his pajamas, seated in a threadbare Barcalounger. He was watching *The View*. A cop watching Joy Behar and Whoopi Goldberg had to be depressed! I was worried.

"So, Louie, I saw the memo. How're you doing, *really?*"

"Rhino, I guess it could be worse, right? I knew Casey was gunnin' for me when we spoke. As far as he was concerned, I was an embarrassment, and maybe he's right. Since I lost my mom, things just haven't been right. Tammy's great, but man, I miss her so much. She raised me alone…was always there for me. Now, she's gone. This would've hurt her."

Luis choked up, and I switched off the TV. "Lou, I never knew you were so close to your mother. You never even shared that she'd died. She must have been a great lady. When did she pass?"

"About two months ago. I was her only kid. My father left us when I was just two. Momma worked two and sometimes three part-time jobs to raise me when I was growing up. When I was thirteen, some buddies tried to jump me into Sur 13 in Stockton, and she basically kicked their asses right out of my life. She kicked my butt for even thinkin' about joining a gang. I admit it—I was more afraid of her than I was of those assholes!

"After I got out of the army, she pushed me to go to college. When I joined the SO, she bragged to all her friends. Last two years the diabetes got worse, and she lost a leg. She died at home, all alone, Kevin. I should have been with her that day! When I close my eyes, I can still smell her homemade tamales." Luis began to sob.

After a couple of minutes, I asked, "So is that why you started hitting the bottle at work? Man, just before you had your crash, I smelled it on you, and Biff and I were going to give you a back-to-Jesus...but you beat us to the punch. I'm sorry we didn't talk sooner, Louie; I'm really sorry."

"I don't know if it would've helped. You knew I liked to drink, Kevin—you *know* I liked to drink. I just always kept it after work; hit the hooch at home. After Mom passed, I just wanted to be numb. I didn't care. I almost lost it all, man, but prayer works! I never prayed to the Man so hard in my life. Mom would have been proud! A month without a paycheck will be tough, but I have a good woman, and we'll get through this. I'm done drinking, too, baby!" Luis looked toward Tammy as he said this. "I figure if I do good back on patrol, and a year passes, I can reapply for the bureau. Hell, you'll probably be king shit there by then—put a good word in for me! I think the hardest part will be havin' to report to Walters. He told me he's gonna have me piss in a cup anytime he wants. I have a feeling I better keep my bladder full!"

Laughing, Luis perked up. I made him promise to shower up, put some real clothes on, and never, ever watch that friggin' *View* again! Having to pay a $2,000 court fine, on top of losing pay, would affect his savings, but Ocampo would survive. Interestingly, his yearlong driver's license suspension came with this clause: "Probationer may ONLY operate a motor vehicle in the performance of his official duties." Thanks to Sheriff Billingsly, the judge agreed to that unusual exception. Tammy drove him to and from work. At night he attended AA meetings and met with the department psychologist as well. I knew my friend—his mom would make sure his drinking days were over! She'd raised a good son, after all.

Chapter 8
DON'T NEED NO WEAK LINKS

"Where's my numbers, *ese?*"

Jesus Santiago sat in his Camaro at 3:00 p.m. in the busy industrial parking lot in Santa Ana. Dennis Fitch sat nervously in Chuy's passenger seat, while a bright-eyed twenty-year-old Hispanic chica sat attentively behind him, watching. Fitch glanced back at her suspiciously.

Chuy pointed a finger her way and said, "She's with me. Yoli, *saludos a* Big D (say hi to Big D)."

"*Hola, como esta?*"

"*Bien.*" Fitch waved back at her, and cocking his head toward the new addition, he gave Santiago a quizzical look.

"She's cool. She's hanging wit' me. She's one of my runners." Then he added, "She don't speak much English but gives one helluva blowjob, if you know what I mean!"

Both chuckled as they continued their business, and Yolanda Tafoya understood that word that El Gerente used quite frequently—when they were alone in the backseat of his Camaro.

"So, I ask you again, *ese*, where's my fuckin' numbers? You ain't brought me shit for the last two weeks. What's the matter; you go on vacation or sumthin'?"

"Man, I dunno what happened, but in the last two weeks I've had problems getting people to cooperate. And, well, one dude hasn't even returned the skimmer."

"Say what? My shit's *gone*? It's hangin' out there somewhere? I think you're fucking with me, dude. Maybe you're calling in the numbers yourself. Maybe you're thinking I won't care. You goin' 'round me, *pendejo*?"

Santiago quickly pulled a chrome nine-millimeter pistol from under his plaid Pendleton shirt and pointed it directly at Big D's balls as he sat next to him.

Throwing his hands up, Dennis exclaimed, "Whoa! Whoa, Chuy. I'm not fucking with you; I'm just in a slump. Havin' trouble getting you numbers. I'm workin' on it. I promise by next week I'll be back on track. I promise!"

Fitch quickly exited the car, and the perky Latina hopped into the warm spot left behind. Chuy uncharacteristically chirped the tires as he drove out of the lot. Fitch knew he had problems now. He had to trust Santiago, but working with him was like petting a pit bull for the first time. He wags his tail, but you know he might take off a finger (or worse) if you look at him the wrong way! Big D was a killer, but he'd never carried a gun. The Driller was rethinking that now.

In the last two weeks, not one but two of the marks he'd left notes for had returned the empty envelopes to their windshields the very next night, not wanting any part of earning "extra money." Those fuckers actually had some semblance of moral fiber—or were just too chicken to give it a try! One young thing who said she'd work with Fitch returned the skimmer with just five numbers in it—*five!* Maybe she had gotten cold feet. Who knew, but the scam barely covered his operating expenses! The Driller's purse was getting light, and sweet Mother Brenda was relentless in her requests for cash.

Then there was that twenty-something assistant manager at the Del Taco in Burbank: Morey fuckin' Anderson! Anderson actually took the offer, gladly accepted the skimmer. Had it for over three weeks now! Never left a note, never said a fucking word about why he hadn't returned the damn thing after two weeks as instructed. Did he call the cops? Did he tell the owner? Fitch didn't think so and wasn't worried anyway because the kid didn't know who he was, and he always handled the notes and skimmers with gloves on. Chunk hadn't been seen either when he placed the notes and skimmer on Anderson's car. Big D never saw the telltale signs of any law enforcement interest in Del Taco. Nah, Morey Anderson was just fucking with the wrong dude. Ol' Morey needed a talking to!

Fitch and Gaylord sat across from the Del Taco for another week, waiting. They were there every night that Anderson worked, watching the little turd as he came to and from that grease pit. No communiqués were left on the windshield, no packages returned to the tire. So, on day nineteen of the "contract," Big D, with Chunk as his sidekick, followed his skinny ass home.

The kid drove a good-looking newer BMW. Morey drove that Beamer onto the narrow streets above Ventura Boulevard, way up the hill into the high-rent district. At every turn, the Driller was on his tail. Fitch had a hard time parking his black Miata close enough to watch as Anderson pulled down a one-lane street and into a narrow driveway. The kid walked up to a modern, multilevel home that was tucked behind a manicured lawn, lined with bonsai trees.

Luckily, it wasn't long before Dennis and Chunk knew why the asshole was up here. A well-dressed older woman trotted out as he arrived, kissed him on the forehead, and walked him through the front door. Little Morey was home!

Big D turned to his brother and chortled. "It's fucking Missus Cleaver!" The binoculars revealed that Dad and Mom were in their sixties, and their millennial son was undoubtedly mooching off their generosity.

As the brothers sat across the alley, getting a good eyeful of this happy family scene, Gaylord said, "Betcha his mom is nice. I bet she doesn't call him names. I sorta wish I were him."

As Dennis started the Mazda, he turned a sorrowful eye to Chunk. "It is what it is, my brother. Shit happens, and then we gotta clean it up!"

The Del Taco on Glenoaks Boulevard closed promptly the next evening at the stroke of midnight. All the worker bees left the business beforehand, and Morey Anderson began shutting down the lights. Big D entertained the thought of making Anderson take him back inside to empty the contents of the safe, but he figured it was too close to his old MO. Going from professional safe cracker to a mere armed robber was beneath him.

As Morey reached the driver's door of his BMW, Dennis Fitch, outfitted with gloves and his black mask, came up behind the unsuspecting Del Taco employee. The blade tip of his knife was pushed firmly between Anderson's shoulder blades. It made Anderson freeze in his tracks. Speaking in a low guttural voice, Big D said, "Hi, Morey, don't look back! Get in and slide over."

Once seated in the driver's seat, with Anderson sitting catawampus on the passenger side, the black-masked assailant continued, "You know who I am...I'm your *friend*. Don't even think about running away...you'll die before you open the door. Where's my property, Anderson? Where's my box?"

"How'd you know my name? I don't have it, man. I gave it to the police. You better leave me alone, too— they're watching!"

"You know you *never* called the cops, Morey. The only one watching you is my partner…right, partner?"

James Gaylord, listening on the Motorola handheld, flashed the headlights of his Honda twice from across the street. His car was parked between two others, conveniently blocking Anderson's view of it. The shaken assistant manager saw the lights flash the high sign and quickly snapped his head back toward Fitch. The crook's wild eyes visibly narrowed toward the scrawny kid.

"Where's my friggin' skimmer, Morey? I want it back, *now!*"

"I threw it away. I don't have it. I swear to you, it's gone!"

Thrusting the knife to within inches of the shaking man's face, Fitch screamed, "You're a fucking liar! I want it back, or I swear I'll cut you right here!"

Morey Anderson just sat there mute, shaking. Big D tapped the knife on the top of his head, parting the kid's greasy locks with the edge of the razor-sharp blade.

"Maybe we need to drive to Dupont Court—8353 Dupont. Yeah, let's go see Mom and Dad. Maybe they can tell us where my skimmer is, eh, asshole?"

That did the trick. The nut was cracked. "I got it, I got it—it's in the trunk. I was gonna give it back to ya; I just didn't know how! Please don't hurt me. Leave my parents alone, *please!* I'll get it for ya, OK?"

"Come out my side…and remember what I said about dying. Now that I know where the box is, I'd just as soon gut you here and leave you bleedin'. If you get it for me, I jus' may let you drive outta here."

A trembling Anderson slid over and out the door behind the menacing Driller. After quickly opening the trunk, he handed the masked man a brown paper sack that contained the black plastic device.

"How many numbers did you get, asswipe?"

"Dunno. I tried to count them as I did 'em. Maybe two hundred."

The previously intimidating eyes of his assailant were now wide with disbelief. "You telling me you got *two hundred* numbers stored in this? SO, what were you *really* gonna to do with this thing? Admit it, fucker—you were gonna sell them off yourself, right? Don't lie to me. Tell me the truth, and I'll cut you some slack."

Staring mute for almost half a minute at the big masked man, Morey Anderson said, "Ah, um, yeah. I ordered the software to download the credit-card information, but I'm still waiting for it." Big D just glared at him.

"Well, kid, you're one lucky motherfucker 'cause if you'd downloaded the numbers already, I'd have killed you. Those numbers are *my* property, understand? Now, I'm asking you one more time—and I'll know if you're fucking lying to me. Did you sell the numbers or even download 'em?"

"I swear on my parents' lives, I didn't!" Morey's face smacked of the truth.

Crumpling the bag around the skimmer and sticking it into his jacket pocket, Fitch said, "Drive off, and don't look back. This never happened. We're square."

Anderson weakly replied, "So you're not gonna pay me?"

Moving back close to Morey, the big man said, "Your payment's that you still have two healthy parents. Now drive away, asshole—don't fuckin' tempt me!"

As the BMW drove out the lot, Fitch turned and discreetly pulled off the mask and gloves in the dark parking lot. When Dennis returned to his brother's car, James Gaylord said, "Holy shit! You made that kid shit his pants, D! That was great!"

Dennis Fitch sat there, drenched in his own sweat, trembling. "You may think it was great, but, Chunk, it scared me shitless. I didn't want to hurt that little asshole. He's just doing what we're doin', lookin' out for himself. Shit, maybe he just wanted to get away from home. Maybe he's tired of his fucking mother, too. Let's go, brother. I need to think this out. I need some sleep."

Two days later, back with Santiago and his now frequent female passenger, Chuy plugged Anderson's skimmer into his laptop.

"Odelay! There's two hundred and twelve friggin' numeros in here, ese! Whoever got these for ya, you keep him happy, comprende?"

Looking tired, Dennis Fitch replied, "You know, Chuy, it's been almost two and a half months now since the DMV, and I think I need to go back to doin' what I do best. These skimmers are great and all, but sometimes it's a pain in the ass trying to find someone to use 'em. I've been lucky, but I don't want to push it. I'll just go back to checks. Here."

Handing Santiago a bag containing his four black skimmers, Chuy accepted them with a quizzical look on his face. "You sure, *ese*? You got a good thing here...I got a good thing here. You'd be stupid to blow it, don' ya think, amigo?"

"Money isn't everything, Chuy. Satisfaction is worth something. I know what I'm doing."

"Big D, I think you got a fuckin' screw loose, but OK. When can I expect some checks? My paper business has been a lot slower since you stopped drillin'. I got other sources for checks, but shit, *ese*, I had to lay off some o' my people 'cause there wasn't as much work for them ta do with you staying outta places and all. You the mother-fuckin' Driller, man!"

"I need to do some planning, Chuy. I need to stay out of Southern California. You know they're gunning for me around here, dude! I think I'll be taking a cruise up the coast. Maybe even go up to Frisco, Oakland, or maybe Santa Barbara. Don't know exactly, but I'll let you know when I know. I figure you owe me, ah...$16,960 for these numbers. You got that much on you?"

"Fuck no, my man! I gotta get it. Meet me in two hours, right back here. This place is cool."

Although Jesus Santiago was a long-standing member of Santanas, he hadn't been allowed at any of their usual gatherings or at their clubhouse for almost two years. He didn't socialize with other gangsters, nor did they acknowledge him on the street. He only saw them inside the walls of Dragon Cleaners. The Shop was a profitable business, so it was critical to keep its manager cool—keep him on the down low. All this protocol prevented the cops from drawing the nexus between him and STS, lest the Shop and their business ventures end abruptly—at gunpoint. Because of this El Gerente had little to worry about when he drove around the Southland, including his trips to the cleaners.

An hour later, El Gerente, with his Latina squeeze by his side, drove into the employee parking lot behind Dragon. With the young chica on his arm, he walked into the front lobby and up to the counter. Shin Wu lifted an outstretched palm in protest.

"Chuy, you know what you do here?" She eyed Yolanda. "She should *not* be here. You know rules."

"I make the rules, old lady. She's cool. She's with me. Now hit the fuckin' buzzer!"

Wu was not pleased but slid farther down the counter and, reaching underneath, pushed the small white button twice. El Gerente and Tafoya walked down the long hallway to the back wall, and he parted the red and blue curtains. Chuy punched in the electronic code on the door's keypad. He had the wherewithal to put his back to his girlfriend, keeping Yoli's prying eyes away from the numbers. The door snapped open, and the pair strolled inside. All eyes immediately snapped toward the Latina as the door slammed shut, and Peanut Hernandez strode quickly up to his boss. Hernandez was a trusted STS lieutenant, but Santiago was the shot caller.

"Jefe, can I talk to you...ah, over here?" The men walked over next to the acetone trays.

"Boss, isn't that Yolanda? She's a runner, right? What in holy fuck is she doin' in here? Nobody's supposed to be in the Shop! No one but da crew and us. No low-level outsiders. What gives, *ese*?"

"Look, Nut, she's with me. She's been with me for a while now. She doesn't know nothin' 'bout what's going on. If she doesn't know nothin', she be cool. Don't worry. Leave her up to me."

"Man, just don't let your dick lead your brain, Jefe. If I were you, I'd leave her home from now on. You don't need no crew talking 'bout this behind yo' back. We don't need no weak links, Jefe! Just fuck her at your crib, ese, not in here!"

El Gerente left Tafoya standing with Hernandez and sauntered to a locked back room that held his safe. Peanut just stood there, giving Yolanda the evil eye. Opening the heavy door with the combination, he took a large stack of hundreds from the shelf and counted out Big D's pay in greenbacks. He left four large cellophane-wrapped bundles of hundred-dollar bills on the shelves, the remaining cache measuring almost two feet square inside the strongbox.

That was just the standby operating capital for the Shop's operation. Routine laundering of cash was accomplished through Dragon Cleaners to their bank in China. Chuy liked to keep a hundred grand, liquid, inside the safe at all times. You never knew when operating capital would be needed—or a stash for a quick getaway!

Santiago, holding a hefty brown paper sack of bills, escorted his squeeze out the steel door and back out the front entrance of the cleaners. Shin Wu glared as they passed. Upon entering his Camaro, he turned to Yoli and opened up the bag. With a devious smile on his face, he tipped the gaping mouth of the bag toward her and whispered, "*Mira* [look]."

With eyes as large as dinner plates, Yolanda Tafoya's breath escaped her lungs. Almost indiscernibly she whispered, "*Oh Dios mio!* [Oh, my God!]"

Chapter 9
A HERO FALLS

Will Phillips had been on the job in CID for almost four months. The kid had been doing a decent job on his cases, occasionally asking questions. He always seemed to know the answers beforehand. If CID was a utensil drawer, he was one of the sharpest knives in it. Will knew it, too, but was smart enough not to get too cocky. He still periodically provided all of us with a morning repast as well: a parade of doughnuts, pastry, and the occasional bagels with a schmear! *What a kiss-ass.* Our three secretaries loved him; my burgeoning waistline, in protest, did not.

"Hey, Kev, there's pastry over there. I stopped by Birkholmes in Solvang on the way in. I got a butter ring. I know you love that shit, partner!"

Giving him the look, I replied, "Goddamn it, Phillips. You know I'm trying to watch my waistline! Stop bringing that crap in, OK? You don't need to buy off the sarge with food—you need to get on your cases. Bringing in this shit looks like a bribe to me."

"I just thought...well, I just want to get to be part of the unit. Fit in, you know."

"Look, you're doin' great, Will; just back off on the brown-nosin' and get your work done first, OK?"

"Got it, boss man. By the way, I gotta run down to Ventura this morning. The Central Coast Lock and Safe School is going to provide me a listing of its students, but they want me to come down in person—they wanna make sure I'm legit. Wanna go with me?"

I had to think. I was pretty much caught up on my own follow-ups. I had to do a warrant return from the search of a burglary suspect that turned up nada, but that could wait a day. "Sure, Will, but, you know—the driver always buys lunch!"

Phillips smiled. "Oh, I got to bribe you to come with me? I get it. Ah, an' don't forget that butter ring over there—*gordo!*"

After chowing down on that Danish delight and dripping some frosting on my tie in the process, we signed out and left for Ventura around nine thirty. Traffic was heavy. As we traveled southbound, at Garden Street the radio squawked, "Thirty-one David Ten, Control Thirty." They were calling me for some reason.

"Go ahead for David Ten."

"Ten-nineteen ASAP for David One." I paused, wondering what was so important that I needed to return to talk to the sergeant.

"Ten-four."

Phillips turned to me. "What the hell is that all about? Sounds like you need to get the Vaseline out, partner!"

I chuckled with Will, but my stomach started to grind a little. Maybe it was the rich pastry, but you know the feeling. I figured I'd screwed up. I just didn't know how yet!

It took us nearly twenty minutes to get back. After parking the unit, I walked into the back door to see several people standing near Bob Roberts's office. One of them was Ron Casey. All my brain could think was, "Holy shit!" As I got closer to the door, the others standing nearby looked nervous and dispersed. They rapidly disappeared into their cubicles like rats deserting a sinking freighter. I figured I was in for it for sure.

Casey and Roberts ushered me into the sergeant's office. The lieutenant's look toward the trailing Phillips made it clear this was a meeting for which he had no invitation. Will peeled off and sat down at his desk as the door clicked slowly behind me.

Ron Casey started. "Kevin, please sit down." I looked at him, sweat now glistening on my balding head. "You need to call your wife, Kev; you've got an emergency at home. You can call from here."

Suddenly bright flashes of white and red bounced behind my eyes. The room seemed to be closing in around me. I took the handset that Casey handed me, and I moved closer to the phone's keypad. For a second I had to remember my own home telephone number. I pushed the numbers on the handset rapidly with my fumbling finger; I misdialed once.

The phone rang one time. "Uh, hello?" It was Julie.

"Honey, it's me. What's the matter?"

Sobbing loudly, hardly catching her breath, my wife could only manage, "Come home, Kev. Come home now!"

My psyche was exploding. "Why, Julie? What happened?"

"It's Tommy, Kevin. Two army captains are here. Come home!"

"Is Tom...*dead*? Please tell me he's alive!"

"They say he is, but he's been wounded in Paktia Province...they medevac'd him to the base; they're working on him now. Please come home. I need you here, Kevin."

I managed to say OK, but for the first time in my life I didn't know what to do. I vaguely remember the lieutenant telling me how sorry he was and that he'd have Will take me home—not to worry about my cases; just go and be with my family. Someone must have told Phillips what had gone down, too, because he was there, leading me around by the arm. I'd forgotten where my desk was. It was all I could do to stumble back there, grab some things, and accompany my partner out to the car.

I had a vague recollection of seeing sad faces as I walked toward the exit. Shock had me in its steely grip. I couldn't think, and my vision was a red blur. My heart pounded, and the pain in my head was almost unbearable. Somewhere near Gaviota, I got a grip on my emotions, and my racing mind began firing off questions. Questions I had no answers for. *My boy! Will he live? Will he be able to function? What happened? Will they amputate anything? Will he walk? Where will they take him? Julie! Oh my God, Julie!*

Phillips got me home as quickly as he could, but I don't remember the drive. I ran from the car door as we pulled in, before the car came to a stop. My legs, like two columns of concrete, failed me as I stumbled to the front door. I was met by two uniformed army officers, who feebly tried to speak to me as I pushed past them to run to my wife. We embraced and sobbed, shaking, for several minutes.

I had always feared this day. Along with the pride of having a son who volunteered to serve his country was that ever-present, nagging dread and fear that he would never come home and that guilty doubt that I should have never let him go in the first place. After I managed to calm down—and it wasn't easy—I helped Julie to the couch, where we both crumpled in emotional exhaustion. The two stoic officers sat across from us on kitchen chairs. They began the story.

"Corporal Rhinehardt's squad was patrolling a portion of eastern Afghanistan known as the Shah-e-Kat Valley. The mission of the Eighty-Seventh Infringement of the First Battalion was to squeeze out the Taliban and al-Qaida factions from that area and create a safe zone for our troops and to support the locals there. It's a very dangerous area—a tough mission—and unfortunately we've taken numerous casualties.

"Your son was riding in an armored Humvee patrol unit, which ran over an IED. After the explosion, their unit came under heavy enemy fire. Your son was only one of two in the vehicle who managed to survive the attack. We lost a total of eight men in that firefight."

Julie sat wide-eyed, but I had many questions. "Will my son live, Captain? What kind of injuries does he have? Where is he now?"

"Sir, all we currently know is that he was shot and sustained some injuries from an IED explosion. Word was he bravely managed to return fire, but honestly I can't tell you the exact nature of his physical injuries. He was choppered out after the area was secured, and we spoke to the doctors in the province on the SAT phone where he's being treated, just before you arrived. He's in critical condition, and frankly they couldn't provide us with any other details. We're very sorry."

The officers gave us a telephone number for the military family support unit. We could call anytime, but family support admittedly only reported on periodic medical updates. The men also told us that if Tommy perished, they would be back, in person, to provide the news. I thanked them but ended the meeting saying, "I don't want to see you two...ever again. Do you understand?"

"Yes, sir, we certainly do." As they walked out the front door, they turned in unison and saluted Julie and me. I closed the door, and we both began weeping, trembling in each other's arms.

After about thirty minutes, I managed to compose myself and dialed Jimmy's cell phone. It went to voice mail immediately. He screened the call. He didn't want to talk to us. I flashed with anger, but the flame quickly extinguished. My mind quickly turned back to worrying about my patriot. We called the family support unit every hour on the hour. No news to report from their end, no idea if our son was dead or alive. It was pure torture.

There have been countless reports of what humans experience as they are dying. Some say they see a brilliant white light; others claim that their past played out like a newsreel on the video screen of their mind. Some swear they float above their body, watching what is transpiring below them in their last moments. Still others claim they were greeted by those loved ones who'd passed before them. Tom experienced none of these things before his consciousness left him on that Afghan ridgeline the local Muslim residents called the Whale.

Corporal Rhinehardt remembered the punch line from a bawdy joke his now-dead sergeant had just finished telling the occupants of the SUV: *"Hank, get a bucket, the dead guy in room 105 is full again!"* Then he remembered feeling a hot flash and remembered the Humvee was flying. There was no pain, just a sudden, annoying swarm of bees buzzing around him. One almost knocked off his helmet…then eerie blackness, interrupted periodically by the cussing from a young corpsman trying to stick a needle into the top of his left wrist. He remembered watching the needle, in slow motion, pushing in and out of his flesh several times. He thought it was comical. The very last recollection twenty-two-year-old Tom Rhinehardt had was a very bright, concentrated light, shining directly into his eyes. He came to on the operating table in the MASH unit.

The morning after the worst hours of Julie's and my lives, we got a call from the support unit. Our son was out of surgery. His condition had been upgraded from critical to serious but stable. They had more information on his actual injuries and the battle. We wanted these details, but they were very hard to absorb. Tom had sustained shrapnel injuries to his left ankle and leg. Although his injuries were serious, the nurse said she believed they didn't threaten the "sustainability" of the leg. Then came worse news. He had been shot after the Humvee came to rest on its top after the explosion. Tom had one round from an AK-47 hit his right shoulder, next to his vest; it had narrowly missed the bone and artery. It traveled out, through and through. Another .223 bullet had struck his helmet on the right side—the helmet had saved his life. However, the projectile splintered and ricocheted off the Kevlar, destroying the top portion of his ear. That didn't bother me so much—he'd just look like an alley cat. But would my son ever walk again? Could he use his arm?

The nurse, Marian Stipes, a naval lieutenant, told us that of the five occupants of Tom's vehicle, only he and another private survived. Witnesses said that after the explosion, once the vehicle came to a resting position, Tom crawled out and, despite the injury to his leg, engaged the enemy by firing his M-16 from a prone position next to the Humvee. His actions probably saved the life of the other soldier since it managed to keep the enemy pinned down until the rest of the patrol caught up to them and engaged the Taliban insurgents. However, as Tom was valiantly firing on the enemy, he was shot in the shoulder and helmet, and he lost consciousness. It was a miracle the bullet missed bones as well as his carotid and brachial arteries.

We asked her opinion as to whether Tom would ever walk again, unassisted. She told us she couldn't give us a straight answer. The unknown was the worst...it sat like an elephant on my chest.

"I've seen worse walk in six months, and I've seen lesser injuries result in an amputation. I wish I knew definitively, but it's always in God's hands." Her acknowledgment of the Divine comforted us. We'd been praying to Him for hours.

Our younger son, Jimmy, returned home the day before, about three hours after my original attempt at trying to get him to answer his damn phone. For once in his postpubescent life, he was quiet after hearing the news, since seeing our emotional state preempted any smart remarks or confrontation with his parents. In fact, he made us dinner that night and remained with us throughout that evening and into early morning as we sought updates on his brother's condition. After we got the news about Tom's actual condition, the fact that he'd survived with a better prognosis than expected brought Jimmy's tears of joy along with our own.

Later that next morning, sometime after speaking with the nurse, I was sitting on our back porch sipping lukewarm coffee. Jim slid open the glass door, and peeking his head out, asked, "Dad, can I talk to you?" I waved him over.

Sitting next to me in a lounge chair, Jim leaned in close and touched my hand, saying, "Dad, I just wanted to say..."

A flood of tears cascaded down my boy's cheeks, and he cradled his face in his hands as he sobbed uncontrollably. Through tears he said, "I'm sorry. I've been a dick. I'm sorry I didn't understand how brave Tom was when he enlisted. I was jealous of how you talked about him. I jus' thought you were being hard on me. I didn't care about our family, but I know how much you and Mom care about... not just Tom but about me. I'm sorry; I'm really sorry!"

I reached out and grabbed my younger son, pulling him hard to my chest. I figured I was all cried out, but the waterworks began anew.

"Jim, you and Tom are the most important things in Mom's and my lives. I hope you know that. If it was you lying in that hospital, I don't know what I'd do...I love you. Please never forget that. And one more thing: You may *not* enlist in the military; you hear me? My heart can't stand this shit ever again. You gotta promise!"

Chuckling and raising his tear-stained face, Jimmy said, "C'mon, Dad, I may want to join the marines...hur-rah!" His grin faded quickly when he saw that I wasn't amused.

———

Three days after I'd nearly collapsed at work after speaking to Julie, I called the office and asked for the lieutenant. Although I didn't like Casey, he was my boss, after all, so I gave him the courtesy of an update on my situation. He was surprisingly pleasant. He made sure I knew I had two weeks of family leave coming to me and almost ordered me to take all of it. He even tried mending our fence.

"You know, Kevin, I realize I was hard on you about Ocampo, but it was my job to get all the details on that IA. I was hard on him, too. When you get promoted, you'll have to do things you'd rather not do, too."

"Well, it'll be a cold day in hell that I'll ever want your job, LT. I appreciate you telling me that, though. How's Phillips doing on the Driller case? I hate to leave him hanging out there. What's been happening?"

"Will's doing just fine. I spoke to Roberts, and it looks like your partner has a list of several people who received safe-cracking training in the state last year. He's checking on them all. When you can, and things calm down at home, just give 'em a call. But for now just hang in there.

Let us know how your boy is doing. I can tell you we're all praying for Tom."

After assuring Casey I would call and update the department on Tom's condition, I called Phillips. My friend was genuinely concerned, even offering to come over and mow my lawn or run errands. Like I mowed the lawn! He'd be doing Jimmy's job. I told him not to worry about that but to come over for a beer anyway when he had time.

He came that very afternoon. I appreciated his concern, as well as the company. Seems that it took some time, but Phillips had begun running down all the people who had received lock and safe training in California that past year. There were a bunch, too: 122, to be exact. As we had previously discussed, he focused first on those who said they lived south of San Francisco. This reduced the totals to around eighty, sixteen of whom had not completed the course sufficiently to receive certification.

Additionally, Will had received a teletype communiqué from Sergeant Stiles of Orange County, informing the task force members that within the last ten days the Driller was believed to be responsible for yet another safe burglary, after a lapse in the crimes of about eight weeks. This last safe job was in San Luis Obispo County, at the AJ Spurs restaurant in Grover Beach. This was an eerie coincidence.

AJ Spurs are upscale steakhouse restaurants, employing a cowboy, rustic atmosphere. There were only three of them: the one hit in San Luis Obispo County, one in

Templeton, and one right here in Buellton—our area. I'd been to the one in Buellton many times, and trust me, you always needed to bring a chubby wallet 'cause the menu was high end all around! Great food and lots of it, but you paid top dollar for the privilege of dining there. Phillips told me our boy managed to make off with over six thousand bucks in SLO, as well as their bimonthly payroll checks. Same old MO, but now he was back in our neck of the woods!

Will and I kicked around the idea of staking out AJ Spurs in Buellton. Stakeouts are always hit-or-miss propositions unless you have good information they're going to pay off. A stakeout takes at least two people, and since you can't take patrol units away from their normal assignments, cops working them are usually paid overtime. "Overtime" in any municipality is a dirty word! Phillips said that he was going to pitch the idea to Bob Roberts if I agreed to back his idea. I like overtime, and I like thinking outside the box, so I told him to go for it. I'd know more about when I could help once we knew more about Tom.

When my partner pitched his idea to Sarge, Roberts was skeptical: "What makes you think this guy will hit AJ's? Do you have a damn crystal ball, Phillips? Does that crystal tell you how I'm going to get the boss to pay for this fishing expedition?"

Phillips stood his ground. "Look, Sarge, I talked this over with Rhino. He agrees that the Driller has a pattern in his jobs. The crook likes consistency. Once he knows the layout of a place, he feels comfortable. He knows AJ's now, and he scored big, so we figure it's a fifty-fifty chance he hits our place in Buellton or maybe Templeton. We're betting on the home team—we think it'll be Buellton. We can narrow the dates and times down to when they put out their payroll; we want to do two surveillances this month. I can use reserves to help out, if you want to save some bucks. It's worth a shot, Bob…whaddya say?"

"Will, this guy's a killer now, so I want at least two on the inside, one outside. I'll pitch it to Casey. No bets on whether he'll go for it, but I'll back you—this one time. Now get the hell outta here and arrest somebody."

One week after Tom was ambushed, we got word that he'd been stabilized enough to ship back home for continued medical treatment. Two days later, Julie, Jim, and I stood in trembling anticipation on the wet tarmac at the Point Mugu Naval Air Station in Oxnard as a lumbering C-130 Hercules transport landed. Tom and one other injured soldier were taken off the plane first.

Tom, with a large white bandage covering most of his right ear and heavy bandaging visible on his shoulder and leg, was conscious and smiling as he held our hands. They wheeled him, lying on a gurney, to the holding area, with us following along like ducklings waddling behind their mother.

A light rain began to fall. As we stood in this covered spot, waiting to hear where our soldier would be taken next, I happened to glance back toward the plane.

An honor guard of six marines solemnly walked an American flag–draped coffin down the wide ramp of the transport, slowly accompanying it to a black hearse waiting alongside a nearby building. Rain was dripping off the brim of their BDU caps. The flag almost shimmered from the moisture. Another family, looking hauntingly similar to ours, stood under umbrellas next to a funeral home's vehicle. I could see them sobbing and holding on to one another as they gazed down at their own loved one—forever hidden from them in his wooden sarcophagus. The sight of this knocked the very wind from my lungs. I quickly looked away. I had to concentrate on my Tom—my living hero.

Chapter 10
COLD STEEL

My two weeks of personal leave were up. Tom was taken to the Long Beach Veterans Administration Hospital, and we were all there with him for most of that first week. My heart broke with his every moan, with every painful cry. He was the bravest man I'd ever known, and to see his torment was almost as unbearable for us as the pain he was experiencing in his shoulder and leg. It seemed like that as his father, but I knew my anguish was a pimple on the ass of the torture he had to be going through. Julie and I cried a river of tears in private each night for him. Jimmy stood by his bedside. He held his brother's hand, and when Tom wasn't too medicated to understand, Jimmy told him how proud he was to be his brother. That renewed sibling bond was the only bright spot in all of this tragedy for me.

The Veterans Administration was totally incapable of handling the volume of casualties from the campaign in Afghanistan. Tom was receiving adequate care, but his family was left out in the cold. Apparently no one ever figured a soldier's family was an extension of their combat warrior. Our savings account was dropping like a stone, all due to the high expenses incurred while staying close to our hero. There was no stipend, no discounted family housing made available to us. It was all on our dime. When we asked about help, no one seemed to know any answers. We were referred to people who never called us back. This abandonment was a nightmare we kept from our wounded son. Thank God they took good care of Tommy because they really didn't give a rat's ass about his family!

As my family leave came to an end, Tom was in much less pain, and with his agreement, we decided to leave Long Beach to travel home. He was a military man, and his bond with the other patients and his caregivers was much stronger than in civilian circles. His mom came back to spend every weekend with him, and I joined him at the hospital as often as I could as well. Jimmy made a commitment to take care of his mom in my absence. She was a strong, perfectly capable woman, but Jim needed to feel useful, to flex his testosterone. I appreciated his newfound concern for his family. It was as refreshing as a summer breeze.

On the weekend before my return to work, I reached out to another friend in need: Luis. His monthlong suspension had ended more than a week before, and he was now working patrol in South County. I visited him on one of his days off and was greeted by a happy ex-detective.

"Yo, Rhino, hi! I was hoping to see you and tell you how sorry I was to hear about Tom. Word is he's improving—is it true? Will he be OK? Please, come in, come in."

I stepped inside. "I appreciate that, Louie, and yes, he's getting better every day. He hasn't gotten on that leg yet, but the therapists think he'll walk pretty soon. They're spot-on with his rehab. He dodged a bullet—not literally, I guess, but the round that hit his shoulder caused no permanent damage. He'll have full mobility up there for sure, thank God. Not his ear, though...they repaired it, but I think he's gonna need some follow-up plastic surgery 'cause at the moment he sorta looks like Mr. Spock on that side. His friggin' ear actually comes to a point! It's the only thing we can joke about. So, how are *you* doing? How's patrol?"

We sat down in the living room. Tammy brought us some cold iced tea. I'd intended on visiting with him more regularly, but our family crisis had put a monkey wrench in all my plans. Ocampo looked like a changed man. He was thinner, bright eyed, and well groomed. Nothing like the last time we had spoken, when a beaten, depressed friend in pajamas spoke to me. Luis looked healthy and happy.

"Rhino, I love patrol. I forgot how much. No more lingering cases hanging over my head, no more pressure...just domestic-violence calls and drunks! I get to come home with a clean slate every night. I've found out that Sergeant Clancy appreciates my experience in CID, though, maybe a little too much! Seems like every incident that's above a simple report call, he assigns to yours truly. Any assaults with a deadly weapon, or child-molestation cases are automatically assigned to ol' 31–22; that's my permanent beat. But you know, amigo, I don't care. I'm happy for the first time in a long time…it's great!"

I was happy to hear that, but I knew he was attached at the hip to our son-of-a-bitch chief.

"So, I hear Walters is your probation officer. How's *that* going?"

"Well, that's the only wrinkle in an otherwise clean sheet. He jumped my shit on day one, calling me into his office. He said he'd be watching me 'personally' every day. Walters even made me give him a pee test on day one! You have no idea how embarrassing it was to have to walk down the hallway from the shitter, carrying that little yellow bottle of piss back to him! I'd actually expected him to follow me into the john and watch where the surf met the sand, if you catch my drift," Luis said, laughing.

"Well, Lou, you know what a prick he can be. I sorta expected that from him, didn't you? You only have to put up with his crap for a year, right? Then you'll be off probation, your license will be reinstated without restrictions, and you'll be good to go! You could even apply to come back to the bureau."

"I don't know 'bout that bro. I'm sorta liking where I'm at. No caseload, no hassle. I haven't touched a drop since I creamed that parked car in Goleta. I guess it was a good thing, in a weird fucking way! I've been going to

AA meetings twice a week and gotta see Doc Thompson once a month. He seems like a stand-up guy. He says the traffic collision finally made me confront what I knew was a problem with my drinking. I was using booze to avoid facing issues. I'm looking ahead now, not back!"

I knew Dr. Carl Thompson personally. Luis didn't know it, but just eight months prior, during the Phantom murder case, I had spent several confidential sessions with Carl. His counseling hadn't been ordered by the department; I'd gone of my own accord. I had PTSD-driven dreams—dreams that haunted me for countless nights over a period of several years. These terrifying nightmares were all due to my guilt over how I had treated the parents of a small boy who'd drowned in Lake Cachuma. I recovered the young boy's cold, limp body myself and then refused to allow the father to touch him. I was angry because he'd left the child unattended—something every parent does. But I was holier than thou—jury and executioner for the parents—and it ate at me back then; almost every night I relived it in my head. The stress of tracking down the Solvang killer back then was like throwing gas on my PTSD fire! Thompson got me over it. The dreams stopped with his help. He's a good guy, for a shrink.

"So, Kev, how's the Driller case going? I hear Willimena's doing a good job."

"Willimena? Where'd you come up with that handle?"

"Before I left the bureau, he farted one day in the break room, and, as usual, it almost peeled the paper off the walls. I said, 'Real professional, WILLIMENA,' and he got all bent—really got pissed off. I got him good!"

"Hmm...I'll put that in the back of my 'how to fuck with Phillips' file! Thanks."

I probably neglected to mention the fact that Will Phillips has a habit of passing noxious ass gas at the most inconvenient times. I hadn't noticed that penchant much after he took to wearing a suit, but back in his patrol days he was legendary! He could clear a room with one toot and did many times during the Phantom case. He'd been keeping his fumes to himself around the bureau for some reason. I knew it couldn't last, though. Willimena, eh!

I left the Ocampo residence feeling great for Louie. His attitude would get him through this rough time. I could only hope he kept his shirt white, as we say in the bureau. He couldn't afford to muddy it with any other screw-ups.

I returned to my desk the following Monday and learned that Phillips had already worked one stakeout at the AJ Spurs restaurant in the central stations area. The bosses had approved it, and Will managed to recruit two level-one reserves to work alongside him: one inside the place as his partner, the other covering the outside in plainclothes.

Level-one reserves were a dedicated breed. Most departments used them. They were screened the same as regular police officers, and they had to go through a full, yet slightly modified, police academy. After they passed their year of probation, they functioned the same as any regularly employed cop. However, these guys and gals went back to their regular jobs every day. Reserve law-enforcement officers were your local mechanics, plumbers, dentists, and secretaries. I'd had the pleasure of working with many over the years. The only drawback was they didn't do this dangerous job every single day. This lack of experience could cause hesitation, and hesitating was not a good thing when seconds could cost you your life or some-one else's! You got to know the good reserves, and you hesitated to work with the others. The good ones were out there in the field with you a lot. They loved it as much as you did. The others put in their one day a month to main-tain their part-time police officer status. These weekend warriors excelled at directing traffic at parades. Lack of experience wasn't usually an issue while stopping cars with a whistle.

Will and his reserve partners were in AJ's for six long hours that first night, and all they had to show for it were bloodshot eyes. What'd they expect from working a "stake-out" at a steakhouse! (I couldn't resist the pun.) However, upon my return that Monday, Phillips was busy working a felony assault case involving a Goleta councilman and his gardener.

Seems that the week prior, Councilman Dan Jackson was accused of striking his employee John Tanaka with a garden trowel. This heinous assault occurred after a heated argument concerning how the Japanese gardener had failed to trim Jackson's trees to his liking. The hospital reported the incident after the guy showed up at Cottage Hospital for treatment of a broken orbit and facial lacerations.

Tanaka hesitated to finger his boss at first because he needed the job. It seems that the tenacity of a certain Goleta patrol deputy got him to fess up to the dirty details of his injury. Yup, Deputy Luis Ocampo got the gardener's statement, and Detective Phillips appreciated his comprehensive investigation.

Fortunately for Will, the good councilman was very concerned about security at his beautiful one-acre ocean-view homestead. Mr. Jackson had cameras *everywhere*, including one pointed toward the front yard where Tanaka said he got clobbered. Will noticed the camera when he interviewed the councilman, who denied ever touching his groundskeeper. My astute trainee never asked lying Jackson for permission to view the digital recordings from the camera. Will knew damn well the man would tell him to go pound sand and destroy them...so a simple piece of paper, a search warrant, allowed Phillips to seize the machine containing the images during a search of the house a couple of days later.

With the aid of our technical-services division, Will printed a dozen eight-by-ten-inch images from the camera's recordings of Jackson whacking the diminutive Tanaka in the kisser with the garden tool. A couple of other pics showed Jackson returning later to retrieve the trowel after the assault, to dispose of it. The case was neatly packaged by young Willimena. A shiny gift box to the DA, with a bow on top. I read Will's reports. Damn good job!

He discussed the case with me, including his intent of driving down to the superior court to get a Ramey arrest warrant from a judge to pick up Dan Jackson later that day. A Ramey warrant! I quickly cooled his jets.

"Partner, have you discussed this with Roberts? You do know this guy is a Goleta city councilman, right?"

"Well, Roberts assigned the case to me. He knows who he is, so yeah."

"Have you bothered to let Bob know that armed with the evidence to prove the assault, you intend to get a Ramey for the guy today…this influential, rich councilman guy?"

"Well, er, no. I thought he'd approve of the fact that I did a good job getting the goods on Jackson."

I'd been a detective for eight years. I'd arrested attorneys, celebrities, even had to interview a superior court judge once for committing a crime…the one thing I knew was you needed someone else, someone with a higher pay grade than yours, to approve you slapping cuffs on the suspect in a high-profile case. It didn't matter if they'd done the deed or not—sometimes you wanted the district attorney to make the call. Let the state's attorney issue a criminal indictment and obtain a bench warrant based on your investigation. A Ramey warrant was a "probable cause" arrest authorization signed by a judge, based solely on a sworn affidavit from a peace officer. Obtained by an overzealous detective, a knee-jerk Ramey warrant arrest could cause unnecessary publicity for a department and usually pissed off the DA since you'd circumvented them entirely. We all knew shit rolled downhill—my new partner wouldn't like brown caca on his new suit!

"Trust me on this one, Willimena. Go see Roberts. Give him your case file, and see what he wants you to do. Betcha he compliments you and tells you to file the case with the DA today. The victim's safe, the councilman isn't going anywhere, and you'll get an attaboy for handling a sensitive political case wisely. Take it from one detective that has stepped on his penis more than once! You'll get to make an arrest when the higher ups want you to. You still get the credit for good work. This way, everybody's happy."

Will Phillips glared at me immediately after I mouthed his cute Ocampo nickname, but his look of disdain faded quickly into one of acknowledgment that he'd received sound advice from his mentor. He nodded affirmatively and walked toward the sergeant's office with the file folder. Another ass saved from the fire, and another butter ring in my near future.

Turns out that after fresh-faced Phillips returned from the DA's office, he gave me the lowdown on how happy staff was that he had come directly to them. Lieutenant Casey called Sheriff Billingsly, and everyone was salivating about the fact that Dan Jackson was going down for a felony. Apparently the heavy-handed Goleta councilman had been a vocal antagonist against the law-enforcement contract between the city and the sheriff's department. He was always complaining about the overtime costs and was known to encourage frivolous complaints against our deputies. That butter ring Phillips owed me had magically turned into a steak dinner!

Phillips said he was supposed to brief Chief Walters on the case tomorrow. Something about a sheriff press conference pending CID's arrest of a certain political official. Will was concurrently working on having the secretary staff do computer runs on all the people trained throughout Southern California by the lock and safe schools the previous year. My protégé was a very busy boy. I was glad for him.

I knew from our conversation about the Driller case that the task force had reported yet another restaurant burglary since the one at AJ's in Grover Beach. One week afterward he hit an Olive Garden in Bakersfield. In Bakersfield! Boy, he was slumming now. He'd dropped a carbide drill bit at that job, too, and only got $2,350 in cash—no checks. Serves him right for hitting the armpit of Fresno County!

Will told me he wanted to do a second (and final) surveillance at our AJ's since their payroll was due in two days. It would be our last hurrah since the boss wouldn't authorize overtime to watch the restaurant for another month. He just had a feeling about it. I figured our boy had moved on, but considering how determined and busy my partner was with his other cases at the moment, I volunteered to help him out with this surveillance. He appreciated the respite.

I called around and had a difficult time finding reserve volunteers to work that next Thursday night. I managed to get Tom Barnes and Vince Bullard to agree to come in to help. Barnes was a trooper. He said he'd take a vacation day to do it. He was a new dad and hadn't been getting much sleep lately due to his new baby teething and all. He could at least lose sleep while working with me! Vince Bullard was another guy who I knew could be counted on. He worked patrol about four times a month—every chance he got. My crew for the evening was set.

Vince, Tom, and I met to brief at 10:30 p.m. the evening of the ops at the Buellton station. I asked Vince to work the plain car outside the restaurant. I'd scoped out the area and told him to park across the street, where he could have a view of most of the exterior of AJ's. A pair of binoculars would help him keep a close watch. Tom would be inside with me. Will had clued me in on where he and his partner had stayed inside the restaurant last time, so Tom and I agreed to set up similarly. After all, why reinvent the wheel? At nearly eleven o'clock, Tom and I walked over to the place and knocked on the side door. We identified ourselves, and the lone night manager unlocked the door to let us in. This guy was cool.

"Do you guys know where the ice cream's at? I showed the other guys. Come on, I'll show ya. Look, just take what you want. We appreciate your help. I made a fresh pot of coffee, too. It's in the side kitchen, over there. We appreciate your help trying to catch these guys. Corporate told me to thank you personally."

The manager let himself out, locking the deadbolt behind him as he did. Of course the alarm system was not set, because the restaurant's system included multiple motion sensors downstairs, which we'd be setting off as we snuck around drinking our coffee and chowing down on the free ice cream!

I stationed myself on the second floor, down the hallway from the office that held the prize: the standing Major safe. All three of us had handhelds (portable radios), with earpieces as well as hand microphones clipped to the lapels of our green sheriff jackets that were buttoned up over our bulletproof vests. Vests are like insurance policies for cops. Ya never leave home without one!

We all agreed that Vince would do a radio check of us on the hour, every hour, for two reasons. First of all, those damn walkie-talkies are notorious for having a short battery life and, second, as a safety check for us inside. If we didn't hear from Vince, we could check the battery and change it out if necessary to let him know. If he didn't hear from us, he would wait five minutes and start checking again, calling in the cavalry if necessary. Calling for help was a last resort, because experience told us that more than likely the guys on the other end of the radio either had a bad battery, had the volume turned down, or had their head up their ass. Of course, in my personal case, it could *only* be a battery or volume issue!

The first two hours went slowly. A guy can eat only so much rocky road and drink so much java before he's bouncing around looking for the head. Spending too much time in the pisser was not a good tactic during surveillance! Our radios were working fine. Then at 2:08 a.m., I heard Tom's cell phone ring downstairs. Damn! Put that fucking thing on vibrate, Tom! A minute or so later, my partner crept up the creaking stairs to my position.

"Hey, Rhino, I got a little problem at home. My wife called and said our baby girl has a fever of 103, and she's worried. She wants to go to the hospital, and I really need to bail to go back home to watch our three-year-old. I'm sorry, man! Can you get someone else to help?"

Patrol was short (as always), and things were moving fast and furious at AJ's (not), so my response was a no-brainer. "Hell, Tom, don't worry; it's slow. I can handle it. I'll let Vince know it'll be just him and me. Leave me your radio. Go up to the second-floor exit by the stairs and leave. It's one of those push-bar doors. It's not locked from the inside—I checked. Just pull it closed behind you. Look, I appreciate the help, so take off. I hope your baby's OK."

Tom left about two minutes later, and I radioed Vince to let him know what the new plan was. I decided to stay downstairs since I could see a lot of the outside grounds through the windows, and it was closer to the coffeepot!

About twenty minutes later, my bladder was bursting, so I headed to the bathroom. When I exited the downstairs head, I heard a clunk. Sounded like it had come from upstairs. There was an older chest freezer up there—the one that held the ice cream. When I was up there earlier, it had been making some creaking noises, so I wasn't too concerned, but I decided to stroll up there anyway. I needed to stretch my legs. Maybe try a scoop of strawberry swirl while I was up there.

I wasn't creeping quietly. I was striding up the old wooden staircase, which squeaked with every footfall. I mused to myself, *Good thing I didn't need to sneak up on anyone!* At the top of the stairs, I shone my flashlight down the hallway, which had recessed doorways on either side. The office door stood illuminated in the thin beam of my torch. The manager said he'd left the door of the office unlocked for us, so I began slowly walking toward it. I wanted to check out the massive safe a bit better—I'd heard it was a big'un!

I walked by the first doorway to my right and slowly meandered toward the second one coming up on my left. Suddenly, in the haloed beam of my light, a tall figure burst into view to the left, his face obscured by a dark hood. The heavy Kel-Light fell from my right hand as I quickly reached for my gun inside my raid jacket. My fingers managed to circle the grip of my Glock .40 when a fist slammed *hard* into my jaw.

The stunning blow to my face bounced me sideways and off the wall to my right. The thin sheetrock was close enough that it acted like a spring wrestling mat, propelling me quickly back toward my assailant. Adrenalin pumping, I hit his black-veiled face as hard as I could with a right cross, driving him solidly against the opposing wall. Throbbing with pain, I thought I'd broken my hand; I hit him that hard.

What followed was a flurry of mutual blows, pushing and grappling, as we fought down the hallway, bathed in oblique luminescence. We careened back and forth against the two narrow walls. Fists were flying, but this guy was much bigger than me, and I was losing steam fast. I knew my pistol was still holstered, but I was way too busy fending off his fists to grab for it. After what seemed like minutes but probably amounted to thirty seconds or so, I couldn't breathe. He'd hit me hard on the side of my rib cage. My knees buckled, and suddenly I was going down. I remember trying to call out, but the breath wouldn't come. I fell to the floor gasping, barely able to move.

I tried to get off the greasy wooden floor. I couldn't budge. My nostrils, pressed against the grimy floorboards, filled with the odor of rancid oil and putrid meat. The last thing I remembered was seeing my assailant's pants legs running away. The bright light of my flashlight, lying next to me, grew dimmer and dimmer. Consciousness gave way to darkness.

"All units, Code 33...thirty-one David Ten...thirty-one David Ten, respond, RESPOND! This is Control Thirty! Units responding to AJ's, David Ten isn't answering. Unknown circumstances, respond Code 3."

My head was spinning; I couldn't catch my breath, but I managed to regain consciousness enough to hear that last transmission from dispatch. They were calling me, so I feebly attempted to respond. I weakly fumbled around on the ground. *Where's the radio; where's the damn radio?* My earpiece had pulled out of the walkie during the melee, and the broadcast blared loudly through the microphone itself. It lay somewhere on the floor nearby. I slowly moved my left hand along the floor and felt for the extender mic, which was no longer clipped to my shirt near the neck. I tried to move, but my body kept undulating in something wet and slimy on the floor beneath my torso.

I fumbled around more with my hand in the dampness and found the loose handset, still attached to the radio lying near it like the outstretched tentacle of an octopus. I grabbed the microphone, now squawking with loud radio gibberish, as best I could with my wet hand. The room was dark and spinning as I managed to bring it to my lips. The slimy plastic slid around in my palm. The light bouncing off the wall illuminated it in my grasp. The black microphone was covered in thick red blood…my blood! The room spun out of control. I remember garbling, "David Ten…eleven-ninety-nine, I'm down. Help me."

Everything went black again. My consciousness was next roused to attention by a loud crashing sound followed by multiple footfalls. Radios blared in the background as I saw more pants legs. They moved in slow motion, this time toward me…it's the last thing I remember.

Chapter 11
CHRISTINA AND THE SNAKE

Stumbling, then scrambling down the hallway, the Driller suddenly stopped shy of the exit door. *"Fuck, where's my bag...?"* Running, almost stumbling back down the hallway, past the form on the ground, he came to it. He scooped it up from where he placed it in the alcove, once he'd perceived that someone was mounting the stairs. Some asshole coming up to obstruct his plan. It seemed abnormally heavy now as he quickly hoisted it up onto his shoulders, to run for his life. He was exhausted; his pulse raced as he exited through the push-to-open door and ran down the back stairs to the rear of the building below.

Fitch managed a steady trot despite the throbbing pain in his nose and head, due south across the back parking lot. He managed to slide, feet first, down the dank embankment of the drainage bordering the back of the business without breaking his neck. Sloshing through the muddy estuary, he began trudging up the soggy opposite downslope. Falling to his hands and knees then back upright again, David Fitch felt as if he'd finally screwed the pooch...and that junkyard dog was nipping at his heels.

Chunk Gaylord had parked his red Honda in the back of the Flying Flags trailer court, situated due south and across the drainage from AJ Spurs. Sitting back there in the darkness, Gaylord was inconspicuous in the sparsely occupied trailer housing, comprised primarily of ramshackle RVs. He'd heard the commotion inside the restaurant via his radio, but despite James's calls for his brother to answer back, Big D wasn't responding. Over the radio earpiece, James could hear labored, rapid breathing as Dennis Fitch ran toward the getaway car in the inky blackness.

Vince Bullard had positioned his cover car due north of the restaurant, and although the reserve deputy had an excellent view of the north, east, and west sides of AJ's, he couldn't see shit on the south end. The Driller had managed to walk up the stairs there and exit the same way, avoiding the watchful eye of Rhinehardt's partner. The spurious brothers had no idea the cops were watching when they approached on that side, parking the car in Flying Flags. Fitch's angle of approach was fortuitous for him and quite unfortunate for the good guys working the stakeout.

"Move, *move*! Get outta here!" Dennis blurted out, as he cranked open the door and slid into the Honda.

"What happened, D? You're bleedin'!"

Dennis Fitch could feel the moisture soaking his balaclava, and reaching up to yank it off, he saw the red festooning his gloved hand. Thick, gooey blood began dripping down the front of his leather jacket.

"That asshole *broke my nose*! My goddamn nose...*fuck*, I think he's a cop! He had a flashlight, and I think I saw 'sheriff' on his jacket!"

"Brother, is he OK? What'd you do?"

"I, I put him down...he's down, OK! Jus' don't worry about it. Move; get us the fuck outta here, Chunk. *Drive!*"

Driving faster than the ten-miles-per-hour posted limit for the park—quite a bit faster, actually—James Gaylord took a left on Avenue of the Flags and headed south toward the US 101 freeway entrance. After a right turn, Chunk Gaylord floored the Honda, roaring into the stillness of the night. The headlights, fleeing the park, never alerted the reserve deputy sitting a block away since at that point all seemed fine inside the business.

At exactly 3:00 a.m., Bullard began his attempts at doing a scheduled radio check of his partner. He and Kevin were on the main frequency's "simplex" channel: they could hear everyone else, but their traffic couldn't be heard over the sheriff's repeater system elsewhere. After ten minutes of no response from Rhinehardt, Vince, somewhat reluctantly, contacted dispatch on the primary frequency to alert them that he had lost contact with his partner. That did it; all hell broke loose.

Sergeants and watch commanders began calling in cars from as far away as Santa Barbara to respond, Code 3, to Buellton. CHP was asked to assist. The throaty roar of police interceptors, along with the blare of their yelping sirens, accompanied the response as multiple units acknowledged and began rolling toward AJ's.

Vince Bullard stood at the locked main door to the steakhouse, banging and yelling for his partner. He was praying that Kevin had just fucked up or maybe fallen asleep—that Rhino merely rubbed against the radio's volume dial, muting the calls. Just as the first black-and-white roared into the parking lot, as the sheriff chopper illuminated everything from above with its night sun spotlight, Kevin's eerie call for help broadcast weakly over the primary radio channel. "Eleven-ninety-nine"—*officer needs assistance*.

Kevin Rhinehardt was in bad shape; his weak mutterings brought tightness to everyone's chest and a fast lump into their throats. The three female dispatchers in the communications center muffled cries and choked back tears as they responded to radio traffic.

Deputy Randy Randolf, all six feet three inches and 230 pounds of him, was first to the front door. One boot kick above the doorknob, one shoulder following it, and the distressed, heavy wooden portal came crashing in: oak splintering, almost dislodging the plank from its hinges. Four deputies, along with Bullard, with weapons drawn, began a frantic search for suspects and, more importantly, for their comrade. Up on the second floor, Vince found his partner, unconscious and lying in a pool of vermillion that oozed like a melting ice pop outward from beneath the immobilized detective.

The morning hour of 7:00 a.m. found Julie Rhinehardt in her bathrobe, hair askew, sitting in the den with her iPad, checking e-mail. Browsing the news on AOL, she mused to herself, *Maybe I'll make waffles. Kev should be home soon.* Teenage Jim had just begun the long, tenuous process of gathering enough energy together to get his butt off his mattress for school.

She heard a car enter the driveway. It had to be her husband. Then there was a knock at the door. What? *Kevin wouldn't knock...*Julie opened the door and saw two men, one wearing a suit, the other holding a radio, standing stoically there; somber expressions painted their faces with uncomfortable emotion. She recognized Sam Walters right away—not her favorite person...*huh, wait a minute—NO...NO!* Before Lieutenant Ron Casey and Chief Sam Walters could utter a word, Julie Rhinehardt's hands went to her face, contorted in terror, and she dropped without warning to her knees on the cold, hard tile floor of the entryway. She knew why they were there. Every cop's wife knew what this meant. The love of her life was gone!

The knock on the door and then his mother's screams brought Jim Rhinehardt running to the home's threshold. He arrived in time to hear Ron Casey address Julie loudly,

"Mrs. Rhinehardt, listen...*listen to me.* Julie, he's not dead. He's not dead."

Casey and Walters helped young Jimmy bring Julie, weak-kneed, to the couch. All the emotion, all the fear cascaded in waves over her as she sat there, holding tightly onto her young son. Sobbing, vision and mind obscured, she managed to comprehend the lieutenant when he said, "He's not dead." But after enduring the recent war trauma to her son Tommy, she just knew her beloved Kevin was either dead or standing at its door. Nothing this pair of paper pushers could say would allay that fear.

Walters spoke. "Mrs. Rhinehardt, Kevin was working a surveillance in Buellton. We don't know the circumstances, but he fought with a suspect inside the restaurant. He been either shot or stabbed...we don't know the circumstances exactly of what happened at this point, but he's alive, and he's at Cottage Hospital in Santa Barbara. He's getting the best care possible, Julie—may I call you Julie? We're here to take you there if you're up to it."

Nodding through tear-stained tissues, with a runny nose and bloodshot eyes, Julie Rhinehardt was helped to her feet by her son. Jim walked her to her back bedroom to get dressed. Shortly thereafter the pair emerged, disheveled, demanding to leave immediately. The group entered the backseat of the lieutenant's white Ford Crown Victoria and began the trip from Lompoc to Santa Barbara. Pulling up to the stop sign at the end of their cul-de-sac, the lieutenant clicked down the turn signal and made a cautious left turn. Traveling down D Street, going thirty-four in the thirty-five-miles-per-hour zone, he got about two blocks down the avenue when James Rhinehardt broke the silence from the backseat.

"*Excuse me*, but my father's probably dying in Santa Barbara. *Turn that fucking siren on and get us there, OK?*" The young man was, after all, Kevin Rhinehardt's son. His mother turned his way and smiled, for the first and only time that day.

Ron Casey reached down, flipped the switch on the car's Unitrol to the ON position, and accelerated the Crown Vic up to about fifty-five. They sped through the streets of Lompoc with the car's red, blue, and wigwag lights flashing, punctuated by the loud constant wail of the yelping siren. Sam Walters tapped his subordinate on the arm, giving him a negative head shake, a quick look of disapproval. Casey glared back at him. "Don't wanna hear it, Chief." Casey continued south on Highway One, kicking it up to almost eighty.

Mother and son sat behind them, holding firmly on to each other, awash in worries. Julie's subconscious thoughts drifted to nightmares about their future: dreaded flashes about planning a funeral, having to break the news to Tommy, a life of longing, of loneliness without her man. Jim held his mother tightly with each tremble, dabbing away flowing tears.

Earlier that morning, at about 2:45 a.m., heading south on Highway 101 just north of El Capitan Beach, James

Gaylord looked into his rearview mirror, and the image back there slammed his asshole shut—hard. Staring back at him was a sea of bright, pulsing red lights. A police car.

"Dennis, *shit*, we're getting pulled over. *What do I do?*" Fitch had calmed down by this point and told his brother to stay calm and just pull over slowly.

California Highway Patrol Officer Stan Waterman made the T-stop, cautiously approaching the red Honda under the bright illumination of his cruiser's spotlights. He came up on Fitch's passenger side, after sizing up the pair sitting quietly inside the Honda upon his approach. His flashlight revealed nothing out of the ordinary. Nervous driver, passenger dozing in his seat. He briefly thought, *Boy, the passenger's shoes are sure muddy!* After checking both occupants visually, he addressed the driver.

"Hello, sir, were you aware of your speed back there? I clocked you at seventy-eight…the limit is sixty-five. Where you guys going?"

Big D had donned his Angel's baseball hat and a pair of dark glasses after leaving the trailer park. He'd cleaned up the blood, changed pants, and at that point his face didn't look all that bad. He'd stashed the tool bag inside the black carry-on, which sat perched on the rear bench seat. He was in his cover mode.

Trying to appear calm, the lunky driver said, "I gotta get my friend here to the airport in Santa Barbara. He's flying out this morning early. Sorry, I didn't see how fast I was going."

Stan sized up the pair. *The passenger seems fine, I guess, but the driver's nervous. Maybe just worrying he's gonna to get scratched...guess they're OK.*

"Sir, can I see your license, registration, and proof of insurance, please?"

A visibly sweating Gaylord reached over and opened the glove box under the bright flashlight beam and careful gaze of the veteran traffic cop. Waterman thought, *Good, no weapons.*

"Here you go, Officer."

Back in his cruiser, Officer Waterman ran the lunky, perspiring driver up the DMV and CLETS (California Law-Enforcement Teletype) flagpoles, and Chunk came back clean. Moseying slowly back to the red Honda, he handed Gaylord back his wad of papers.

"Tell you what, Mr. Gaylord, just slow down. Not much traffic out here this morning, so it's just a warning this time. Have a nice night." Backing away cautiously at first, the trooper eventually turned and walked back to his unit. Once out of earshot, Chunk mumbled, "Wow, I thought we were fucked...*for sure!*" Dennis slumped farther down into his seat. "Drive away, Chunk...just keep it under sixty-five from now on, you moron!"

By noon there was quite a contingent of Rhinehardt entourage at Cottage Hospital. Most huddled around Julie and Jimmy, like a pod of whales nurturing young calfs. Of course, Sheriff Billingsly himself made a perfunctory appearance. He spent most of his time chatting with

Walters. Ron Casey made it clear to Julie that he wouldn't leave her side until her husband's condition was known. About three that afternoon, the surgeon finally made an appearance. He walked out to the lobby in his green scrubs and spoke up. "Rhinehardt family?" His eyes widened as about fifteen people—Jim and Julie, men in suits and sheriff uniforms—all bum-rushed him.

He addressed Julie. "Well, Mrs. Rhinehardt, he's not out of the woods, but he's off the critical list for now. We've downgraded him to serious but stable. We had to go in to repair the damage to his chest wall and left lung, but everything went fine. He has two broken ribs, and you'll see he has a chest tube in there to drain the blood and fluid from his chest wall. All routine, I assure you."

The MD continued, "Someone said he was shot? Well, he wasn't shot—he was stabbed, three times, actually. When we peeled off his bulletproof vest, we could see where two of the knife wounds penetrated only about a half inch into his left chest because they'd hit the thick material. It didn't stop the penetration, but it really slowed it down. Those two punctures went in only a small bit. However, the third knife wound missed the vest by about a half inch. Went into his chest in the gap where the material didn't cover. It penetrated the chest wall about four inches or so. The force of the stab broke two ribs on that side, and the blade deflated his left lung. The wound missed his heart, thank God. He was lucky. We've done our best to repair the damage, but your husband may lose about twenty percent lung function on that side. It's not that significant, though, and he'll get used to it. As long as there's no infection, healing is normal, and his lung inflates, he should recover fine in around a month or so. If he drains and his lung inflates, he could get out of here in a week to ten days."

I guess everyone gave a sigh of relief. I had no idea, though, since I was in the throngs of morphine-induced sexual hallucinations down in the ICU. I vaguely remembered something about a big yellow snake and Christina Aguilera—yeah, she was my genie in a bottle, baby! Sometime the next morning, Christina faded away, and through the cheesecloth haze that seemed to obscure my vision, I perceived a warm hand clutching my own. A bright light loomed above, and I had an urge to walk toward it! Slowly coming back to consciousness, I saw a cute brunette napping next to me, her head uncomfortably perched on the bedsheet next to my left side. I feebly shook the hand, held loosely in my own.

Wiping the cobwebs from her eyes, she awakened. God, I was happy to see she didn't have that snake! It was my lovely Julie, and the wide smile on her face was all I needed to make me feel instantly better. Her smile was all I'd ever needed. I managed to slur, "Hi, baby..." My throat was raw from the breathing tube they'd stuffed in there earlier while working on my chest.

Choking back tears, she loudly proclaimed, "Hey, Kevin's awake!" Despite my drug-induced euphoria, I realized we weren't alone. One by one a parade of faces floated in front of mine: Jimmy, Tommy (he really wasn't there, but my brain produced him), Will, Luis, Biff Corbett, Vince Bullard, Bob Roberts, and, oh yeah, good ol' Ron Casey. I slurred a few words. I believe I told Casey I was glad to see him. When you float above your body, high on drugs, you love everybody.

About two hours later the love fest came to an abrupt halt. *Son of a bitch!* The legal heroin (morphine) had worn off with a sudden, burning reality. I screamed profanities and cried out loud for more drugs as waves of immeasurable, searing pain engulfed my entire body. I felt like passing out. The hospital staff hadn't managed to stay in front of the eventual return of the pain freight train. Nurses ran in, pushing friends and family aside, stuffing needles full of shit into my IV tubes. I remember one young thing asking, "On a scale of one to ten, what's your pain level?"

"Fucking fifteen!" It took about five minutes for the screaming meemies to begin to subside. Here came the relief...oh yeah, baby, now that was *much* better. I started looking around for Christina and that anaconda again! After witnessing my girly-man tantrum, many of my visitors made their way out the door with perfunctory excuses. "We'll leave you guys alone" translated actually means "We're getting the fuck outta here!" I didn't blame them in the least!

That afternoon, while I rolled around in la-la land with the singer and the serpent, Ron Casey called a meeting of South Coast CID. One of the sheriff's own had nearly been killed, and the Driller case now took priority over all others. Casey was building creds with the guys. He made it clear that no one hurts one of our own without paying for it. The entire detective bureau would be made available as necessary to identify and catch this asshole. This was no longer just a property crime case. The ante had been raised, exponentially.

Lieutenant Gilstrap of Orange County SO volunteered to assign one of his brightest people, Detective Susan Wilcox, to work with Will Phillips up north. She was assigned on the Orange County end of the task force, but at this point it was one for all and all for one. She'd be coming up the next morning and would bivouac in Santa Barbara until the case was resolved. This made my good friend Will Phillips more than a tad nervous.

Unbeknownst to me, Willimena had been seeing a certain female acquaintance of mine. He'd finally hooked up with the lovely reporter Rachael Storm. Rachael was flat-out beautiful. She had a figure like Gina Lollobrigida and porcelain skin akin to Jennifer Aniston's. Well, perhaps I exaggerate, *a little*, but you get the message. Phil knew that working closely with a woman partner at this point in his burgeoning relationship could be an issue and not necessarily with him. He started sweating over having to tell his paramour he'd be working with a woman!

Phillips popped in later to visit me after work. I was still enjoying my visit with Christina but could comprehend most of what he had to say, about Casey making the investigation of my assault a priority, about Will getting a temporary lady partner, about his dating Rachael Storm. Back up—*say what*? Will and Rachael? No shit! But I should have known it. I remembered the telltale signs: their looking at each other with doe eyes, the mutual flirting, her leaving her blouse unbuttoned around us. At the time I thought she might have done that for my benefit, but I should have known better! Way ta go, William!

Julie and Jimmy stayed with me all that first day. She slept on a divan at my bedside. As she sat close to me, I could see the anguish in my lady's eyes. The pain of almost losing Tommy was still raw and now—almost losing me! I know it's corny, but she and I are soul mates. We're yin and yang. Sure, I'm a guy, and I may occasionally look at a younger woman as one bounces by. Hell, even a Rembrandt owner goes to art exhibitions, right? Funny, when Julie catches me looking at those bouncing chests, and I use that rationalization, she never buys it. All kidding aside, I don't know what I'd do without her. Twenty-five years and the love story's still the same between us.

That day at the hospital, I knew young Jim had turned the corner in his maturity. His relationship with Tom changed after his brother was wounded on that Afghan road. Today, as I saw my son holding his mother, crying at my bedside, I knew that even if I hadn't made it, my family would have been fine. The tree of my kin was made of strong branches. Even if one limb withered, the hardwood stood firm.

———

The Saturday following that ill-fated Friday morning on the second floor of AJ Spurs, the Driller's clan sat around their sixty-inch flat-screen television in that cul-de-sac in Seal Beach. CNBC channel four, KABC seven, and Fox channel eleven all ran stories on how a detective with the Santa Barbara Sheriff had been viciously attacked by an unknown assailant during the apparent commission of a burglary in Buellton. Although the sheriff's department would not comment further, the reporters dug up information from an "inside source" that members of the Orange County Sheriff burglary task force would be assisting in the investigation. The reporters hinted that the cops were working some kind of "crime spree."

Dennis Fitch was nervous, with good reason. His nose was misshapen and bulbous. One eye was quite swollen: black, blue, and red all over. That fucking cop gave him a run for his money, but Big D did what he had to do. He kept thinking to himself, *fuckin' A, I took care of business!* Secretly, Fitch couldn't help but fear his days were numbered. He was just glad he hadn't killed the pig. After all, it would be one less murder rap should things turn south. Most times normal people don't care if a cop gets hurt; after all, it's part of their job, getting in fights, right? The

Driller's thoughts were interrupted by an unmatronly drawl.

"Dennis, *baby*, whatcha gonna do now, seein' as you screwed the pooch! How much you got stashed away for that rainy day, darlin'?"

Brenda Gaylord sat beside her son on the sofa, her brown nicotine-stained fingers holding on to a smoldering Marlboro, the ash ready to fall into the glass tray hugging the top of the armrest beneath her right hand. James sat nearby, wearing a dingy white T-shirt riddled with moth holes. His large frame sank deeply into the cracked vinyl recliner that cradled his fat ass. Chunk's big head and unwashed hair hung low down the front of his chest. He knew he was part of something bad. Something he never wanted to be part of. Regardless, they were his kin. He'd stick it out. Did he even have a choice now?

Fitch lashed out defensively at his momma. "Look, I didn't mean to shank that guy, Mom! He nearly knocked me out. I couldn't get arrested, could I? I just had the friggin' knife in my hand...when we went to fighting, and I hit him a few times...forgot it was even there. Look, shit happens, Ma. I waited out back in the bushes for over an hour before I went in. I saw someone walking around inside there in the dark, but when that dude left out the back stairs I figured it was the same guy I'd been watchin'. I figured everyone was gone. How the fuck was I supposed to know there was another guy waitin' in there—a fuckin' cop, even!"

"So answer me, son…how much cash do ya have stashed? Are you goin' right back to work, back to the skimmer shit or doin' safes? Like before baby, you gotta have a plan. We need to have a friggin' plan!"

Looking at the video headline flashing across the bottom of the television screen, "*Deputy Stabbed—Manhunt for Suspect in Santa Barbara*," Dennis Fitch touched his face, throbbing and swollen, and weakly replied to his mother.

"I still have about thirty Gs, Ma. We'll be OK for a few months. I gotta stay low for a long while, though. We'll just sit tight. I gotta think this thing out."

A sullen James Gaylord, sitting nearby, got a shot of sudden chutzpah. "*You got to think this out*? What about me, bro? This is the second time you've lined me up for a prison fall…fucked up my life. I'm tired of you sayin', 'You fucked up, Chunk! You moron, you retard.' It's always my fault, right? Well, *you're the retard*! Gotta think things out, MY ASS! I oughta fuck you up, brother. I owe it to myself to do it an' just get the fuck outta here!"

Crushing her cigarette out in the ashtray, Brenda Fitch struggled to rise off the couch, her weight and physical deterioration impeding her. Shuffling slowly toward Gaylord, still deep in his recliner, she pointed a bony finger at his pockmarked face, wagging the wrinkled digit as she sauntered toward him. A deep furrowed scowl spread across her countenance like a pasty rash.

"You listen to me, *boy*. Your brother's done a lot for this family. What the fuck have you done, eh? You do what he says, that's what! He says, 'Jump,' you say, 'How high?' He says do this, you step and fetch, 'cause you don't know how to do shit on yer own. That's how it is. You touch my boy and you deal with *me*! Now, knock off this bullshit about leaving. With your brother hurt and having to lay low, you need to step up your own damn game 'round here. Ya hear me? *You* need to go out there and bring back some dough for us to live on...ya hear me?"

"But, Ma, I don't..."

Reaching out quickly she slapped James's face. "You don't, *my ass*. Shut the fuck up, Chunk. You better come up with something y'all can do, or you're right: you *will* get the fuck outta here. My son and I would be better off without ya anyway!"

James Gaylord sank farther down into the weathered chair, almost as far down as his own self-confidence. Her words rained like daggers thrust deep into his brain. *My son and I would be better off without you!* He realized she was correct. Brenda Fitch had never treated him like a son, just like some irritating neighbor kid who'd hung around for supper way past dark. He'd worn out his welcome in this family years ago. He was her condom mishap—the result of an unfortunate pinhole in Brenda's past. If he had any doubts before, the reality was crystal clear now. The hulking boy-man looked her right in the eye and weakly replied, "OK, Mom, I'll try."

Chapter 12
CHECKMATE

Two weeks had gone by, and Chuy Santiago hadn't heard from Big D. His calls to the Driller went directly to voice mail, and the Santanas' shot caller was getting pissed. He wasn't stupid. He figured Dennis was the one who had stuck that pig up in Santa Barbara. It wasn't Chuy's problem, though. Fitch had provided a steady stream of hot paper to the Shop, but suddenly that tit had dried up.

El Gerente's business associates had noticed the lack of productivity on the Shop's end, too. Acid-washed checks, altered and cashed for high dollars, meant good income for both gangs. The West Side Lopers converted that cash to Mexican heroin—dope they slung to the salivating users in Southern California. This trickle-down-cash drought prompted a request for an impromptu meeting between Santiago and his Loper counterpart, Manuel Quiroga. They met in a nondescript parking lot in Santa Ana.

Manny Quiroga, also known as *Martillo* (the Hammer) did not maintain as low a profile as his STS counterpart. Tatted up with "Loper" and "13" monikers inked over his hands, arms, neck, and back, this head-shaved banger had heavy ties to the Mexican Mafia. He was Mi Familia, through and through. The three dots on the web of his right hand let everyone know Martillo was an OG (original gangster), a veteran of the mean streets. The dark teardrop below the corner of his right eye telegraphed that he was a killer.

This fifty-something OG had made his bones by shooting an Orange County White Tiger when he was just fourteen. He walked up from behind and shot the *cabrón pendejo* in the head as the kid *puto* marked over *Locos Para Siempre*, which Quiroga and his homies had just finished spraying across the side of the Taco Tio in Costa Mesa. Known among his homies for two other unsolved homicides over the subsequent thirty-five years, Martillo Manny Quiroga was one hombre no one fucked with in Orange County.

Quiroga called the shots for most of the west siders. His Lopers had bankrolled El Gerente and his Santanas homeboys to begin Dragon Cleaners and start up their original operation. It was proffered in exchange for a 50 percent cut of the Shop's ongoing proceeds. Martillo and the Lopers had gotten quite used to a regular cash infusion from Chuy, but lately the STS *putos* hadn't been kicking them down their fair share.

This meeting made Santiago sweat because the Orange County Special Investigation Bureau's gang detail knew Quiroga all too well. Santiago didn't want to be seen with Manny in public, lest he be classified by the cops and entered into the Cal Gang computer system. Once classified, he was fair game to every *placa* (cop) in the state. Once put under the microscope, he would have to give up the Shop. El Gerente would be no more.

Quiroga didn't waste time. "So, what's up, *puto*? The boys and I be wonderin' why you're not kicking us down much green lately? Nobody got jammed up on your end. We know the bacon been leaving you 'lone. So why you keepin' dat *lana por sí mismos, ese: [that money for yourselves]*?"

Santiago tried being tough right back at the Loper: "Not keepin' da cash for myself. No, *ese*, we jus' hit a snag in supply...*chuco*! Dats it. *Claro, puto [Understand, fucker]*?"

Quiroga glared at Santiago, but the banger didn't back down. Epithets were traded, and in the end El Gerente seemed to satisfy his tattooed associate that things would pick up soon. Santiago was glad when the *pinche cabrón*, that fucking asshole, drove away. Santiago stayed put, parked there in his Camaro, a watchful eye out for the *policia* to roll up, for the bacon to fry him. He gave a sigh of relief after twenty minutes; it was cool.

Before going back to the Shop, Chuy stopped by his apartment on the east side of Garden Grove. Santiago was always respectful of his neighbors in the Sunnyside Apartments. Most of the other renters there were older gringos. He actually liked them, so he didn't want to draw unnecessary attention to himself by having loud parties, especially with his STS homeboys. Chuy owned a bull-mastiff terrier called Bruno. Bruno never caused a ruckus, never barked. El Gerente made sure of that by having a vet cut out Bruno's voice box. It didn't seem to bother the canine, who slobbered incessantly and loudly squeaked his voiceless approval.

Nowadays the neighbors noticed that Chuy Santiago even had a female companion, a nice Mexican girl. He introduced her around as Yoli. Yolanda Tafoya didn't converse much. Her grasp of the English language was slim to none. Greeting Santiago at the door that afternoon, Yoli kissed him hard as the door closed behind him, her wet, sensual tongue caressing his, entwining, penetrating deeply. She squeezed his shoulder, her other hand firmly cupping the cheek of his ass. Her exploring hands slowly teased their way downward to his crotch. She giggled as she grasped his maleness. He grew larger with her exploring touch.

She telegraphed her willingness, her expectation. He smothered the tops of her exposed breasts, jutting firmly out the top of her low-cut blouse, with sloppy kisses. His lips eagerly seeking her nipples—hungrily. At the front door, he picked Tafoya off the ground; her legs gripped firmly around his waist. She was ready to ride! Laughing and kissing they moved to the back bedroom; he tossed her backward onto the bed. Yoli opened up like a blossoming flower, ready for pollination by her hungry bee. "Oh, *da-malo, mi novio!* [Give it to me, lover!]" They groped and titillated each other's bodies as the items of clothing slowly peeled off. Bruno gave out a deep sigh, plopping down on his bed in the corner of the room.

As he got dressed afterward, Chuy informed his lady that he was under pressure to provide a new source of stolen checks. He'd come up with a plan to supplement the Shop's regular supply—normally provided by that guy he had introduced her to once: Big D. She remembered the tall, muscular gringo quite well. *El vato estaba muy guapo*— [he was very good-looking]—although she'd never tell El Gerente that! She figured Big D had to be a good thief nonetheless. She'd heard Chuy talk about him more than once, saying this guy scored all that paper while doing something with safes. She didn't ask any more questions— she didn't dare to.

Santiago laid out his plan as they sat, holding hands at the kitchen table in the darkened apartment. "Novia, I want ya to take a crew."

He would pay her well, and she wouldn't have to run checks nearly as much anymore. It'd be quite a raise! She and her boys would target mailboxes in western Orange County apartment complexes. He'd thought it all out. There were lots of apartments in that part of the county, with lots and lots of community mailboxes. He promised to get her a couple of STS guys who'd open the locks for her. She would be responsible for coordinating the times and places they hit. He would sort the stolen mail to pull out any checks—checks his magicians at the Shop could alter and prepare for a lucrative payday.

Turns out normal people living in apartments write a lot of checks to pay for stuff—checks to cover bills, big checks to the state or the feds, and even some to little Billy on his birthday! Chuy had heard of another similar operation in the Rancho Cucamonga area. Word around the 'hood was those pendejos were doing pretty good for themselves up there! Santiago wanted the Shop in on the action, and maybe this would get that fuckin' Martillo off his ass! Maybe even fill their own *pantalónes* in the meantime.

As he sat in the Shop's office later, lining up Yolanda's crew, he thought to himself, "Fuck Big D. I hope that dude just goes away. That gringo never did nothin' El Gerente can't do better!"

A day later, come 10:00 p.m., Chuy kissed Tafoya good-bye. She'd work the night shift tonight. Exiting out their apartment complex, Yoli spotted a newer white Ford Windstar van parked curbside, driven by Peanut Hernandez. Santiago had chosen his lieutenant because of his mastery of Spanish and his commitment to silence. Not all his guys could speak the language of their own country, but Peanut's parents raised him right, making him learn English but speaking only Spanish at home. He could converse with Yolanda the best of all of them.

Santiago also made it crystal clear to his lieutenant that although Tafoya would *think* she was in charge,

Hernandez was to make any key decisions. Peanut was sworn to secrecy to the other members of Santanas about the fact Yoli was even involved in this type of job. Mexican gangs are notoriously chauvinistic, oozing testosterone-driven machismo. Hernandez agreed to El Gerente's wishes. Inwardly he didn't trust this *chola* bitch at all. He questioned working with this *puta* in the first place.

The Shop had three of these nondescript transport vehicles. El Gerente knew that California is awash in a sea of white—it's the most popular vehicle color in the country, for all makes and models of cars. A white van would be difficult to describe by potential witnesses to his crew's handiwork. Each of the Shop's vans had three sets of magnetic signs stashed behind the front seat: *Johnson Electric*, in bright blue with a lightning bolt centered over the wording; *Bixby Plumbing*, in bright red with a muscled arm holding a wrench over the title; and *Bimbo Bread*, in brown, with a big-ass loaf of bread floating over it.

Santiago told all his drivers to put a set of these signs on their vans before they cashed checks or pulled other jobs, and, after they'd finished the deed, to drive a block away and pull them the hell off. Witnesses would only remember the logo, and cops would give them a pass as they drove away in their plain white vans. El Gerente laughed. "Stupid *placas*, they won't know shit!" His plan was tried and true; it worked well, job after job.

Yolanda pulled out her Thomas Guide map book and perused it under the dim illumination of the penlight perched between her pearly whites. The new female "crew chief" barked turn-by-turn directions, guiding Peanut toward the one thousand block of Palmyra Street in the city of Orange. Hernandez drove into the night, inwardly loathing her perceived command.

Tafoya had done her homework. Palmyra was the center point of a ten-block area in Orange, littered with low-rent apartments. Large complexes that had at least two, and up to four, hulking commercial mailboxes periodically dotting their streets, like the occasional zit on a teenager's face. The cool part for the Shop was that, although each of these large mail receptacles contained up to thirty-six locked mail cubbies for their residents, only one or two USPS locks protected them all from attack from the rear. Once this USPS access door was breached, all the boxes appeared like cells in a bee's honeycomb, each cell holding a few pieces of honey, which these crooked bees wanted to fly off with. The Shop crew could scoop out letters from all those cubbies in less than a minute and be off to rip off the next honeycomb.

El Gerente had done his own research before sending them off. He spoke to an old west sider, who'd served federal time for mail theft. The dude clued Santiago in on the fact that the best time to rummage for checks was on the first of the month, the second Friday, and the last day of the month. This was because people liked to pay bills at the beginning or in the middle of every month. Good citizens were creatures of habit. Those with tight budgets reluctantly wrote their checks at the very end, hoping their accounts didn't choke and bounce those rubber bank notes like soccer balls at a FIFA match! Tafoya and Hernandez were sent out that early morning on the second, hoping to find a treasure trove of waiting paper!

Pulling into an alley under the cover of overgrown trees, Peanut Hernandez affixed the Bixby Plumbing signs to the doors of the van and put a rag over the license plate. He then slowly motored around the corner into the Palmyra Gardens Apartments and up to one of their two mail containers. They'd driven through the complex moments before and knew the layout. It was now 12:30 a.m., and working folks were snug in their bunks.

Parking legally in the stall next to their first mailbox, the pair pulled bandannas up over their faces and exited the van. Some complexes had video cameras. Most of the greedy, albeit cheap apartment owners never bothered putting them in. The lux lighting around the complex was more than adequate to illuminate their nefarious deed. Peanut immediately went to work, quickly drilling out the two round USPS locks with a quiet DeWalt cordless drill. The small aluminum locks, made of cheap pig metal, literally disintegrated at fifteen hundred rotations per minute. Hernandez pulled the remaining shards of hanging metal out with a small set of needle-nose pliers. The doors swung open. Tafoya then started yanking mail from the honeycombed cubbies; scooping the letters rapidly into the open mouth of a bag held by her gangster counterpart.

The entire operation took less than three minutes. When they drove to the next box around the corner, a citizen's car was slowly exiting a nearby garage. They made a slow pass around the block and came back a minute later. Car gone. Get out, drill, scoop, *vamos*. Another quick job. More bills due that wouldn't get paid on time. *Too fucking bad, pendejos!*

That night Tafoya and Hernandez raided three complexes before traveling back to Garden Grove at 5:00 a.m. Two large green cloth garment bags containing the bulky mail sat perched on the backseat of the van like lime-colored birthday presents, each waiting to be unwrapped by curious criminals. Yoli found this much more exhilarating than passing checks. After all, she was the jefe now! Her sweet Chuy would be very happy.

As they drove back toward Sunnyside Apartments on the return trip, Peanut reached over and tapped Tafoya on the shoulder to get her attention. She turned to listen to him. His menacing Spanish was clear.

"I want you to know sumthin'. Chuy's my brother; *Gerente es me hermano*. If you betray him, you're dead!"

This caught her off guard. "*No*, never, he's my lover. I would never do that. Why are you threatening me?"

Hernandez just stared at her and, lifting his hands, threw an STS gang sign. "I protect my brothers; remember that!"

Twenty minutes later Peanut Hernandez pulled the van to the curb in front of Santiago's apartment complex.

As the girl exited, she looked over at the stoic Peanut as he pulled two clenched fingers across the line of his pursed lips. "You know better not to tell Chuy. Remember what I told you: *usted sabe mejor no decirle a Chuy. Recuerda lo que te dije.*"

As the van pulled away, Tafoya, who had earlier perceived she was the crew boss, the *jefe*, now understood who held the reins. She entered the apartment silently and gently slipped between the sheets with Chuy. She wouldn't say a word. She loved El Gerente, but she feared Señor Peanut.

Santiago went to the Shop at ten the following morning. He met Hernandez near Dragon's loading dock. They carried the two heavy green bags into the dry cleaning business and past Shin Wu, the scowling gatekeeper. Each banger wondered what they'd find inside those sacks, hoping this new enterprise would pay off. Sitting inside the back room, secure behind the heavy steel door, the two Mexicans sat cross-legged on the floor, greedily ripping open envelopes. Of the 472 gum-sealed vesicles, seventy-seven of them held the prize sought by Chuy. Seventy-seven possibilities for a Santanas/Loper payday!

El Gerente reached over and slapped Hernandez on the back, "My man! How long you say dis took you and Yoli las' night?"

"We got goin' 'bout half past midnight…stopped just shy of four thirty. We was humping, *ese.*"

Smiling, Chuy said, "She's sumtin' else, eh, Peanut? I picked a good one in her! Whatcha think?"

Feigning a grin, Peanut paused and said, "That's right, brother, she's one *muy buena chica*!"

El Gerente had to call in three more trusted workers to help with this new treasure trove. Olegario Zepeda supervised the delicate acid washing of the checks, carefully removing the legitimate ink with an acetone bath, taking care not to rub the bleached paper too hard, causing it to appear worn or unnatural. Armando Martinez was the Shop's pen master. He and one other forged the information on the rejuvenated conveyance to match the IDs manufactured for those running the paper. The dollar amounts listed were carefully set not to alert the store clerks to whom they were presented: face values of no less than $250, no more than $500. Why be greedy, after all?

He kept Olegario and his two cohorts off to one area of the expansive back room, separated by a floor-to-ceiling plastic curtain. A year ago Santiago installed a vacuum hood and vent fan over there, adjacent to their workstations. It kept the carcinogenic fumes relatively contained and filtered them out into the much larger main work area of Dragon Cleaners. *The chumps working out there were used to noxious fumes!* The venting was a necessity since Olegario's nose began bleeding, and debilitating headaches kept him homebound on several occasions. He started bumping into the walls! El Gerente made it clear to everyone that the Shop had no workman's comp insurance! If anyone got too sick, they got a bus ticket to

Tijuana, or perhaps euthanization via nine-millimeter (it was Chuy's call). It was in the Shop's best interest to keep Zepeda healthy.

Within the next four weeks, Hernandez, Tafoya, and one other STS grunt hit apartment mail in four separate cities and scored another 317 checks. Santiago made it a strict rule never to go back to a city within the same month. No use turning up the heat on any one jurisdiction. The cops might get pissed and burn your ass! Yoli did the initial planning but acquiesced to the menacing Hernandez when real decisions had to be made. Other than picking the cities and targeting the apartment complexes, she kept her mouth shut.

The Shop's manager had to deal with *uno mas problema*. Of the three crews of check runners, four of the twelve Hispanic shills used in the past to pass the altered paper had left the area for parts unknown. One other "bronk" got picked up for a DUI in East LA. He got a free ride, care of Border Patrol, back to his native soil, and it wasn't a round-trip ticket. In the months that the Driller had been on sabbatical, Chuy never had a need for most of the runners. There were just a few checks trickling in from some other suppliers, so why pay for loads of wetbacks to sit around? It was just good business to cut back on the Shop's overhead. However, now, to his chagrin, the workload exceeded the workforce!

Reluctantly, Santiago reached out to Manny Quiroga, asking for a couple of his Loper new guys with big balls.

He needed to make sure they didn't have a lot of tattoos and could speak fluent Spanish. They needed to be followers, not arrogant wannabes. Quiroga produced three new gangsters, all under twenty-one, recently jumped into the Lopers. Martillo vouched for them, and his word was his bond. All three knew if they opened their mouths, a Loper OG would permanently shut it for them. If necessary they would take the fall and say *nada*.

El Gerente now had three full crews of check runners, and run they did—all up and down Southern and Central California. Mom-and-pop stores, small markets, and check-cashing business were all taking it right in the ass. While Santiago, Tafoya, and his gangbanging henchmen were celebrating with Cuban cigars and silver Tequila, their game playing was not going unnoticed. Another prolific gang in Southern California—better armed and extremely motivated—was paying very close attention to the goings on. This gang owned the chessboard and were just a few moves away from taking their king!

Chapter 13
HOMER

"Are you fucking kidding me, Casey?"

"Chief, what can I say? We need him."

Lieutenant Ron Casey stood in the office of Operations Chief Deputy Walters, pleading his case. Walters sat defiantly behind his red oak desk glaring at the detective lieutenant. A picture of a smiling Walters standing next to then Lieutenant Todd Billingsly sat on a shelf behind him. It depicted the pair at a fundraiser that Sergeant Walters had thrown for the sheriff's candidate ten years prior. Walters had made chief deputy by the end of Sheriff Billingsly's first term. Everyone knew how. Walters's reputation as a self-aggrandizing prick was well known to everyone working under him. Payback was a bitch, it seemed, for everyone but Walters. Ron Casey now stood before the scowling chief with a somewhat unusual request.

"Look, I know Ocampo screwed up, made us all look bad with that deuce arrest, but you know he's been kicking ass out on patrol. You must admit that although you make him do a piss test, almost every week, he's been clean. I checked: he's been attending AA meetings regularly, and the shrink says he's made excellent progress. We're down Rhinehardt on this Driller case, and the Orange County task force supervisor is telling me they believe there's a Mexican gang connection here somehow...who better to help us out than Ocampo, our best bilingual?"

"Hell, Ron, you recommended Ocampo's termination, for Christ's sake! What kind of message will I be sending the troops if we just put him back into the bureau? I don't like it. I'm against it."

"Chief, you know damn well that you made me suggest his termination! It made me look like a total asshole when the sheriff balked at it. Look, make it TDY...just until this case is over. Just temporary, until we get a better handle on things. Look, I should've never agreed to suggest his firing; after all, he's been around a long while and did some great work in CID before he screwed up. I'm not supposed to know this, but a little psychologist birdie told me that Luis had some pretty serious issues when he lost his mother...that might have been the reason for the drinking. I'm willing to vouch for him now. If he messes up again, blame it on me."

Walters stood up and pointed a chubby digit toward Casey, who was feeling the ever-growing moisture in his armpits beginning to leach into his suit jacket.

"OK, have it your way, *Lieutenant*, but you said it, not me. If Ocampo so much as farts a 0.01 BAC, he's out, and you, my friend, will be counting spoons over in the jail. Am I clear?"

"As a bell, Chief. Can you cut the order today?"

"I will. Now get the fuck outta here, and don't come back until you catch that asshole! Oh, yeah, and tell the Mexican that I'll be watching him like a hawk."

The order came out thirty minutes later from the operations chief, sending Luis (TDY) from patrol to CID. TDY means "temporary duty yonder"—an old military term, still used today. Luis was working the south beat in Goleta when he got the cell phone call from Casey with the news. The deputy pulled the squad car to the side of Turnpike Road and just sat there looking skyward. With tears staining his weathered face, he whispered, "I love you, Mom."

At 10:00 a.m. Sergeant Roberts mustered most of CID into the squad room for a Driller case briefing. As Will Phillips entered the room, he couldn't help noticing a tall, somewhat muscular black woman sitting in the back corner. She wore a green blazer bearing a five-point sheriff badge with "Orange County Sheriff" embroidered below it, and suddenly the scales fell from his eyes. So THIS is Wilcox!

Detective Susan Wilcox normally worked vice-narcotics, and was a thirteen-year veteran of OCSD. Standing five feet eleven inches tall and weighing 150 pounds, she was…well, a female stud. Her bobbed haircut sent a certain message. Under her blouse, her diminutive breasts and large biceps revealed that, like Sergeant Randy Moore of LASD, she, too, spent time (a lot of time) pumping iron at her local gym. As Phillips approached her, she extended her hand and said, "I bet you're Will...heard a lot of good things about you." As she firmly shook Phillips's hand, it began to ache a little. He wondered if that was her intent.

Ron Casey began the meeting. "I just got a update on Kevin at Cottage Hospital...he's improving, and Julie wanted me to tell you all that he appreciates all the cards and visits. Visit when you can, but I'm telling you we need to double down to catch this asshole. You also probably saw the order cut this morning...we'll be joined soon by our own Luis Ocampo. He's back in the bureau temporarily, and he'll be working with the Orange County contingent since they expect a replacement in the OC for their Detective Wilcox, who is joining us for a while...Susan, stand up."

Wilcox almost snapped to attention and, pivoting around, waved like Queen Elizabeth to her British subjects. Will thought that was a little weird but told himself to give their pairing time. Sergeant Roberts then handed out team assignments, indicating that Phillips and Wilcox would continue following up on the leads that Will had developed toward identifying the Driller through the training records of the lock and safe schools in California. The other members of the team were to communicate with their Orange County counterparts and provide assistance and follow-up as needed.

An hour later, Ocampo had managed to change into his street clothes and stood ready in Sergeant Roberts's office. Ron Casey sat quietly in the corner. Seeing him perched there made Luis sweat.

The sergeant started it off. "Luis, you're back in the bureau because, with Kevin being down, I need someone we can devote specifically to the Driller task force. Orange SO is loaning us a body, and they expect one in return. They've asked for a Spanish speaker...now you know why you got a reprieve. I've been speaking with Ron, and you need to know that he went to bat for you with Walters today, and as expected, it wasn't easy getting you back into the bureau. This isn't permanent, and you still report to Walters as your special probation officer. I know that's not an easy pill for you to swallow, but shit happened and it is what it is. Please keep sober, and keep doing a good job. A fuckup could cost you everything."

Bob Roberts then looked over at the lieutenant, stood, and left the room. Luis was now alone with the man who was personally responsible for his demotion. Ocampo had read Casey's recommendations in the internal investigation. He knew this guy suggested he be fired. Luis expected an ass chewing from the guy. Instead, Ron Casey started it off with, "Louie, I'm glad you're back."

"Look, I want to tell you that even though I got you demoted—hell, almost canned—I was just doing what I felt I had to do. You embarrassed the department, made all of CID look bad. I admit that I started off the investigation pissed off from the get-go. That was wrong. Even though I heard about what great work you did here in the past, I was under tremendous pressure from higher-ups to, well, make it clear to everyone else that screwing up like that could get them fired. You brought it on yourself, Lou, but I'm here to admit that you were a scapegoat. What happened to you was meant to send a clear message to the troops. It did.

"Now, however, I want you to realize that this assignment is a very good thing for you. I expect you to bust your ass to help bring this asshole in. Go home and pack enough clothes for a couple of weeks. The two sergeants in charge of the Orange County Task Force are expecting you. Report to Sergeant Randy Moore, who's with LA Sheriff but working down there. He's on the end of the investigation that has connected our Driller to a bad-check ring they believe is centered in SoCal...they're passing the paper he's been stealing from his safe jobs. They're all connected somehow. They have intel that it may involve Mexican street gangs down there, and they need your help with interviews and translation...everyone knows you can sweat those beaners like nobody else."

"Beaners? Lieutenant, you do know I'm a beaner, too, don't you?"

Casey suddenly looked like he got caught farting in church.

"Relax, Ron, Lieutenant, I know what you meant. For the record, we beaners do like refries! I know you did what you think you had to do with me on the IA, too. And I know exactly who put you up to it. He gets a piss test from me every week."

Shaking his head affirmatively, Ron Casey said, "Er... you know, Luis, I can't comment on that."

Meanwhile, Will and Susan were getting better acquainted. Phillips laid out his research on all the safe-school applicants, including one in particular that stood out: Todd Starnes. This guy provided a Cal ID to the school and attended six weeks of classes. Interestingly, he left before they certified him as a safe and lock technician and could run a live scan of his fingerprints for a background check. Turns out the ID card was fake: no record of that number or name in the DMV files. Phillips obtained a copy of the card, showing an address in Orange County. That meant a road trip.

Detectives Biff Corbett and Ed "Ditch" McCormick got the job of combing the evidence from AJ Spurs to turn up any leads. Biff stood six feet five inches tall and Ed only five feet seven inches. Talk about Frick and Frack! Corbett liked to stand next to McCormick and lean a forearm atop Ed's shoulder. To add insult to injury, a local photographer had captured that very image at a homicide scene a couple of years back, and the paper printed it on the front page.

Good ol' Ditch! McCormick got that nickname several years back when, on a stakeout, he chased a youthful burglar and fell headfirst into a drainage sump, emerging muddy from head to toe. The guys had called him

Ditchwalker ever since. Always wearing cowboy boots with his suits, Ed normally worked burglary cases, but his expertise in warrants made him stand out among his peers. Ditch spoke with a low midwestern drawl.

Biff Corbett was the go-to guy on crimes against persons. Robbery/homicide was his forte, and his work on the Phantom murders helped crack that case. Biff's normal partner, Ted Banner, had recently been promoted, so Corbett was occasionally working with Kevin on major crime cases. With Rhinehardt laid up, Frick and Frack had become an item. Corbett was by far the tallest detective the agency had ever employed. With jet-black hair and chiseled features, he looked like a giant Clark Kent. The only drawback was that his ego matched his size. Otherwise he was one of the best.

Frick and Frack met with Sergeant Ron O'Hara of forensics the day after Rhinehardt "got the shaft" at AJ's, to go over all the photos and examine the evidence. They found DNA—drops of the crook's blood at the second-floor exit door. Kevin apparently fucked the boy up in the fight. Good for Kevin. The sample had been sent off to the Department of Justice. If the Driller was a convicted, violent felon, he'd be in their data bank. No fingerprints were found, however, and eventually the DNA proved fruitless as well.

No forced entry into the building was observed either. Forensics had determined why. They found that, into the depression of the strike plate to the upstairs emergency door, someone had pushed wet paper, which hardened when it dried—like a block of cement. The latch would not catch in the plate once the door was closed. To everyone other than the crook, the door seemed secure. When the inside bar was pushed, it opened as usual, but the door could be pulled open from the outside without effort. The alarm sensor on the door had been disabled as well. Forensics found a thin magnet taped across the recessed sensor in the door frame. The door could open, and effectively the magnet kept the alarm circuit closed all the time. The Driller must have scouted out the restaurant beforehand and slipped upstairs to set up the door for his upcoming burgle. Unfortunately, AJ's didn't have video cameras upstairs, so that was a disappointing dead end.

The stairs and asphalt parking area gave up no clues, but the Driller tore a path through the drainage on the south side of the restaurant, directly toward the Flying Flags trailer park. Once over there it was gravel, and the trail ended. Biff and Ditch proceeded to interview every resident of the park and got a list of all the folks who had rented space the morning of the burglary. None of the residents they found had heard or seen anything suspicious that morning. No shadowy figures, no unknown cars. No video. No leads. Two days after their canvass of Flying Flags, things changed.

Josh Bellamy was a vagabond traveler. At seventy-two, he and his cocker spaniel traveled the California coastline in his 1984 Dolphin class C motor home. He was on a bucket list spiritual quest. He'd stopped over that night at Flying Flags on his way to Big Sur. He had only a post office box for an address, and since the form asked for it, Josh left his cell phone number.

"Hello, is this Josh Bellamy?"

"Why, yes, who's this?"

"I'm Detective Ed McCormick with the Santa Barbara Sheriff's Office. We obtained a registration card from the Flying Flags trailer park in Buellton with your phone number on it. Did you stay there on April third of this year...less than a week ago?"

"Why, yes, did I do something wrong? Am I in trouble?"

"No, no, sir. There was a crime that occurred around two a.m. that morning, right across from the trailer park at AJ Spurs restaurant, and we're asking anyone who was there in the trailer park if they noticed anyone or anything suspicious in the early hours of that morning or anytime during your stay there, for that matter. One of our detectives was severely injured that night, so we're asking for the public's help."

Bellamy paused on the other end of the line. "You know, detective, I do remember something. My dog, Tinkle, growled that morning, early—just after two in the morning. Sort of woke me up enough to pay attention, so I glanced at the clock. Think it was about 2:25. I heard some kind of commotion off in the corner of the park, the part closer to that restaurant. I had the shades closed, so as I tried to look out I heard a car start up over there and kinda rev the engine. It was a distance away from me, but I saw it speed off, out the main street past my rig. I figured it was some other resident leaving the park in a bit of a hurry."

Ditch sensed a lead, and his voice piqued with curiosity. "Did you get a look at the car—the color, make, or model? Did you see anyone near it? Could you describe the occupants?"

"Well, it was pretty dark. Can't tell you what kind of car, but it was maybe compact or midsize. Let me think— yeah, I think it was red. I saw red as it went by a light on one of the trailers over there. Sorry, though, I couldn't see who was in it. Is your officer OK? Gosh, I hope so."

Ed McCormick reassured Mr. Bellamy that Kevin was recovering and gleaned as much information as he could from the gentleman. It was obviously the Driller: right time frame, right area of the park. Now the team had a color and an approximate size. Better than no leads at all.

Frick and Frack relayed the vehicle description to the team. Sheriff FIs (field interviews), calls for service, and citations were checked the prior night and that morning for any connection to a red compact or midsize vehicle anywhere in the county. Disappointingly, deputies had no contact with anyone in a similar vehicle that night. Biff Corbett sent out a BOL (be on the lookout) request for information regarding any agency having contact with individuals in a red compact or midsize car during the time frame of Rhinehardt's assault. Days, then weeks, passed with no responses from allied agencies. It was a dead end.

While en route to Orange County, Will and Susan discussed the case file regarding the suspicious lock-school student. The photo on the driver's license for Todd M. Starnes, DOB 2/22/1984, was a bit grainy. It depicted a dark-haired Caucasian man in his late twenties, six feet one, 175 pounds. The address listed was 25525 Main Street, Lake Forest, California. As the pair traveled the congested 101 and 405 freeways to check out the address, they discussed each other's backgrounds.

Will recounted his recent rise from patrol deputy to detective and the fact that he was Kevin Rhinehardt's partner at the time Kevin was almost killed. Reluctantly, Will confessed some survivor's guilt over the fact that Kevin was doing him a favor by taking the stakeout that night in his stead. Susan reassured him that she would have felt the same way but that all cops know the job is dangerous when they take it. It's all in the toss of the dice.

Wilcox, now in her third year in vice-narcotics, had experienced the seedy streets of Orange County firsthand. She had worked many a sting operation, walking the barrios in tight skirts, trolling for takers. Her lips smeared with cherry-red paint, she wore Afro wigs similar to those worn in the seventies. Johns apparently like that. Two years ago, while working a black pimp who assaulted random girls, she had to shoot the suspect when he pulled a knife on her. OCSD determined it was a "good shoot," and she was cleared. She did mention to Will that by happenstance she shot the pimp *in the pecker*! That brought some laughter to the car. Cop humor can be a tad dark.

Will mentioned he was dating an *LA Times* reporter, and Susan responded with, "Yeah, I'm engaged. My partner and I live in Laguna Hills." Hmm, short hair, muscles, a kung-fu grip, and she lives with a "partner." Will was a slow learner, but the light finally came on. *Rachael would be so happy*!

Traffic was a real bitch, but Phillips and Wilcox managed to get to Forest Grove at around 2:30 p.m. Not surprisingly, 25525 Main Street was located in a commercial district. The sign above the numbers read *"Home Away from Home."* They entered the dingy outer office and discovered a hallway leading to another small two-hundred-square-foot room in the back. Numbered lockers, with key locks, lined the four walls. Of course! A mail drop! White-collar crooks in particular used them all the time. So, coincidently, this Todd Starnes guy probably got stuff here. The plot had just thickened!

A side door near the front entry bore a very small plaque that read *"Office."* Wilcox knocked a few times, receiving no answer. In her Robocop style, she then banged hard, and repeatedly, with her kung-fu fist, announcing, *"Sheriff, open up!"* After a minute or so, they heard, "OK, OK, don't fuckin' break it; I'm coming." The inside deadbolt was turned, and a safety latch could be heard as it was pulled from its slide. The door cracked about six inches, revealing a very short balding man wearing thick horn-rimmed glasses. "Yeah, *do ya have a warrant?*"

This was Susan's territory. Thrusting a five-point OC sheriff's badge in his face, she announced, "*No,* we don't have a fuckin' warrant, but if you know what's good for you here, you'll open up and talk with us; *understand?*" The little hobbit gave a look of surrender and reluctantly opened the door. He stood there in his dirty wife-beater undershirt and stained shorts, holding a half-eaten bagel. Cream cheese adorned the side of his diminutive mouth, running into his misshapen mustache.

"What's this about, officers? I didn't do nothin'. I run a legit business here. It's not my ex-wife, is it? That bitch's always saying shit about me. I didn't touch her; don't believe it!"

Will Phillips took over. "What's your name, buddy? Believe me, this has nothing to do with your wife…if you answer our questions, you'll be just fine."

"Homer Stimson. I own the place."

Both Will and Susan just stood there, staring at each other. Phillips stifled a chuckle. Wilcox couldn't resist. "Homer Simpson, are you fucking kidding me? You expect us to believe that shit? Hell, you even look like Bart's dad!"

"Come on, you guys, the name's Homer *Stimson*, not *Simpson*. I get crap about it all the time." He reached into his back pocket, producing a California DL.

The detectives both stared hard at the license: Homer J. Stimson. With a broad smile, Susan Wilcox said, "Well, we apologize, Mr. Simpson; we stand corrected."

"*Stimson*, it's S-T-I-M-S-O-N! OK, what do you two want, really?"

Phillips made an attempt at getting professional. "Does anyone named Todd Starnes have a mailbox here with you? We have reason to believe that as recently as a few months ago he did."

Wiping his hand, covered in cream cheese, on the rag he wore as a shirt, Homer Simpson, er, Stimson, adopted an "I'm pondering" expression. As if deep in thought, he tapped an index finger on his lips while rolling his eyes around. "No Todd, but I think I remember a Brenda...yeah, a Brenda Starnes. She stopped payin' on that box about three months ago. I got it rented to someone else now."

Susan chimed in. "What came to that box while she had it? Was she the only one who used it? Did she pay you with a credit card or a check?"

"Slow down, five-O, I gotta remember...check my records, OK? Come in and sit down. Just don't go nosing around too much—my clients have rights, ya know! I'll cooperate."

The pair of investigators walked into the dingy office apartment. A twin-sized, disheveled bed occupied one corner. The sheets were, to put it mildly, *used*. A kitchen table littered with pizza boxes occupied the other, with a sink full of unwashed dishes smack-dab in between them. Susan Wilcox gave out a stifled scream as a cockroach, big as a crab, skittered across her shoe. Apparently the kung-fu queen had some phobias!

Stimson went to a rusty four-drawer file cabinet sitting next to his threadbare couch and pulled out a file folder, filed under "S." The application for the box was not so surprisingly devoid of a lot of pertinent information, like address, phone number, and so on. *"Pays Cash*—Box 17" was written in black felt pen at the top of the form. Stimson noted a date, two months earlier, on the bottom with the notation *"Moved Out."*

Wilcox was pissed. "Are you fuckin' kidding me, Homer? You get no address, no info from this lady, this Brenda Starnes? What did she look like? I don't suppose you remember that tidbit of information, do you?" Surprisingly, Stimson seemed to brighten up a bit.

"As a matter of fact, I do remember her. She was around fifty-five or so, a white lady. I found her attractive. About five foot tall, a bit heavy—I like that in a woman. She had light brown hair and smoked a lot. It was her only drawback. I know she had a son, too. Said he was a good kid, and he lived with her. I think she said they lived in San Diego. She mentioned she was picking up stuff for him here, but I don't remember her ever tellin' me his name. Wait, you know, it might have been Todd, yeah, Todd Starnes was the addressee on the packages—I remember now. She ate lunch with me here once…she was a very nice lady."

Will continued picking the hobbit's brain. "Do you remember what kind of packages this Todd Starnes got here? Names of the companies mailing to him, that kind of identifying stuff?"

"Let me think." Homer went into his cerebral lip-tapping memory mode. "I don't nose around people's packages here. It pays not to, if you catch my drift. Some of the boxes were pretty heavy, though. I remember that."

Once back in the detective unit, Wilcox ran Brenda Starnes, fifty-five years old, living in San Diego, in CLETS. No match. Nothing even close. She ran the Homer "Stimson" DL number, too. The dispatcher came back with "Homer *Simpson* is clear." Giggling was heard in the background. Phillips couldn't resist and, grabbing the microphone from Wilcox, he stoically proclaimed, "That's *Stimson*, Homer J. S-T-I-M-S-O-N."

"Ten-four, he's also clear on CLETS and NCIC, as well as with Springfield PD."

Mic clicks peppered the Orange County Sheriff airwaves, along with the occasional ***Doh***!

Chapter 14

ON THE MEND

About ten days into my extended vacation at Cottage Hospital, I was feeling better—a lot better. The doc came in early and told me he was ordering my chest tube removed. I was ecstatic! I had watched my lifeblood oozing through that damn thing, filling a gnarly plastic bag for way too many days. It was an ugly reminder of how screwed up I was!

About an hour after the doctor gave me the good news, the three stooges came in. I should have known something was going down, something bad, when I spied these ladies bounding into my room. Not the usual cute, petite nurse staff, these harpies all looked like Broomhilda from Sweden—they were rather large-framed ladies. They looked like they went to Arnold Schwarzenegger's tailor! The lead nurse—I could swear her name was Cratchet—said, "Mr. Rhinehardt, we're here to take your chest tube out—isn't that wonderful?"

With that comment, the three of them surrounded me like cops ready to take down a perp. The one boss lady ripped off the surgical tape that held the tube securely to my chest. She just yanked it off without warning. Then she clipped off the stitches that held it in place.

"Ow, that hurt!"

Then the other two behemoths laid hands on me; they pinned both my arms down onto the bed! As my head swung side to side nervously, my eyes wide with dread, I wondered if they intended on doing an exorcism or just give me the last rites. Then the head honcho barked an order. "Now exhale, Mr. Rhinehardt, *hard and long*!"

I began to mouth, "*Excuse me?*" I was actually thinking *What the fuck?*

"Here we go. *Exhale, Kevin.* Do it **now**!"

Holy shit. It felt like they were pulling all twenty feet of my small intestine out that friggin' one-inch hole! I feebly pushed every ounce of life-giving breath out of my weakened lungs with a loud hiss. The burning, ripping sensation seemed to go on forever as the mere ten inches of crimson-stained plastic tubing slowly wormed its way out of the left side of my chest! I felt like an actor in a real-life sci-fi movie. I was birthing a tubular alien!

"Sorry, Mr. Rhinehardt, but we couldn't pull it fast, and we've learned to use the element of surprise!"

Surprise? The bitches ambushed me! I must admit it felt a whole lot better afterward, though. I couldn't resist chipping back at 'em as they left. "Do you ladies work out?

We could use you on the sheriff's arm-wrestling and tor-ture team—*shit!*"

The trio feigned smiles as they clomped out of the room. Once I settled down, I realized that I was breathing easier now, and a heavy weight, a constant pressure, had been lifted from me. Thinking back now, that was the day I turned the page on my recovery. My day got much better as the afternoon unfolded.

"Look who's here, Kevin!" Julie was talking as she walked into my room, extending her two hands back toward the opening in the door as if mouthing a magi-cian's "ta-da!" My son Tom was wheeled in by Jimmy: two wounded warriors meeting face to face! I couldn't help it: I began to cry. It hurt my chest like hell, but I couldn't help it.

"Knock that shit off, Dad! You'll get me started." Tom was wearing an army logo polo shirt, altered to allow for the huge cast on his shoulder and arm. Below his gym shorts, another cast encased his left lower leg. Tom's face was bruised but held a wide smile. Jim, pushing behind him, shared the same broad grin as did my honey, Julie. It was like a shot of adrenalin, straight to my heart. All the Rhinehardts together once again! For the first time in a couple of days, I actually wanted to get out of bed. So we all sat around talking and laughing until fatigue hit both Tom and me like an unappreciated Christmas present.

I rejoiced in the news that my veteran son would be re-ceiving physical therapy in nearby San Luis Obispo. Thank

God! He could stay home with us during his rehab. The cast on his shoulder would stay put for a couple of months, but his leg would heal much sooner. His docs told him he could soon begin the arduous process of learning to walk unassisted again. Don't tell me miracles don't happen! My son would soon be walking, and I was alive to see it.

Jim wheeled Tom out of the room, but Julie lingered behind. She handed me a paper bag. Opening it, I cautiously withdrew three paperback books: *Supervision of Police Personnel*, by Nathan F. Iannone, *The Santa Barbara Sheriff's General Order Manual*, and the *Barron's Police Sergeant Examination* study book. I looked at her quizzically and asked, "What's up with these?"

"I got a visit from Ron Casey yesterday, Kevin. You know, he's been pretty great to us, calling every day, and I know he visits you all the time, too. He's even coordinated some of the wives who've brought us meals. I really appreciate that. Well, he gave these books to me and asked me to tell you that he wants you to take the sergeant's test next week. You haven't applied yet, so there's an application in there for you to fill out right away. He figures you'll be out of here by the time the written exam comes around, so he 'ordered' me to tell you, 'No excuses.' Ron said you're a good cop and that he'd like to see you get to a position to help other guys develop into good cops, too. He seemed very sincere, Kevin. I think you oughta take the test."

"Crap, Julie, I don't know. I love my job. I don't love this part of it—you know, the getting stabbed part. You know what I mean. If I get a promotion, it's back to patrol. Twelve-hour shifts, nights, weekends...are you OK with that?"

"I love you, baby, and I know you deserve those stripes! I say go for it."

Julie left me alone with my thoughts and with that paper bag full of books. I'd taken the promotional exam twice before, but honestly I'd never actually studied for it. As a result I was never a serious contender, either! I knew that Ted Banner, my ex-partner, had told me that it wasn't until he got serious and put his nose to the study grindstone that he finally got it. All kidding aside, Ted deserved it, and his patrol squad loved him. Maybe I could make it, too, and the extra cash for retirement would be an added benefit. I slowly retrieved the sheriff sergeant application form and called the nurse for a pen. I'd give it a try. Hell, even a blind squirrel manages to score a nut now and then!

Two weeks later I was home and had *Supervision of Police Personnel* memorized cover to cover. I'd just finished taking the written exam and was receiving daily briefings by Phillips on what was happening with the hunt for the Driller. I was blown away by how many resources were being expended to catch that asshole now! About twenty investigators with Orange and LA counties and Will and Luis were full time on it. When I heard Ocampo was TDYed to the bureau, I called him personally to congratulate him. There wasn't a doubt in my mind he would shine—he was a greater resource to the department where he was. I figured that even rat-faced Walters would see it soon enough! Luis had spent the last couple of weeks staying in Irvine, working there with the SO in a mutual aid capacity. Our loss was their gain. My oral exam for the sergeant was in five days. I was feeling great, and I was hoping to be medically released to come back to work soon afterward.

Immediately after their revealing interview with Homer J. Stimson, Will Phillips and Sue Wilcox beat feet back to Orange County Sheriff headquarters. They called for a meeting with Sergeant Chuck Stiles and gave him the news. Phillips let Susan deliver the glad tidings (she told Will she wanted to since she worked for the guy).

"Chuck, we may not know his name, or where he lives, but we have a picture of the Driller!"

The duo laid the photocopy of the fake California ID on the sergeant, depicting a younger Dennis Fitch, also known as Todd Starnes. It was a small grainy picture, though, thanks to the crummy copy machine used at the Stanley Lock and Safe Academy in San Jose. It wasn't great, but it was enough to light up the detective sergeant's face.

"Good work, you guys! Get this to forensics and have them blow it up and make up a professional flyer. Have the flyer sent out to every agency in California, including parole and probation. Someone's gotta know this asshole. I'll pass this along to the Sheriff personally, Susan. Again, good job, Wilcox!"

Will walked away from the meet more than a little pissed. After all, it was he who had developed the lead in the first place. Kung Fu Grip was taking all the damn credit! *I'll pass this along to the sheriff, my ass*! Wilcox never bothered to tell her boss the truth about the lead, never spoke up when *she* got the accolade. Young Will Phillips was experiencing his first bitter taste of professional back-stabbing! As with any bad culinary experience, that lousy taste would linger.

Will kept his angst to himself, at least for the time being. He called me later in the day to vent, and I reminded him that he was the new kid on the block and cautioned him not to let his mouth overload his ass. Perhaps she hadn't meant to take the credit. My own ass had been over-loaded by my tongue many times over the course of my twenty-two-year-long career!

I complimented him on his work with Bart Simpson's father and suggested he begin checking with lock and safe equipment companies for any dealings with our crook, Todd Starnes. It might just lead back to the mail-drop address, but who knew, some good old-fashioned shoe leather might just break the case. My partner told me that since my dance with the Driller at AJ's several weeks ago, the prick had gone underground. No more safe jobs, any-where. I had faith the punk couldn't stay low forever. He and I would meet again, and the next time he might be the one on the floor in his own pool of red!

Meanwhile, Luis Ocampo was enjoying his work with Sergeant Randy Moore and the LASO gang enforcement team. Along with the Orange County Sheriff CAT (Criminal Apprehension Team), they'd been working a tip that the OC Lopers were involved in recent mail thefts plaguing the cities of OC and LA counties. These pervasive and prolific mail thefts, primarily from larger apartment and condominium complexes, had caused a local media blitz.

The losses even raised the interest of the US postal inspector's office. Two postal inspectors were working closely with the task force. The twenty-man unit, in three separate surveillance teams, had been keeping close tabs on known Lopers, hoping to catch one of them in the act or in any act, for that matter. A couple of the bangers had been picked up but adhered to the gangbanger code of ethics: "I got nothin' to say, *puto!*"

Mom-and-pop grocery stores, liquor stores, and any smaller business that routinely cashed workers' payroll checks were taking big losses as a result of the checks stolen from the victims in the six-week-long mail theft scheme. Despite all the flyers and the publicity, the employees of these markets just kept getting fucked over by the Hispanics passing the damn things. Time after time, the victims of the bogus check scam told the detectives the same story. "If we stopped taking checks or made it harder for our customers to cash them, we lose business. They hand us what looks like legitimate identification!" It was hard to feel sorry for the store owners; it was all about money, after all—greed by the crooks to take advantage of the victims and greed on the part of the merchants to draw in more customers; it all fed the fire. It was the age-old formula: the quest for the almighty dollar. It keeps law enforcement in business.

The task force troops were getting restless and frustrated, as well. One brave LASO detective spoke up in a meeting: "Why are we busting our humps, night after night, when these store owners keep doing the same shit? They keep allowin' these assholes to fuck 'em over? I say let them suffer. This latest batch of checks doesn't have a fucking thing to do with our Driller either...wasn't this party started to catch that prick in the first place?"

Randy Moore's face became flushed, and his thick neck swelled further. He was quick to quell the potential mutiny: "*Shut the fuck up*, all of you! We're cops; they're crooks—it's that simple. Is this Driller asshole directly involved right now? No, maybe, I can't tell ya for sure. Are these the same fuckers who were dealing with the guy just a month or so ago? Yes. When we catch the assholes stealing the mail, we catch the assholes passing the checks. Chances are, they're one and the same...and, by the way, you morons, those pricks can identify the Driller! If any of ya don't wanna continue working with this crew, I can arrange for you ta go back to pushing a black-and-white and answering barking-dog calls. Feel free to start that diet, and put those tan and greens in the dry cleaners. Anyone else wanna one-way ticket back to graveyards?" It got very quiet in the room.

Will Phillips and Susan Wilcox had a long drive back to Santa Barbara in heavy traffic after their briefing with Sergeant Stiles. Will was uncharacteristically quiet during the trip. He dropped her off at her room at the Turnpike Lodge and drove back to his apartment in Buellton. It was late, but Rachael Storm was waiting with hot spaghetti and red wine, her long hair loose, her blouse unbuttoned. After they embraced, and Will gave her a perfunctory peck on the cheek, she called him out for his lackluster attempt at affection.

"Boy, that was a breathtaking welcome, my less-than-attentive lover! My God, I'm all hot and bothered now—let's screw! Take me now baby—NOT!"

"Sorry, Rachael. I'm tired, and I already got fucked over once today. Don't know if I could handle another one, quite frankly."

"All right, tell Momma all about it. Come here, little Will."

"Arg, just don't *ever* call me Willimena."

"Ah, that's cute—why?"

"Just leave it…I got my reasons."

On the couch, sipping wine and cuddling, Phillips laid out how exhilarated he had felt when his intuition about checking the safe and lock schools had paid off. How they now had an actual picture of the bastard who had stabbed Kevin—the guy who was responsible for one of the biggest crime sprees he'd ever heard about. And then Susan Wilcox basically took credit for it all. He felt like strangling the bitch.

"You told me about this Wilcox chick. What's her angle? I betcha she just wants to hit on you. I don't know how I feel about this new partner of yours, Will. Should I be worried?"

Stifling a grin, Phillips said, "Ah, you see, lovely Rachael, my only worry is that she never meets you."

Looking puzzled, the curious reporter sensed a story. "Now, come clean. Now I gotta know. Why the hell can't I meet this woman? What the hell are you hiding?"

Openly laughing, Willy laid it out for her. "Rach, I think she flies the rainbow flag over her and her partner's place in Orange County. If she met you, she might like my gorgeous lady just a little too much! I figure my muscular, tall female partner roots for the other team, swings on the other side of the vine, if you get my drift. I don't give a shit about that, though. Hetero or homo, the backstabbing still hurts."

After a good laugh, and more venting, the spaghetti went down quickly, thanks to the lubrication of a nice bottle of Merlot. Rachael was sleeping over more and more at his place now. Will made her feel special. As beautiful and successful as the *Times* reporter was, she'd never before felt appreciated or wanted for anything other than her looks or her work ethic. This guy did it all for her. He was her reason to come home now. She didn't want the carousel ride to stop.

As they finished cleaning up after dinner, the rookie detective eased in behind his beautiful lady standing at the sink, her hands still full of soapy dishes. Running his gentle hands up from her thighs, slowly tracing her perfect lines with his fingertips up to the magnificent swell of her breasts, he whispered, "Well, maybe getting fucked one more time today won't hurt me!" She turned around and held his face, framed in the suds, their lips melding, their tongues exploring.

Chapter 15
SHARKS AND MINNOWS

The white van pulled up outside Jesus Santiago's dimly lit apartment complex promptly at ten thirty. Traffic was light that time of the evening, and Yoli Tafoya slowly walked up to it on the deserted street. The excitement of her new job had worn off weeks ago. Dressed in blue jeans and an oversize gray hooded sweatshirt, her long hair tucked inside her black baseball hat, her feminine curves were disguised well. Peanut Hernandez glared at her from behind the wheel as she slid the side door open to climb in.

"Hey, Yoli, how ya doin' tonight, home girl?" The greeting came from the grinning passenger sitting shotgun, Gilbert Moreno. Moreno was a Loper recruit, fresh off initiation, too green to have yet been classified by the Orange County gang task force and too naive to know he was pissing off Hernandez by chumming up to Tafoya.

Moreno turned back toward her and, pulling up his shirt-sleeve, showed Tafoya a fresh street tattoo on his left inner arm: LWS, for Lopers West Side. Fresh Vaseline still glistened over the letters. When Peanut saw the newbie raise his sleeve to proudly show off the gang moniker, he promptly reached over with his right hand and backhanded the youngster, knocking him solidly against the passenger window.

"Fucking A! Why'd you mark yourself, *ese*, when you know we caperin', *you dickhead*! You fuckin' better hide dat tat until you're done workin' wit' me, *puto*, *cabrone*! No cops better jack you cuz of it, and if they do, you better act like your mouth's fuckin' sowed shut. *You hear me, pendejo?*"

"Hey, man, nobody said nothin' dat I couldn't get no tat! Gimme a break, man. Besides, who says you're the fucking *jefe*, man? The bitch told me she's in charge."

Hernandez decelerated rapidly, pulling the van to the curb on the quiet residential street. He put the shifter into park. He slowly turned in his seat and faced the young gangbanger, perched to his right, still reeling from the face slap. Yolanda shrunk deep into the right corner of the rear bench seat; she feared what might happen next.

Peanut sat there for a few seconds, staring quietly at the passenger in the dark, his hands folded together at his crotch. You could almost feel the sweat oozing from Moreno's pores as he stared back, trying to look tough. Suddenly in one swift motion Hernandez reached under his ass with his left hand, coming up with a chromed .38-caliber pistol, his right simultaneously reached out and grabbing the new Loper by the T-shirt collar. The STS lieutenant pulled the kid's face right up to the business end of the gun's barrel. The whites of the new gangbanger's eyes were so big, they almost lit up the darkened van.

"Now listen close to me, fuckhead. You're nuthin' round here, got it? You got no boss but me. I'm your daddy and your mommy. I'm your fuckin' worst nightmare, too. You jus' do your job. Don't talk to me, and don' fuckin' talk to this *puta*, either. She's taken, and not by me. Her daddy will fuck you over big time if he knows you flirtin' wit' her. Am I clear, *ese*?"

Moreno, his shaved head glistening with sweat, shaking, just said, "*Si, mon!*"

The lieutenant pushed the kid back into his seat and then turned to the back, looking at the cowering Tafoya. "You got somethin' to say, Mrs. Jefe? You tell this mothafucker you're in charge here? Look at him now. You tell this piece of shit who's the real fuckin' boss here, tonight and every night."

Tafoya knew enough English to understand what he said. She understood that should she say the wrong thing, she would feel his heat. Weakly, she straightened up in the seat and, looking into Moreno's eyes, she said quietly, "Peanut. He the boss, *no mio*."

Hernandez turned, shoving the .38 back under his ass in the seat, and pulled the shifter down into drive. The night was young but already it seemed too long to everyone but the driver.

About five minutes later, as he merged onto Interstate 5, Hernandez spoke Spanish to the cowering woman in the backseat. "So, Yoli, where d'ya wanna go tonight? *A donde?* I figure we do three or four places then get some food and call it."

"My choice is Westminister tonight."

"No, *puta*! I would rather Costa Mesa, because we did good there last week. Remember who's boss!"

Tafoya sat back in her seat, stifling the anger rising inside her. Jesus Santiago had made it clear to her that *she* needed to research the cities to hit, and never, ever hit the same cities within a close time frame. Cops might be looking for them there. She had made sure, up to tonight, that the group never hit the same city, or complexes, within the same month. El Gerente made it very clear. Hernandez was calling the shots now, though. Jesus had never laid a finger on her, but Lieutenant Peanut was itching for the opportunity.

"OK, you're the boss. Costa Mesa it is."

Yolanda sat back, afraid to stand up to the driver. She was afraid they were doing something stupid, for which her lover might blame her as well. They had definitely been on a roll lately, though, scoring enough stolen mail to keep the Lopers happy and STS rolling in cash-fat altered checks. El Gerente, ever the appreciative boss, had given everyone involved a $1,000 bonus. Yolanda got two thousand, but unbeknownst to her, Hernandez received four grand and a bottle of Don Jesus silver tequila.

Santiago oversaw the check-cashing operation himself, closely controlling the runners and drivers. There had been fuckups but no close calls because they always spread the wealth—cashing the checks—around the tricounty areas. They had been ahead of the *puto placas*, those bastard cops every time. One time in Agoura, one of the runners even saw an LA sheriff bulletin, talking about their check-cashing ring, plastered right on the outside of the cashier's cage! Playing it cool, the Mexican smiled, presented his false ID, and scored his cash. Stupid was as stupid did! As careful as the check-cashing end had been, young Tafoya feared her side of the operation was literally heading down the wrong road.

Hernandez, in his ultimate wisdom, decided they needed to rob the same grouping of apartments they had visited just ten days before. Inwardly, he was tired, and since he knew where these apartments were already, he didn't want the hassle of finding a new place. He was lazy. Besides, he didn't have to listen to this bitch. As soon as he drove up to the first apartments, Yolanda objected.

"Shut up, bitch! We're doing this one again, got it?"

No one was around there, but the trio scored only a limited amount of mail from the boxes. Tafoya felt vindicated. She just knew the tenants were taking their mail personally to the post offices. They weren't stupid like Hernandez! This didn't deter almighty Peanut, though!

He next drove directly to the Desert Inn Apartments on Ponderosa Street. Yolanda recognized them right off from just a few days ago. She knew it was a bad choice, but she kept her mouth shut, did what she was told. It was about 1:00 a.m., and all was quiet. The gang parked the van nearby, exited, and quickly went about their business at the grouping of tenant boxes. Slightly more tenant mail here. It made Hernandez feel good.

"Ida One, we got a white van entering on the west side...on Quick Springs Drive. It's a Ford Windstar and got a red magnetic sign on the side...wait, says 'Bixby Plumbing.' No plates."

"Cat Seven, keep us posted. I'm set up on the north exit."

"Cat Two, I'm on the south."

"Sam One, I can go either way."

"Ida One, they're stopping at the west boxes. *All, copy. These are our guys.* Three total, out with bandannas on their faces, wearing hats. One's smaller, five one, thin, with a gray hoodie, maybe a female, sittin' in the back. Driver's male, five-ten, black hoodie, medium build. Right front passenger is male, five eight, chubby build, brown hoodie. They're at the boxes now...stand by. We got a bingo. They're cleaning the boxes. Sam, you copy?"

"Sam One, all units hold. Ida One, give us a direction when they leave. All units, be ready to take the point when they leave."

Tafoya finished scooping out the boxes into the green dry-cleaning bag, and the trio hopped back inside the van.

Hernandez knew better than to chirp the tires when leaving the parking lot. He slowly drove out north while the three of them removed their bandanna disguises. Moreno and Tafoya adjusted the bag of stolen mail in the back of the van. Hernandez was too pumped up, oblivious to the law enforcement shark in the white Nissan Murano, who pulled away from the curb to follow him from a block behind. Sharks were in the water, and the van was lunch.

"Ida One, do you have a signal?"

"Ida One, affirmative; now they're northbound on Andros."

"Cat Seven, Sam One, you got them?"

"Cat Seven, I'm on them, north on Andros, turning west on Palau."

"Cat Two, I'm trailing."

"Ida One, follow Cat Two and monitor the signal. I can see Cat Two ahead about three blocks. Let me know when you're behind me, and move around."

"Cat Seven to Cat Two, move up...take the point. Wait, WAIT, the van's pulling over. BACK OFF!"

"Cat Seven, I'm going around..."

"Cat Two, I'm over; I've got a visual. Driver's out... walking around, taking the signs off. Hell, he's putting some other signs on. I can't see them...someone else got a visual?"

"Sam One, I can see 'em. Shit, the new signs are blue; they say...ah, 'Johnson's Electric.' Hell, they're rich! Plumbers and electricians." The mics clicked. "The driver has no bandanna on now..."

"Cat Two, they're moving again…now eastbound on Baker, toward Harbor Boulevard."

Inside the Dragon Cleaners bag tucked under the bench seat, one piece of the stolen mail was a USPS overnight-shipping envelope. "Ida One," or Tom Parker, the postal inspector assigned to the task force, had placed a small gray device inside it disguised as an Acco-brand garage door opener. This high-tech unit broadcast a GPS locator signal in real time to Ida One via a laptop computer. Even if they lost the van, Ida One could pick the signal up in short order, and the four-car team could resume their hunt.

Sergeant Randy Moore, or "Sam One," and his task force members had spent many a night set up on random apartment complexes in Orange and southern Los Angeles counties hoping for a bingo. His four separate surveillance teams of detectives had spent boring weeks of eating fast food, drinking coffee, and urinating in bushes while watching metal mailboxes all night long. Tonight, however, his sharks would feed!

As Moore and his team trailed the white van, it traveled north on Interstate 405. He called in the other three teams from their Code 5 (surveillance) positions to assist. By the time Peanut got off the freeway in Westminister and pulled into the Chieftain Village Apartments on Trask Avenue, the three crooks had a total of sixteen sharks circling the dark waters in the unlit streets around the complex. The teams watched the van drive in and let the crooks do their thing with total impunity.

Bringing down a large criminal organization requires patience. It had previously been decided, further up the law enforcement food chain, that once the suspects were located they would be tracked, photographed, followed to their respective hideouts, and later identified. At this point the plan was to release them without contact. These crooks only stole mail—mere paper, after all. No lives were threatened tonight, and moving in too quickly could cost the identification of much bigger fish. These minnows were not the masterminds. A quick arrest could fuck up the entire operation! Many an investigation had been screwed up, or *fubar*ed, by jumping the gun. Every cop knew what *fubar* meant: *fucked up beyond all recognition*. Every veteran cop has a fubar story. Chuck Stiles would not allow one here, allowing the bigger fish to swim away. That was for damn sure!

After the Chieftain Village was pillaged, Peanut must've got a hankerin' for some pancakes because he drove directly to the IHOP on Goldenwest Street. At ease now, the trio removed their jackets and even their hats. Luis Ocampo and his partner watched from the parking lot as the mail thieves lathered raspberry syrup atop their Fresh 'n Fruity breakfasts! Using a long lens, Luis snapped photo after photo of their faces, usually stuffed with a mouthful of flapjacks. One of them depicted syrup dripping down the younger guy's chin. The photos were all suitable for framing.

Luis watched through the camera lens as the attractive female Hispanic slowly ate her meal, never smiling. She was hauntingly familiar to Ocampo. The van's older Hispanic driver liked to chew with his mouth wide open, and Ocampo flicked a nice pic of the "LWS" tattoo on the third Mexican's inner arm; it was red and looked infected. Other members of the task force got a good look inside the van and managed to see a corner of a big green cloth bag tucked under the backseat. They copied down the VIN number found on the dashboard. All three gangsters gobbled those flapjacks down quickly, leaving the restaurant in just thirty-five minutes. It was now 3:40 a.m.

"Cat Twelve, the primaries have started the vehicle; they're driving out the east entrance. Sam One, copy?"

"Sam One to Cats Fourteen, Ten, and Eight, takeover point. Some of us are a little toasty at this point. Sam One and other Cat units will monitor and trail. If they hit the freeway, let's all move up closer. We want to keep it loose, but let's maintain a visual. Ida One, do you still have a ping?"

"Ida One, loud and clear. I got 'em on Goldenwest."

"Sam One to all Cats: let's stay on 'em." A litany of mic clicks followed as the pack of great whites followed the minnows as they drove away on the surface streets of Westminister. Back on Interstate 405 and heading east, twenty minutes later the van signaled and got off on Euclid Street in the city of Garden Grove. The litany of unmarked cop cars followed loosely behind—not too close, not too distant—stalking their prey.

"Cat Ten, going right on Lampoon Avenue. We've got a fresh green. Cat Eleven, move up."

"Eleven, I've got 'em, now continuing eastbound."

"Cat Eleven, they're slowing and turning right onto Twin Tree Street...looks like they may stop. There's apartments here. Someone move up, move up; we need eyes on an address. Someone's getting out."

"Cat Twelve, I'm parking and going out on foot. I think I can see through the bushes on the side inside the complex."

"Sam One. All other Cat units, we need to follow from here. Cat Twelve, you stay behind and get a visual on the secondary. Make sure you make that address."

"Cat Twelve, you got it."

Pulling the van to a stop in front of the Sunnyside Apartments, Yolanda grasped the handle and slid the side door of the Windstar open with a loud clunk. Getting out, she hesitated for a split second, looking back at Peanut. She desperately wanted to tell the fucker off, wanted to exclaim that she intended on diming him off to his boss, her lover, about what an ass he had been to her tonight and every night, to reveal how this self-proclaimed jefe refused to follow El Gerente's directions and disrespected his woman at every opportunity. Her look of anger quickly faded to one of despair. Tafoya slammed the door shut and slowly walked away toward Santiago's apartment door. She pulled off her baseball hat, loosing her long brown hair. The van drove off.

Detective Ray Williams, Cat Twelve, stood concealed by the blanket of darkness on the east side of the Sunnyside complex, his radio's volume turned down to avoid detection. He used a monocle for a close-up view. The young Hispanic girl with the nice body walked toward the row of medium-income apartments. This secondary walked up to the door of apartment A-3. The porch light was on, illuminating her face. After inserting a key, Cat Twelve heard a single squeak-like bark coming from inside. Once she had entered and shut the door, the squeaking ceased, and the porch light was extinguished. Williams's work was done. The sharks had a place to feed at another time.

"Sam One, who's got the van?"

"Cat Ten, it got back on I-405, but I got two semis blocking me. Stand by."

"Sam One, for Christ's sake, don't lose them! Any Cat unit with eyes on, advise."

"Cat Seven, I got a white van way up ahead. Wait, I'll get a visual. It's an older Econoline up here; that's not it."

"Ida One, you still got the ping. Where the hell are they?"

"Ida One, hold on...Sarge, the signal's gone. My end is working, but maybe the battery's dead in the unit, or maybe they're outta range!"

"Are you fuckin' kidding me? *Keep looking!*"

Murphy's Law applies to every part of life—law enforcement is no exception. Despite thirty minutes of exhaustive searching, the Cat units and their sergeant came up dry. Seems that the watch battery in the sending unit was indeed old, and Peanut Hernandez made a sudden three-lane turn on the freeway after Gilbert Moreno informed him he was about to miss the off ramp to his parents' house. That quick move, ahead of the two semi trucks, blocked the view of the van by the trailing sharks. Just as quickly as the noose around their necks had tightened, it slipped open, and the minnows swam off. At 5:05 a.m., back at Orange County SO headquarters, Randy Moore was not amused at the recent turn of events.

"I can't friggin' believe you guys lost the van! A big-ass white van on an open freeway at 4:15 in the morning? Come on! And, we don't have GPS on the bag either. What the fuck?"

Detective Tim Larson of Santa Ana PD, a ten-year veteran, spoke up. "Sarge, look, we're all tired. When the damn van got onto the 405, he zoomed up alongside a wall of Freightliner trucks...he was in the number-four lane. Suddenly the asshole cut right in front of all three big rigs. I dunno. Maybe he made us; maybe not. I just couldn't slow down to see where he went, and once we all got up next to the trucks, well, the fuckin' van just disappeared! He must have made the off ramp; either way, he was gone, and we were way past any exits to go back. Sorry, boss. Shit happens."

Looking at Cat Twelve, Moore said, almost reluctantly, "Williams, tell me you got the address of that goddamn apartment!"

"Sure did, Sarge: number A-3, Sunnyside Apartments, 12110 Twin Tree Street, Garden Grove. Saw her use a key. You want the zip and phone info, too?"

"Don't be a smartass, Raymond!"

"Don't have it yet, anyway. Ha-ha—lighten up, Randy!"

"You will have it before you leave tonight, Ray! Listen up. It's after five, we're all tired, but I want you all back here at thirteen hundred hours—one p.m.—and be ready to move. I have team four already set up on the Twin Street apartment. They'll need relief. We need to take down that little chica away from the apartment, alone if at all possible. Hopefully we get a clean shot at it, but she's our link. We need that girl in pocket. I've instructed team four, and I'm telling all of you, this is our first big break in this case. *Don't fuck it up!* Now go home and get some shut-eye."

As the herd of groggy cops left the briefing room, Luis Ocampo approached the bleary-eyed Moore. "Sarge, I took the flicks of the crooks inside the IHOP. I got real good looks at all three of them. I know damn well I've seen that chick's face before, somehow connected to this case. I just know it!"

"Really, Luis? Let's hit the case book. Let's do it now; it's important."

An audible sigh came from Ocampo and Moore. Despite being dog tired, they still knew it was important to track down this hunch right away. Moore dug out the three-inch-thick binder marked "The Driller." Page by page they read multiple follow-up reports, and then on page forty-seven, the bank surveillance photos from Home Savings and Loan in San Luis Obispo popped into view, showing the woman cashing the stolen check.

"*That's her*!" Ocampo stood up, pointing to the black-and-white eight-by-ten-inch picture printed on the page.

"Holy shit…you know what this means, Luis? This little mail-thievin' *vata* is connected to the entire mail-theft, check-cashing ring! She probably knows *all* the players. Probably can take us right to the Driller's front fuckin' door! You the man, Louie; you the *man*!"

Chapter 16
THE BLIND SQUIRREL SCORES A NUT

One day, before the Cat team sharks took a bite out of the minnows' asses down in the OC, people were talking up in Santa Barbara. The office was all abuzz. The sergeant's promotional list was coming out, and, oh yeah, Kevin Rhinehardt was coming back to work! I was feeling pretty good, too. No more shooting pains in my side; I hadn't taken anything but Tylenol for a couple of weeks now. Yeah, I was good to go. About 8:00 a.m. I strode into the detective bureau wearing a new white, long-sleeved Brooks Brothers shirt and an equally new gray Men's Warehouse suit. I bought it to take the sergeant's oral exam, and, due to an unexpected weight-loss regimen, my other two suits were being taken in, as well. This boy was twelve pounds slimmer and ready to take on the world.

As I walked down the hallway toward my cubicle, person after person greeted me with well wishes, even high-fives. A couple of the hand slaps gave me a shock of familiar pain down my left side, too, but other than the occasional wince, I tried not to telegraph my angst over my less-than-ideal physical condition. Sandy Phillips, one of the bureau's secretaries, came up and hugged me. *Shit, that hurt!*

Bob Roberts came rushing out of his office and headed straight for me. All I could think was, "*For God's sake, don't hug me!*" Instead I think he caught himself midgrab and just held me tight by the shoulders, looking at me.

"Rhino, we've all missed you, buddy. How you feeling?"

"I'm back, and I'm great, Sarge. Put me to work."

"Whoa, Nellie, you need to talk to me first." A voice behind me had me whirling around to spy the lieutenant as he came up my flank.

"Come over to my office and see me, Kevin. We need to chat a bit."

Why did the hair on the back of my neck stand up every time this guy said he wanted to talk to me? I came into the office with a broad smile on my mug this morning. It was starting to fade now as I walked down the hall toward Ron Casey's office.

"Kevin, Chief Walters talked to Commander Hogue. The doctor's cleared you for light duty only. You wanted to come back; you're here, but Walters wants me to make sure you know there's restrictions."

"Like what restrictions—you gonna take my gun away or something?"

"Actually, Walters did say he didn't want you in the field with a weapon."

"*What*! Are you fucking kidding me, lieutenant?"

"Wait, wait…even though Walters said that, I'm telling you to carry it. No cop working for me goes around unarmed! Screw Walters, but do me a big favor. When you're in the office, keep it in your desk; just wear it under your jacket when you leave. I don't wanna get a piece of my ass chewed off if doughboy sees you strapped, OK?"

Doughboy! Casey called Walters a doughboy! "Thanks, you got it, Ron…and, I want to thank you for supporting Julie and my family over the last month and a half. We all appreciate it, and, well, I especially did. I wouldn't have thought to take the promotional exam if you hadn't pushed for it. I scored number three on the written. I had those books you gave Julie memorized line by line! I think I nailed the oral, too, but you never know."

"Yeah, I heard you did good. The list comes out in a couple of hours. I'm rooting for ya, Rhino!"

Back at my desk, Bob Roberts dropped a hefty load of mundane crime reports in front of me. A lot of low-level stuff: burglaries, petty thefts, minor assaults. I felt like it was my first day on the job again! Then as he left, he dropped the hammer on me.

"Rhino, one more thing. You can do follow-up on the Driller case, but you are *not* to take any enforcement action, like making arrests or participating in field operations, until you get full medical clearance. That's straight from the chief. So, go ahead and interview witnesses, file complaints, network with Phillips and Wilson, but if you get hurt out there, it's your ass and mine."

"If they get a break on the Driller, are you telling me I can't be there when they take him down? Come on, Bob, you can't do that to me. It's personal, after all."

"Look, just remember what I said. Let your conscience be your guide; that's all."

Thirty minutes later I was sitting with Will Phillips and his new partner, Susan. I hadn't even looked at those cases Roberts gave me. The two were commiserating on how their LexisNexis computer data bank searches and phone calls had come up empty for any leads to further identify Todd or Brenda Starnes. Despite the fact that every agency from the Mexican border to Oregon had his picture, no one had replied with any kind of actual identification of the guy depicted in the photo as Todd Starnes. Not one of their yuppie keyboard searches over the last few days had revealed anything. That's when I gave it to them with both barrels of the gun I wasn't supposed to carry.

"Willimena, what've I told you about detective work? Did I tell you to solve all your cases while sitting on your ass behind a computer screen? No, cases are solved by footwork: beating the bushes, talking to actual people face to face! You young dudes sit behind that fucking box for hours. Shit, I have no idea how any of us old guys, armed with just a gun and notepad, ever solved a case without a cell phone and the friggin' Internet!"

"Kevin, wait. Susan and I figured that the computer search would…"

"With all due respect to you," I said, pointing at a now-scowling Susan Wilcox, "Will is my partner. I'm back now, and although they think I'm too puny to go out in the field with you guys toting a pair of handcuffs, you both need to listen to me. Get off your asses and knock on some doors! Those computer searches are wrong much of the time. Just go down to the San Diego and Orange County Registrar's Offices, and have them do a hand search for the names you're interested in. You just might be surprised."

The tall, muscular Orange County detective sat mute, glaring at me, but the look on Phillips's face said it all. He knew I was right. We sat for another thirty minutes, strategizing, but I could see that Wilcox didn't like me right off. Frankly, I didn't give a shit. I had a six-inch scar on my side that gave me a right to speak my mind. Every twinge of pain made me want to find this asshole. I hadn't forgotten about Frank Gilroy either. Mr. Gilroy was the real reason the Driller and his network had to go down. That war veteran never made it to retirement because of him, never made love to his wife again. All because of this killer. I was the lucky one, and I reminded both of them that they were investigating a murderer, not just a talented thief. Phillips got it—not so sure about Wilcox.

On the afternoon that Phillips and his OC partner headed down south to do actual police work, California Highway Patrol Traffic Officer Stan Waterman was getting ready to start the afternoon watch out of the Goleta office. Stan had worked graveyard for the last three months, and three days into his daytime rotation he had a little shift-change jetlag going on. It takes a couple of weeks, especially with older guys, to get used to a change in sleep pattern. Fifty-year-old Stan Waterman's ass was dragging.

Working on his second cup of coffee, sitting in the squad room, Waterman was slowly going through the briefing book for any new stuff. Admittedly, Stan hadn't gone through the book thoroughly for more than a couple of weeks. This information normally dealt with traffic and accident trends, officer safety bulletins, and the like. At the far back of the book, stuck to an advertisement for discount car insurance, Waterman found a Santa Barbara Sheriff BOL (be on the lookout) flyer:

Information Wanted in Connection with the Attempted Murder of S. B. Sheriff Detective

On February 2, 1999, an unknown assailant, in the act of burglarizing AJ Spur's restaurant in the city of Buellton, attacked and stabbed a Santa Barbara sheriff's detective who was inside the business working surveillance. Investigation has revealed that, after the attack, the suspect fled south on foot into the Flying

Flags Trailer Park. He is believed to have left the area in a newer-model compact or medium-size sedan, red in color, at approximately 2:00–2:15 a.m. that morning. Any allied agency having contact with an individual or individuals in a vehicle matching this general description is asked to contact Detective Edward McCormick or Buford Corbett with the Santa Barbara Sheriff's Office at (805) 681–4100.

Stan remembered the incident—that a detective named Rhinehardt had been the victim that night. Everyone was talking about it. He'd been sent up to the Gaviota area to cover for the Buellton officers who had responded Code 3 to help the sheriff up at the restaurant. Buellton station CHP officers normally worked the freeway between Gaviota and El Capitan State Beach. He was up there within minutes after the detective got stabbed. The sheriff bulletin started burning off the thick cobwebs caused by inadequate sleep...*information requested on a red compact car on February second. Sometime after 2:00 a.m.?*

Waterman hustled into the back changing room and quickly dialed in the combination to his locker door. His mind raced. *God, I hope I still have it. THERE!* In a bundle of brown notebooks at the bottom, he found one marked, "Jan–Feb '99." Thumbing relentlessly through the pages of scribbled notes, he came upon what he was looking for: *2/2/99 0245 s/b El Cap/James T. Gaylord, DL E5094321, red '98 Honda Accord. Warning 80/65.*

Less than an hour later, Ed McCormick, Biff Corbett, and I stood at the front counter of the Goleta CHP station. *Yeah, I had my Glock .40 on my hip (under my coat).* They called Waterman in, and we interviewed him on his recollection of the traffic stop.

"It was right around 2:45. I was parked by the refinery when I saw three cars heading south on 101. One of them passed the others, so I got on 101 to clock him. I had him at just under eighty as we're nearing El Cap. I called it out, and he yielded right away. Nothing out of the ordinary. I remember the driver, and there was a passenger in the right front, too. The driver, this James Gaylord guy, was sort of a slug. Had long, stringy brown hair, hadn't shaved; I remember he was heavier than the weight listed on his license; he was downright fat. The right front passenger was slouched down in the seat and had a black hat on—it was sort of cocked down over his eyes, like he'd been sleeping over there. I never really saw his face, and his arms were crossed the whole time. He didn't say anything, just sat there. He was wearing dark glasses. I didn't pay much attention to him because quite frankly I was tired, and I intended on just warning this Gaylord guy...that was it. I ran the driver; he had no wants or warrants. The plate came back clear to him, too. I didn't write it down, but I think the registration matched his DL address. I remember it was a bright-red 1998 Honda Civic in good shape. Don't remember any dings, marks, or pinstriping on it. A stock color. Hope it helps."

Ed asked the officer for a better description of the passenger. Other than the fact that Waterman had a "feeling" he might be taller than Gaylord and was much trimmer than the chubby driver, he couldn't help much. He said the guy's face was obscured by a big pair of sunglasses. He thought he had dark, maybe black, short hair under the hat. He remembered the jacket was leather, maybe brown in color. Nothing else. Waterman gave a plethora of excuses for not having called us sooner. We cut him some slack and thanked him. After all, we don't call the CHP "AAA with a gun" for nothing. If it'd been me pulling the car over, I would have asked sleepy-bye guy why he was wearing sunglasses at three in the morning!

As we walked toward the exit door, Waterman ran up from the back. "Hey, I do remember one more thing. His shoes were all muddy. The passenger's shoes had a lot of mud on them, and I remember that. Hope that helps."

We looked at one another. I said, "Stan, it helps more than you know!"

All three of us ran to records to run our person of interest. I get a kick out of how it's PC (politically correct) now in law enforcement to call a suspect a "person of interest," like they're just some Tom, Dick, or Harry who we just want to chat with over tea! James Thomas Gaylord, born December 23, 1964, was six feet three inches tall, two hundred pounds, and had brown eyes and brown hair, according to his California driver's license. The DMV showed an address of 243 Spinnaker Drive, in San Diego, California.

The license had been issued ten years prior. His DL photo depicted a smiling, clean-shaven Anglo dude with medium-length hair. A far cry from the overweight slug driver Officer Waterman described the night of the T-stop. The 1998 Honda was registered to Gaylord at the same address in San Diego. Ed, Biff, and I burned a copy of his photo and began walking back to the detective bureau. Suddenly, all sorts of people started congratulating me.

"Good job, Kevin."

"Way ta go, bro!"

"Congratulations."

"Start sewing those stripes on, Rhino."

What? By the time I got back to my desk, Roberts and Casey were standing nearby. Casey broke the silence.

"Number two on the list...your days in the bureau may be numbered, Rhinehardt!"

The sheriff's department lists the top-ten candidates for a promotional position in order of ranking on the tests taken for the position. After the written and oral exams, my score was ninety-six out of one hundred, or number two of the top-ten people qualified to be promoted. Deputy Janet Billister was number one. Not too shabby, but it wasn't over until the fat lady sang! In this case, the fat lady was the Sheriff. All the sheriff commanders would meet and send him three recommendations. It looked likely that I would be promoted over the next two years—if I didn't screw up! Billister had a good reputation, but she'd been on the job for only six years. If fighting crime for twenty years counted for anything, I just might have had the edge. But I knew better than to sew any sergeant stripes on just yet.

Down in San Diego, Phillips and Wilson had discovered that one Brenda Sarah Starnes had recently purchased a condominium on Alvarado Street in Chula Vista, according to the county assessor's office. As they drove down Alvarado, a poorly maintained street with overgrown yards and abandoned cars, it made the two cops begin to think that maybe—just maybe—they'd hit pay dirt. They sat parked down the street, eyeballing the dilapidated condo, careful not to tip their hand to any unsuspecting crime kingpins. Suddenly the door opened, and the homeowner, the "person of interest," emerged: a white-haired, hunchbacked woman of about eighty-five, hobbling her way down the front walkway with the help of a three-legged cane.

Exchanging glances back and forth, Phillips and Wilson almost simultaneously said, "*Say what*?" Will started the engine and slowly cruised down the street toward the woman, now outside and closing the metal gate enclosing the weed-infested front yard behind her.

Will slowed as he approached and asked, "Hi, uh, excuse me, are you Mrs. Starnes? Brenda?"

"Why, yes, are you bringing me my groceries, young man?"

"Ah, no, we're just...we're looking for someone else by that name and thought you might be her. We know her son."

"Funny, I don't have a son…never married, just have a cat. I don't get many visitors. Would you two want to come in and chat? I have cookies."

Will slowly applied the brakes on the Ford Taurus, but Susan's robo grip on his right arm stopped him short. Under her breath, she whispered, "Don't stop. We'll be here all fuckin' day!"

"Gosh, thanks, ma'am, but we gotta go. Thank you anyway!" Driving away he cracked a smile. Phillips had never intended to stop; he just wanted to pull his partner's chain.

Just two minutes later, I called them and shared the skinny on James Gaylord. They had a better address to check now: 243 Spinnaker Drive. It didn't take them long to get there. No red Honda and no chubby James Gaylord either, just a thirtysomething man and wife, a family of four. The owners had never heard of James Gaylord or Brenda Starnes. The previous owners were an older couple: Joan and Carl Thomas. The Thomases had sold the house to them six years ago. It sounded like another dead end, and Wilcox wanted to call it a day. Phillips persisted.

"Just for grins, let's go back to the recorder's office. Let's check on who owned the place before the older folks."

Wilcox wanted to take the easy road. "Come on, man. It's late, and I'm frigging tired. Let's just head back. I'm supposed to call my honey tonight, and I don't want us to fight traffic."

"I'm driving—driver's call. It won't take long."

At twenty minutes to five, they finally got what they came for: one Brenda Jane and Richard Fitch sold the house to Joan and Carl Thomas in 1988. A DMV check on Brenda Jane provided them with an old picture, and description, but the lead stopped there. Brenda Fitch's listed DMV address was the old one, on Spinnaker Drive. Her license had expired the year she sold the house, and she hadn't renewed it. As they hit Interstate 5 traveling north, in heavy rush-hour traffic, Will couldn't stop grinning. He wondered how his seemingly conniving partner would spin this to her advantage. Susan Wilcox just sat there, staring out the window.

Chapter 17
THE TRAIN GAINS STEAM

The sun rose, blinding the Cat surveillance team members that morning as they struggled for clarity, sitting in their undercover cars in Costa Mesa, watching and waiting. About 8:00 a.m. they noticed an elderly man drive into the complex. He parked near some utility sheds on the east side. Exiting his older-model Buick, he donned a ratty, torn pair of gray overalls and started raking the leaves piled high on the dry grass a fair distance away from apartment A-3.

Agent Scott Willens of Santa Ana PD keyed his microphone and spoke to Ted Spector, the deputy who was currently watching the front door of the apartment.

"Ted, has there been any movement inside?"

"I haven't seen any...the only one moving is that old guy."

"I got an idea. I'm going out on foot. I want to feel this guy out. Maybe we can use him."

"Keep it cool, Scott. Don't let him know what we're doing."

Scott Willens, dressed in bleached-out blue jeans and sporting a blue and white "Go Dodgers" T-shirt, sauntered slowly into the complex and walked up to the seventy-something gentleman, intently raking up mounds of dead, sun-bleached maple leaves.

"Hi, excuse me, sir, but you work here, right?"

A grumpy Hank Haafkamp, cocking his head, looked suspiciously at the stranger and retorted, "Maybe. Who're you and why d'ya ask?"

Quickly flashing his badge on the down low, Willens tried acting official.

"Well, sir, I work for the police department, and we're doing a confidential investigation on a person we think may be living here. I can't tell you who that person is, but it involves large-scale fraud."

Now softening, Haafkamp squinted an eye toward the undercover cop and said, "I bet you it's that bastard Jarvis. Bob Jarvis in B-4s been sniffing 'round all the widows livin' here—loosin' them up, ya know. I figure he's been tryin' to wring out their bank accounts, that asshole! It's him, isn't it?"

Seizing the opportunity, Scott winked and said, "Well, we just want to watch him—oh, I meant to say, we need to watch someone, if you catch my drift. Can I just sit over there, like I'm with you, and watch for a while?"

"Son, you do anything you want. Anything to get that bastard outta here! I promise, my lips are sealed," he said, pursing his lips and running his finger across the slit.

"Sir, you're a true citizen. Thanks for your cooperation."

Now seated, secluded in the shade, about fifty yards away from apartment A-3, Agent Willens had a front-row seat to anyone moving in or out of the target apartment.

At 9:22 a.m., a sleepy El Gerente exited A-3, locking the door behind him. Yolanda Tafoya was still fast asleep in the back bedroom; Bruno the bulldog lay snoring away in his corner. Jogging down the stairs from the second-floor apartment, Chuy made it to his blue Camaro parked under the carport awning, a mere thirty-five feet from the policeman. The gangbanger didn't give Scott a second look.

By this time there were six plain wrappers (undercover vehicles) dotting the streets surrounding the exits to Sunnyside. Luis Ocampo and his partner were in one of them.

Scott Willens spoke quietly into his handheld radio. "Cats Six, Eight, and Eleven, take this guy out, take pictures, and keep it loose. The primary's still inside. For Christ's sake, *don't lose him!*"

Chuy Santiago had no reason to suspect a tail, so he stopped by Dunkin' Donuts a mile away and sat munching a chocolate-cream-filled doughnut while leisurely reading the *Orange County Register*. He left twenty minutes later. The gangbanger jumped on the 405, transitioned to Interstate 5, and got off on Fourth Street in Santa Ana.

"Cat Eleven. Keep it loose; he's turning down East Third Street...there's nothing but businesses down here. I have point. He's turning into a large complex...Dragon Cleaners, 12113. I'll keep the eye; everyone else back off. Our secondary parked in what I think is an employee parking area on the east side of the building...he's walking in the front door."

After twenty minutes the detectives made the decision that this male Hispanic must work at the cleaners since he wasn't dropping anything off or leaving. Running the Camaro's plate, they came back with the identifying information for Jesus Santiago and the fact that his address of record was apartment A-3 at the Sunnyside Apartments. Two cars were left to sit on him at Dragon while the remaining sharks swam back to the Costa Mesa apartment complex—after all, the real prize was the sleeping chica.

As Ocampo and the others sat waiting for their target to stir in Costa Mesa, Ron Casey was preparing to brief Phillips, Wilson, Corbett, McCormick, and me in Santa Barbara. Lieutenant Sam Gilstrap had called him from the OC that morning and described how his team had scored the previous morning, hoping now to identify the mail thieves. Gilstrap included the fact that his crews had just followed a secondary male to a business in Santa Ana, and the plan was to pick up the female at her place in Costa Mesa without raising eyebrows. It was made clear that no one would jump the gun and make contact with any known suspects at that point. The locomotive was rolling down the tracks now, gaining steam, and any premature arrests would fuck up the train ride—a fubar would cause a derailment. With the final destination in sight, a crash at this point could be catastrophic.

As we waited for the briefing back in the detective bureau, sitting just a few feet away from Sue Wilcox's desk, Will Phillips listened intently in on her telephone conversation. It was obvious to him she was speaking to Sergeant Chuck Stiles, her boss back in the OC.

"So, they scored last night...great, Chuck, great. We did good yesterday down in San Diego, too. I followed up on a lead there and managed to get a name for who I think the Driller's mother is—a chick named Brenda Jean Fitch, also known as Brenda Starnes. I figure the guy I found running the mail place in Forest Grove can ID her photo too...we're planning to go down there this morning to show him a lineup."

Phillips's face was on fire; he wanted to jump her shit right then and there. Angry thoughts ravaged his brain: *I can't fucking believe it! She did it again. I, I, I, me, me, me!* At the tail end of her conversation, he got up and slammed his chair into the desk, glaring in her direction as he quickly walked toward the hallway. The racket immediately got my attention. I could see Will standing there, pacing back and forth, waiting for Wilcox to hang up. She placed the phone on the hook and looked his way.

I overheard him say, "Partner, I need to talk to you *now*." Wilcox stood and followed Phillips as he walked out the door, exiting into the parking lot. Uh-oh! I figured the honeymoon was over. Trouble in River City! I had the urge to tiptoe out behind them for a listen, but for once I used my head and stayed put. I'd sweat the details out of my younger partner later anyway.

Stepping outside the back door, Phillips gave it to Wilcox with both barrels. "What's with you, Susan? You got some problem with me? When we work *together*, we do things *together*. I don't expect a slap on the back or a pat on the ass every single time I come up with a lead on my own. That's the definition of a team: *people who work together*. We share the appreciation. Not once but *twice* now I hear you tell Stiles that you're coming up with all these leads, apparently all on your own. *You* figured out where the guy's mail drop was, *you* found Homer Simpson, *you* got Brenda Fitch's address...it's all *your* work. I'm fucking invisible! I've had enough of this shit! You either start sharing the wealth, or I'm gonna tell your sergeant about your bullshit!"

As Will began his tirade, Wilcox's facial expression went from anger to one slack from shame. It was like her new partner had made her take an inward look, and she didn't like what she saw. A softer Susan Wilcox looked down at her feet and then reached her hand out, lightly touching her partner's shirtsleeve. Her softening demeanor set Phillips back on his heels. The wide, sorrowful eyes. The gentle touch. Wilcox was acting feminine!

"I'm sorry, Will, I'm sorry. Man, you're right...sometimes I can't see it myself. It's just that, well, I'm havin' a tough time at the SO. A year ago I got passed over on the sergeant's promotion, and Stiles made it clear I had to stand out. I had to start shining to get noticed. I knew you were new in the bureau, and I guess I abused that, figuring you wouldn't care if I bragged a little. I dunno, maybe I need to go back to patrol. Working the street hookers in vice was an easy gig. Developing leads, using my head in my own investigations...it just isn't as easy as I figured it would be. I guess I'd be better off back on the street. Forgive me?"

Wow! Big Sue Wilcox, the muscular lesbian, wasn't so tough after all. Will caved. "OK, OK, I accept your apology, but the next time we—I really mean I—come up with something good, give me some credit at least. Is that too fuckin' much to ask?"

"No, man. I'm sorry, and I promise to give you all the creds you're due. Please don't rat me off to Stiles, though. No harm, no foul at this point...OK, partner?"

When my young protégé later described the confrontation to me, the only advice I gave him was, "If I were you, I wouldn't trust her as far as I could throw her, and since my chest hurts, that's not far at all!"

Ron Casey held a briefing ten minutes later. Wilcox made sure she told us about how her partner had made her go back to the San Diego assessor, and it was Will's determination that led to the identification of Brenda Fitch. Perhaps the ebony worm had turned. The jury was still out in my book.

I was told to stay put in Santa Barbara. If anyone needed any paper (search warrants or computer work), I was the designated duty officer. Roberts was still babying me! Corbett and McCormick were running down more leads to find James Gaylord in the county of Orange while the newly revitalized partnership of Phillips and Wilcox headed south to visit Homer Simpson once more in Forest Grove.

The pair found Stimson in his office/apartment, "entertaining" a lady friend. She resembled Ruth Buzzy from the seventies TV series *Laugh In*, just a homelier version of Ms. Buzzy. The detectives later mused that Homer was still wearing the same food-stained wife-beater T-shirt he had worn on their first encounter with the hobbit.

Will produced a six-pack of color lineup photos. Brenda Fitch was depicted in position number three. Using the Santa Barbara jail booking photo records, Will and Sue had to find five other females resembling Brenda's DMV picture for the lineup, and, boy, it wasn't easy! Each photo had to match her basic hair color and features. When God made the enchanting Brenda Fitch, he broke the friggin' mold!

Phillips gave the witness the admonishment required before showing someone a photo lineup. Many years ago, in the *Manson v. Brathwaite* case, the Supreme Court ruled that cops needed to admonish witnesses that they didn't have to pick anyone and that it was just as important to clear innocent people as it was to convict them.

Fortunately, Homer had no trouble identifying the enchanting Ms. Fitch.

"That's her. She looks just as lovely in person." Stimson placed his initials next to Brenda's photo on the sheet.

Leaving the two lovebirds alone, Will voiced his appreciation on the way out.

"Thanks, Mr. Simpson!"

Homer winced. "It's *Stimson*, you asshole, *Stimson!*"

Frick and Frack (Corbett and McCormick) managed a homerun with the Orange County clerk recorder. It seems that there was no record of a Brenda Jean Fitch ever owning any property in that county, but—hold on—a Brenda J. Gaylord was the owner of record of a single-family home located at 5525 Rhapsody Drive in Seal Beach.

Ditch McCormick, on a hunch, contacted his source with the Internal Revenue Service, asking him to search for any current W-4 filings by James Gaylord or Brenda Fitch/Gaylord. As luck would have it, James Gaylord, of the same Seal Beach address, had recently started a new job and filed one. Their records showed he was currently working at a Carl's Jr. restaurant located on Pacific Coast Highway in Dana Point. Our locomotive was roaring now, gaining speed.

After getting the information from the recorder on where Brenda Jean Gaylord, also known as Fitch, lived in Seal Beach, the two detectives did a fly-by at 5525 Rhapsody Drive. Frick and Frack expected to see James Gaylord's red '98 Honda. Instead a black 1997 Mazda

Miata sat solo in the driveway. The current registration came back to one Dennis Ray Fitch, of 25525 Main Street, Lake Forest, California. They called back to Santa Barbara, and after they pulled up his DMV photo the raucous celebration could be heard throughout the building. Ron Casey couldn't wait to tell me. Frick and Frack sat on the house and called for another surveillance team to take over. They heard the unmarked car was soon to arrive, so they left. That turned out to be fubar. When the two other Orange County SO detectives arrived, just six minutes later, the Mazda was gone! Biff and Ditch were in for a major ass chewin'. The Miata never returned.

Right around 10:35 a.m. that very same morning, the Cat sharks down in Costa Mesa smelled blood in the water when the door to apartment A-3 opened and a fresh-faced Hispanic woman exited and locked the door behind her. A dog was heard squeaking his disapproval at her abandonment as she walked down the stairs and out the front walkway toward the street.

Yolanda Tafoya never drove a car; she saw no reason to since her man usually came home around dinnertime. If they went out, he chauffeured her in style. Besides, if she wanted a real license, she'd have to properly identify herself to the DMV, and Santiago wanted none of that. Her pattern was to awaken late morning after working nights and walk over to the Rutt's Hutt taco stand four blocks away. She enjoyed the walk in the fresh air, and the *menudo* at Rutt's was killer. Her stroll in the sunlight that afternoon would prove to be her undoing.

Two and a half blocks from the Sunnyside Apartments, on a long stretch of residential street, a new blue Chevy cargo van pulled to the curb about twenty feet ahead of the strolling woman. A tan Nissan Maxima pulled to a slow halt behind it. Three burly detectives exited the van and quickly approached and grabbed the unsuspecting girl. The man with his hand over her mouth quietly said, "*Policia, estas arrestado!* [Police, you're under arrest,]" as she was rapidly whisked inside the van. It happened quickly, without fanfare, unobserved by any locals. The vehicles drove off in unison; the minnow had been swallowed whole.

As the van, containing a shaking, frightened Yolanda, drove toward sheriff headquarters, Sergeant Randy Moore received a call from the two Cat units watching Dragon Cleaners.

"Sarge, this is Ron over at the cleaners where the Camaro came this morning. The car's still here, but you won't fuckin' believe what just happened. The white van, the one from last night, with the same two guys in it, just drove into the parking lot! They parked next to the other guy's blue Camaro, and the Mexicans walked in the front door. They had two of those big green bags with them, too, and it wasn't clothes in there. It was obviously paper-shaped items; they were full of mail, Randy."

Detective Ron Williams had earlier run down the DMV information on the white van from the previous morning. The crooks had covered their tracks well.

"Sarge, the van comes back to a John Smith, with a PO Box of 432 in Culver City. There ain't no such box there; I checked."

Randy Moore shook his head and said, "John Smith? You gotta be fuckin' kidding me."

"No, Sarge, that's the R/O's name: John Smith."

"If I were you, Ronny, I'd check with Virginia about Pocahontas. She'll know where to find the dude."

Looking bewildered, Williams replied, "Poca—who? How'd ya spell that, Randy?"

Slapping his big forehead with his palm, loudly, the sergeant just walked off muttering, "God, help us…what the fuck do they teach in high school nowadays?"

Arriving at the Orange County sheriff's station, a hand-cuffed, nervous Yolanda Tafoya was ushered back to the interrogation room. Detective Mario Santos, the LASD's best bilingual, was still sleeping off last night's marathon surveillance. Randy Moore had one other choice left to interview the Spanish-speaking suspect: Luis Ocampo.

Luis was finally in his element. Wired for video and audio, he went to work. The entire interview was conduct-ed in Spanish, and Luis spent the first twenty minutes try-ing to gain Tafoya's trust.

"I know you're scared. I understand you go by Yolanda Tafoya, right? Hey, are you from the state of Guerrero?

Tafoya is a popular name in that region, and I have cousins still living there."

Sensing a connection, Yoli opened up. "Yeah, I was born there; my parents, too. I'm from Zihuatanejo."

"Zihuatanejo, really...do you speak Tlapanec?" Luis asked, referring to a dialect native to Guerrero.

"Yes, and Mixtec, too."

"Wow, that's hard to learn. Let's just stick to mainland Spanish, OK?"

After the warm-up, Luis got down to the business at hand. "You know why you're with us, don't you? We watched you rob those apartments of the mail last night... two separate times. You were with those other two guys in the white van. I saw you chow down on pancakes at the IHOP, too, saw you go home to your apartment, where this Jesus Santiago dude lives. We're watching him right now. We got lots of pictures, including this one—he showed her the bank photo—of you cashing a stolen and forged check. We got you cold, Yolanda. Understand?"

Tafoya began to cry. Ocampo knew he had her.

"Yolanda, please read this. It's your rights here in America. I want you to help yourself by telling us your story, but you have the right to stay silent and the right to an attorney here. Read this, and sign it if you want to talk—if you want to help me understand how this all happened."

Tafoya began shaking again as she read the Spanish Miranda waiver form. Her thoughts raced. *What am I gonna do? I can't go back. They'll kill me. Chuy, my love, I'm sorry. This isn't my fault. It was that fuckin' Peanut!*

She spoke up, "If I sign this, are you gonna send me back to Mexico? Am I going to jail? If I go back to Zihuatanejo, the Sinoloa cartel will kill me. I refused to mule their cocaine; I had to run. I'm dead if I go back!"

Luis had heard similar stories before. He had a sympathetic ear for the plight of Mexicans, living in poverty, with no hope for a future outside of the drug trade. Guerrero was one of the worst areas. The cartel of El Chapo was the most ruthless, demanding allegiance from the natives in the region. Help them and they'll take good care of your family. Cross them and you and your entire family will end up minus your heads, your tongues stuffed down your throats; you and your loved ones will be lying side by side in a shallow mountain grave!

"Look, Yoli, I'll do everything I can to make sure the district attorney knows where you come from and the dangers you would face if you go back to Mexico. I can't promise you won't go to jail, but if you cooperate, I'll make sure they know, so you might have a chance at a better deal. No guarantees, but either way if you don't agree to talk to us, I can't help you."

After shedding some crocodile tears, Yolanda Tafoya wiped away the waterworks and defiantly said, "Fuck those assholes; I ain't going down for this. I know all of 'em and what they're doin'. Just promise not to hurt Chuy...I'm pregnant. He doesn't know. I don't wanna raise this kid without it ever knowing its father! I hope you shoot that fuckin' Peanut Hernandez in the face, though. That prick!"

After signing the Spanish Miranda rights waiver form, Yolanda Tafoya laid it all out on tape for Ocampo. The Santanas–Loper connections, the check washing, mail thefts, the check-cashing network, and the thousands in cash flowing in and out of the Shop through Dragon Cleaners. She named names and gave a detailed account of who had done what.

She warned Ocampo about the potential danger, too, with all the pistols and assault rifles. She'd seen them all, carried by drones and shot callers alike. Best of all, she'd visited the Shop; knew how to get in and the layout. Yeah, she knew this Driller guy, too. Described him in detail. She knew his name as Big D; she thought she'd heard Chuy call him Dennis. He drove a black Mazda and was connected to the checks and stolen credit card numbers taken in by the Shop. The comprehensive interview lasted six hours. The last hour was spent with members of Orange County SWAT. They brought with them plans of the Dragon Cleaners building, obtained through the fire department.

The freight train was nearing the station. Any misstep, any miscalculation in speed or direction, could prove deadly.

Chapter 18
GROUND ZERO

About six o'clock that night, Jesus made it home after a long day with his crew at the Shop. He was surprised, because the only one greeting him, with a squeaky wet kiss at the door, was Bruno. After more than an hour of waiting, he began calling around to find his lover. Not one of her usual acquaintances had seen her; she'd vanished.

Chuy hopped back in his Chevy and began cruising the streets of Garden Grove, checking everywhere he knew she liked to hang out. The dudes at the Rutt's Hutt hadn't seen her. She wasn't at any of the local bars or coffee shops; where the fuck was she? He spent two hours driving around, calling his homies on the cell phone, all the while being tailed by four sharks.

"Pick up. *Pick up!* Hey, Peanut, you seen Yoli? I don' know where she is. I'm worried."

"*No se, ese.* [I don't know, dude.] Maybe she wised up and finally left your ass," Hernandez said, chuckling.

"Listen, *pendejo*, did you fuckin' hurt her? I'll kill you, motherfucker…straight out, what happened to her? I know you been dogging her…you scare her. I can see it in her eyes when she's 'round you!"

"No, no, *jefe*! I haven't touched her—no way!"

"Listen, you fuckin' *puto*, call everyone in the crew. I want all of 'em at the Shop at eight tomorrow mornin'. We're gonna find her; you hear me, Nut?"

Peanut Hernandez didn't give a rat's ass about Tafoya, but he knew better than to contradict his boss. "*Si, mon*, we'll all get wit' choo tomorrow."

Around the same time the distraught El Gerente began his frantic search for his lover, Lieutenants Gilstrap and Casey met at sheriff headquarters in Santa Ana. Arranging logistics for a large-scale mutual aid operation is no small feat. Thirty investigators, along with twenty specially trained OC special weapons section team members, received the word to assemble at five o'clock the next morning at the gymnasium of Garden Grove High School.

I was told to pack up right away and travel south to meet with two other OC investigators at their station. My job was to write the search warrant for the known residence and vehicles of Brenda Fitch and James Gaylord in Seal Beach. It was obvious that Dennis Fitch was our Driller, too, based on his description and the details provided by our young female snitch. I typed up a Ramey arrest warrant for Fitch, aka Todd Starnes, Brenda Gaylord (Fitch), and fat boy James Gaylord, all for numerous counts of burglary, one count of murder, and one for the attempted homicide of a peace officer.

Thankfully, I could rely on the investigation of other detectives to establish the probable cause for the searches and Fitch's warrant on the attempted murder charge since, well, I was the one who'd almost been snuffed! When I presented the affidavit of information to the magistrate in Orange County, Superior Court Judge Bill Honeycutt looked up in stark disbelief.

"Detective, this is amazing! Glad you're still with us. You must relish this moment. Tell you what I'll do for this Dennis Fitch fellow: NO BAIL. Half a million for the rest!"

Paper for Dragon Cleaners, the Sunnyside apartment, and all associated vehicles and persons would be covered by my OC associates. A "no-knock" provision was included, indicating that SWAT members intended to circumvent the requirement to notify the occupants that the police were coming in with a warrant. Notifying hiding, armed gang members that cops were on their way in tended to get the good guys shot. We wanted the element of surprise in order to avoid unnecessary violence and prevent the destruction of evidence. Realistically, we just wanted to get in quickly, and if gunplay was in order, we wanted to start the playing!

Five a.m. came way too early. Twelve dozen assorted "fat pills" (doughnuts, that is), along with gallons of java, sat on the table at the gymnasium as more than fifty heavily armored coppers paraded by the food, gobbling and slurping as they passed. There's nothing like a sugar rush before a high-stress, potentially lethal operation! I opted for the coffee. OK, I had an éclair—but just one.

I met with the brass to distribute copies of my warrants. Ron Casey pulled me aside and told me that he was graciously allowing me to help serve the warrants on the Driller and his house. But I was to stand back and let the others gain entry and arrest my nemesis. Someone else had to hook up Dennis Fitch. Casey "reminded" me that I was still a week away from full medical release, and that if I screwed up and got hurt, I would go from number two on the promotional list to number zero! His exact words were "Kev, that promotion is yours to lose." What a way to raise my stress-o-meter ten points higher!

"Everyone, grab a seat. We have lots to cover this morning."

Sam Gilstrap officiously barked the order as he and Ron Casey stood before a sea of tan and green and blue uniforms. At least half the crowd held assault rifles or shotguns, helmets dangling from their gun belts. Most of us made last-minute adjustments on our body armor. We all felt the knot of apprehension forming in our guts.

The SWAT unit members stood in the side aisles wearing camouflage, their helmets and gas masks clipped to rings on their heavy ceramic vests. MP-5 machine guns and .30-caliber gas guns were slung across their chests as many adjusted the Velcro securing their tactical holsters tightly to their legs. They were foot soldiers, prepared for war. OC Sheriff Michael Caranza and Santa Barbara Sheriff Todd Billingsly stood in the background, watching and listening. We all felt their steely gaze. They knew a lot was at stake this morning. Everyone knew it.

Over the next hour and a half, the lieutenants, assisted by Sergeants Stiles and Moore, briefed us all on the violent history of the Santanas (STS) and Loper gangs of Orange and southern Los Angeles counties. A litany of all the known violent assaults, murders, and drug trafficking charges they had been involved in over the last ten years were carefully described. These flips and vatos were a dangerous lot!

Then Stiles and Moore laid out the evidence connecting STS with Dragon Cleaners. Photos of all the known players were displayed, along with a link chart showing the connections between the two gangs. Moore read the search warrant for the business, describing what was to be searched and what was to be seized. All arrests, minus the famous Fitch and Gaylord clan, would be made on probable cause.

Many of those found inside Dragon Cleaners were probably on court probation, so five OC probation officers were attached to that warrant service. Randy Moore would supervise the full search warrant service at the business, but the initial entry and securing of that back room was exclusively controlled by the SWAT commander. Moore and his crew would make entry into the front, using a ruse, and SWAT would then take over to make entry and secure the fortified workshop in the back.

SWAT briefed on their own that morning. It was a somber meeting. Will, Susan, and Luis were all assigned to the outside perimeter containment at Dragon Cleaners. Their work inside started once the place was secure.

Chuck Stiles then addressed me and nine other investigators. He brought out an eleven-by-fourteen-inch glossy reprint of the DMV photos of Dennis Ray Fitch, Brenda Fitch, and James Gaylord. Just looking at Big D brought back memories. I felt a sharp twinge in my left side as I stared at his crooked smile. I could just see that asshole wearing that black mask the night he stabbed me, staring back at me through the narrow eyeholes. I gotta admit I hoped he pulled out a weapon when my partners confronted him. I'd gladly let one of my cohorts pass him along to a higher authority. Go ahead, Fitch, make my day!

Our team would be serving the search warrant on the house in Seal Beach and handle the arrests of Fitch and his relatives. Seven of us, including yours truly, would go directly to the house to handle the crooks and serve the paper there.

An arrest team of three would go to the Carl's Jr. in Dana Point because we knew Gaylord was scheduled for work that morning. Our guys sitting outside the house on Rhapsody said his Honda was parked alone in the driveway. The object was for all the search and arrest warrants to be served within the same thirty-minute period. It was a lofty goal but a tried and true way to prevent bad guys from getting away or calling their coconspirators to tip them off to the proceedings. All teams would monitor the scrambled Orange Country tactical radio frequency, so we all would know what everyone else was up to.

At six o'clock we all left the high school and staged in our respective areas. We still had Dragon Cleaners and the Fitch abode under surveillance. Nothing would happen until the operation at Dragon Cleaners began.

Around fifteen minutes to eight, Jesus Santiago left his pad in the Camaro and drove directly to the business, under the watchful eyes of our guys. Units began getting ready to swoop the cleaners when a Cat team saw another one of those familiar white vans drive down the street. It parked next to the other van, which hadn't left the place from the day before. Six Hispanics got out, many sporting gang tattoos and wearing white Ts and baggy Dickey work pants. Zebra One decided to wait a few minutes more just in case any others wanted to join the festivities.

At 8:45 a.m., Randy Moore gave the go-ahead to start. Detective Ron Williams, dressed in street clothes, would come to the front counter carrying a load of clothing to be dry cleaned. Little Miss Tafoya had told us that a Chinese lady at the front counter, the Dragon Lady, was the lookout. She didn't know how she did it, but she was the one to blow the whistle if the cat was out of the bag. At the corner of the building, Moore and twelve others lined up to make entry and secure the cleaners' side of the building. The

Zebra team, in two assault vans, would come up once the front was secure, to begin the staged entry of the Shop in the back. Of course, there was plan B. Everyone rush in if there was a problem.

After Moore and his troopers had made a stealthy approach to the front corner of the cleaners and were lined up like dominos, Williams drove a ratty old Ford sedan up to the front, parked, and got out with his load of laundry. He even dropped a pair of pants on the way in, cursing in front of the Dragon Lady standing behind the counter. He plopped the eight pieces down, and Shin Wu began counting them out.

As soon as Williams's hidden microphone picked up "OK, mister, you got one, two, three..." Moore gave the signal, and his team swooped quickly in the front door, fanning out down the sides of the building. Moore, in his *sheriff* vest, hopped the counter. Shotgun at the ready, he ordered Wu down on the ground. She crouched down fast at the counter, hands over her head, shouting, "No shoot; you no shoot me!" Moore was listening as the rest of his men corralled the five other Hispanics who were working in the back of the cleaning business. They did it quietly, and once they declared the main building clear, he radioed, "Zebra units, you're up."

Two black utility vans drove quickly into the parking lot and up near the front door. Two teams of ten SWATters each then broke off, with the team sergeant (Zebra One) leading the first entry team. Entry team two was poised to follow them. As they entered the front door and set off the bell, Randy Moore looked away from the cowering Shin Wu long enough for her to quickly reach up and push the white button mounted underneath the counter near her. She held it long and hard until Moore looked back and saw what she was up to. The Dragon Lady saw stars as the butt end of Moore's sawed-off Remington 870 shotgun instinctively struck her head. Problem was, the deed was done!

"Sam One to Zebra One, go, go, go! We've been burned!"

"*Fuck, fuck*...get the guns; burn the paper; dump the acetone!" Chuy Santiago was caught flat-footed as Shin Wu's buzzer rang out the panic alarm. He was in the midst of planning a search for Tafoya—the pigs' snitch.

"*Nut, Manny, 'Gario, Mario*, handle the door—I gotta clean the office!"

Six armed gangbangers ran around the fifteen-by-fifty-foot shop, some throwing down papers under the exhaust hood, dousing them with the highly flammable acetone. Olegario Zapeda lit a match nearby but wasn't ready for the result—the fiery flash of the checks and envelopes blew back into his face and onto his clothing. Now ablaze, the onetime check washer was now engulfed in fire, screaming, running up and down the aisles, and knocking over trays and equipment as he ran. The pungent odor of burning hair and flesh began permeating the room. The fire was now producing black smoke, which began clouding the Shop. Peanut coldly looked Gario's way and, as he stumbled closer, fired a short burst from his 9mm Uzi into the screaming Zapeda. As his coworker writhed on the floor dying, gurgling, Hernandez threw a nearby bucket of water on him to douse the remaining flames. The others saw the steam rising from their friend's body and nervously trained their handguns back toward the door—the only way out or in. As far as they knew, that is.

"Zebra One, shots fired from inside; not us, we haven't gained entry yet."

Jesus Santiago had quickly gone into the office and stuffed a white cleaners bag full of rolled hundred-dollar bills. Each small roll held a thousand bucks, and Chuy had at least forty of them held tightly in the mesh bag as he quickly jogged past the smoldering Olegario, still gyrating on the ground. He ran to the center of the room amid the smoke and hid under a back table. The others saw him do it, wondering what his plan was since he was closer to the steel door than anyone else. His men figured El Gerente was bravely going to be the first to defend his homies.

Zebra Team One had located the Shop's secret entrance and was preparing to enter. Zebra Six, the team explosive-ordinance man, quickly affixed a round explosive shape charge to the right of the digital electrolock, adjacent to the bolt. Quickly inserting a small blasting cap into the charge, he backed the team away on each side.

"*Fire in the hole!*"

He turned the electronic fuse clockwise. The ensuing blast was directed straight out from the small cone-like device and decimated the lock; the door swung open after the blast, smoke billowing, the stench of gun smoke permeating the air.

"Zebra Two...*bang, bang*!"

One by one, the ten members moved up behind the two front-entry team members, as the leading pair immediately responded to the command by throwing flash bang/sting balls inside in either direction. Like a bright, loud grenade, the devices delivered a loud blinding flash and blew small rubber balls outward at five hundred feet per second. They were designed to distract the bad guys and incapacitate them, and the SWAT team used them to facilitate their entry.

As soon as the grenades went off, four of the desperados dropped their weapons and fell to the ground groaning in surrender. The team came in right behind the blast, advancing, machine guns ready, peering through the smoke and dust. Joaquin Hernandez had made a pact with himself a long time ago. "I'm never going down. I'll take the pigs with me." Peanut was true to his word.

He fired a ten-round burst in the direction of the smoky front door from his Uzi, and two of the rounds hit their intended marks. Zebras Four and Eight went down. Before their knees touched the cement, the remaining team members unloaded in the direction of the opposing fire. Fifty-four bullets, fully automatic from five MP-5 machine guns, peppered the area where the shooter hid. After a two-minute pause to let the smoke clear and respond to further gunfire, the injured SWATters were carried out quickly, and the team moved forward. The four remaining bangers in the room gave up immediately. Zepeda lay in the corner motionless, silently smoldering.

When they checked the bloody body slumped over in the corner, where the gunfire had come from, Peanut Hernandez, still cradling the Uzi, sported a total of twenty-two bullet wounds, five of which were located somewhere between his mouth and forehead. The STS lieutenant had gone out with a bang—twenty-two, to be exact.

"Zebra One, Code 4, two officers need medics, one suspect neutralized, four others in custody."

Will Phillips and Sue Wilcox had pulled a cushy assignment for the service of the warrant. Since the blueprints and intel on the Dragon Cleaners building revealed there were no windows or doors on the back wall to the outside of the building, they were assigned to "contain" that area. They were told to come inside after things were Code 4 (no assistance needed) and help seize evidence and then write reports. When the operation began, they stood ready at the northeast corner of the building.

From outside they heard Hernandez shoot Olegario. It sounded like a hand quickly slapping the walls. Then there was the loud explosion of the door breach, the flash bang reports, and then lots of popping machine-gun fire. Will and Sue looked back and forth at each other. Sue just said, "*Shee-it!*" The machine-gun fire sounded like the buzzing of bees, and the multiple slaps of the rounds against the east wall made them take cover outside behind a parked car. Sue had moved to Will's left about thirty feet. He was standing at the far back right corner of the building when suddenly something caught the corner of his eye.

A ten-foot-high chain-link fence ran away from the Dragon building down about fifty yards. It enclosed a large scrap yard, littered with cars, refrigerators, and the like. The sign outside read "Johnson Metals." As Phillips stood poised with his gun drawn, he heard a clank of metal on metal to his right. Looking over toward the scrapyard, he saw a male Mexican, wearing a white T-shirt, emerge from the door of an old Volkswagen van parked against the back wall, adjacent to the Dragon Cleaners building! The dude was in a hurry and was carrying a white bag—it was full of something, too. It took about four seconds for Will's brain to engage and realize that this guy was a guest at their party!

"Sue, *Susan, over here!*"

Phillips, running now in the direction of the open gate, keyed the radio breathlessly: "David Eleven, I've got a suspect running north from the back of the building. He's inside the scrap yard! Send backup, *now!*"

Sue Wilcox was looking away and was surprised by Will's report. She instinctively began running in his direction. Meanwhile, Chuy Santiago, having used his secret underground escape tunnel to leave the Shop, was now sweating these two pigs running toward him. Clutching the white bag of cash tightly, he withdrew the Beretta nine millimeter from his waistband and pointed it at Phillips, who was about thirty feet away from the open gate to the scrap yard. El Gerente pulled off two rounds in rapid succession in the detective's direction.

"*Shots fired, shots fired*, I'm taking rounds," Will managed to broadcast as he brought his Glock up to get a sight picture. As Santiago exited the gate on a full run, Phillips cranked two .40-caliber Winchester Black Talons back at him. Neither of the rounds rang true, and the foot pursuit continued down the parking lot, toward the main street. Now running parallel to the fleeing suspect, Sue Wilcox popped off three bullets of her own at him. All three struck the wall of a commercial building on the other side. She slowed to get a better sight picture, and Santiago seized the opportunity; he fired two at the stationary detective. The second bullet tore through Susan Wilcox's right shoulder, above her vest. She tumbled down to the asphalt.

Will Phillips was about ten feet west of her when she was struck. He actually saw her clutch her shoulder as she dropped and knew her wound shouldn't be life threatening.

"David Eleven, David Thirteen is *down; she's down* in the parking lot—send medics. I'm continuing in foot pursuit toward the front street."

As Santiago neared the end of the commercial complex, Will raised and fired five rounds at him. Bullets ricocheted off the building to Chuy's left and off the pavement next to him, but none found their mark. Santiago heard the barrage around him, turned, and fired off three more at his pursuer. Will felt one zip by his head. He later realized one had actually nicked the fabric of his raid jacket sleeve as well.

The foot bail continued. Will could hear the wail of sirens in the distance, the screeching of tires, but the responding units didn't know his exact location. They kept asking, but Will didn't know street names down in Santa Ana!

Santiago was still running hard, the adrenaline pumping hard through his arteries. Phillips was getting breathless, too, but was keeping a steady distance behind the fleeing felon. Thoughts of getting into better shape flashed across the Jumbotron of his brain. *No more doughnuts!* Looking ahead to see what the backdrop was, to gauge his shots, Will saw that the street ran into a T intersection about one hundred yards ahead of the now jogging Santiago.

Remembering his training, Will made the decision to reload since he couldn't remember how many rounds he'd fired. Pushing the magazine release on his Glock, the partially full magazine dropped to the ground in front of him; he kicked it away as he continued running. Realizing he needed a free hand, he didn't hesitate: he threw the handheld radio aside and grabbed his extra ten-round magazine with his now free hand, loading it up into the weapon. He tap-racked it (a training method of ensuring that the weapon is loaded in a firefight). He knew he had ten good to go now.

272

Santiago had no clue, but he had eight rounds of his fifteen-round Beretta left. He was losing steam fast now. Dog-tired, he looked ahead and saw a McDonald's restaurant. There were kids on the red plastic slide in the brightly colored playground! He figured if he could just get there, he'd have bargaining power...maybe get away from this asshole! Phillips had gained ground, though, running about twenty yards behind the huffing El Gerente. Will saw him crest the intersection and start running in the general direction of the playground. He stopped and began firing before it was too late, before any friendly fire could end the life of a young boy or girl or injure a mother or father.

One, two, three rounds—all went to the right. Chuy turned and began blasting back. One, two, three, four, all whizzing by Phillips's head, close enough to smell. Will got back on target and fired five more. This time his sight picture was true for windage (centered), and although the first two's elevation were low (one bounced off the ground in front of the banger), the second bullet he fired ricocheted upward, striking the crook's left leg. Round three hit Santiago just above the groin, four slammed into his stomach, and number five hit him just above the bridge of his nose—dead center in the brainpan. When a person takes a bullet to the brain, all nerve action ceases. There's no more ability to move. The threat is neutralized.

Jesus Santiago, smack in the middle of the intersection, immediately dropped his gun, the bag of money, and fell backward. Some of those thousand-dollar wads fell out, slowly rolling down the gentle slope of the roadway. It was as if they wanted no part of him. The manager's arms were splayed out to the sides. A later crime scene photo, taken from the Orange County Sheriff's helicopter, depicted Santiago—the great El Gerente—in a biblical pose: his gun lying next to one outstretched hand, a bag of loot next to the other. He looked like the second thief, the unrepentant one, crucified along with Jesus Christ on the hill at Calvary.

Chapter 19

IN THE WIND

We listened intently to the radio traffic over at Dragon Cleaners; the SWAT team was going into a war zone: "Sam One to Zebra One, *go, go, go*, we've been burned!"

Damn! The radios blared: Zebras down inside, taking fire. Then, word from Zebra One that they'd neutralized the suspect. Two dead crooks inside, two cops shot, four others in custody. Not good, but they put out a Code 4 (no more assistance needed), and we breathed a sigh of relief. As we were preparing to begin our own operation, suddenly our hearts jumped right back up into our throats.

"Sue, *Susan…over here!*"

"*Shots fired, shots fired…*I'm taking rounds…"

"David Eleven, David Thirteen is *down; she's down* in the parking lot—send medics. I'm continuing in foot pursuit toward the front street."

There was eerie static and the sounds of a keyed microphone and the labored breathing of a cop running for his life. The deafening claps of repeated gunfire in the background, amid excited, broken radio transmissions. The worry in the dispatcher's voice, and dramatic patrol radio traffic said it all: they desperately needed my partner to give his current location. Will's only response was a breathless, "I'm on the main street...*the main street*; I don't know!"

Then there was nothing but heart-wrenching quiet, dead air space. Silence for what seemed like hours, amounting to just a few minutes—minutes when I prayed my friend wasn't dead or wounded. Yeah, I prayed. I sat there in Chuck Stiles's car, two blocks from the Fitch house with Biff and Ed, with eyes closed, asking the Big Guy to spare my partner, to save Sue Wilcox. "God, I don't talk to you often, but please stand with them. Protect them!" The silence was deafening in the unmarked Ford. I thought a couple of my partners, sitting close, were making the same plea for His help that I was.

Then a loud broadcast from a sheriff deputy, trying to stay calm: "Ocean Twenty-Two, I'm with the detective, corner of Third and Ross...Code 4, suspect's down; eleven forty-four. We need traffic control and a supervisor immediately."

We looked at one another. We all knew what that meant. Will had triumphed. Eleven forty-four was the statewide radio code for a dead body—the suspect wouldn't need an ambulance. One less scumbag, no doubt. Now our job was to put our anxiety on the back burner and carry on.

Stiles radioed the other three-man team, staged near the Carl's Jr., that we were commencing our operation in Seal Beach. We weren't hopeful, however, since earlier we had driven by Rhapsody Drive, and the place seemed buttoned up. No lights were on; no cars occupied the driveway. Our plan was to send Ed (the old guy) up to the front door while we stood back, hoping someone answered. Since we had no reason to believe our Driller was home, we decided to serve the warrant ourselves. If we waited for a SWAT backup—well, they were a bit preoccupied over at Dragon Cleaners at the moment! A marked OC sheriff two-man unit sat parked nearby, out of sight: our insurance, should we need to look official.

After parking our car around the corner, we all walked down the street. McCormick took off his raid jacket, trying to look normal. We stood off to the side, away from view, as he knocked. No response at first, then "Who the fuck is it?"

"Oh, hi, I'm your neighbor down the street...I need a little help."

"Just a goddamn minute...I'm coming."

The door cracked open, and Brenda Fitch's weathered face popped into the gap between it and the doorframe. As soon as we saw the door begin to open, the three of us filled the gap between Ditch and the troll lady. Biff Corbett, all six feet five inches of him, pushed by her as the sergeant proclaimed, "Sheriff's Department, we have a search warrant!"

Mrs. Fitch didn't take the news kindly. Frantically waving her arms, she screamed, *"Fuck you guys! Get out of my house. Y'all can't come in here. I want my lawyer!"*

Well, considering she had said the L-word, right off the bat, we knew Brenda wouldn't be offering up a wealth of cooperation. Oh, no. In fact, as Ditch McCormick tried to calm her down in the living room as we searched for other suspects, she became even more animated. A plethora of naughty words cascaded from her nicotine-etched lips. Sailors would have blushed had they been nearby! It was educational. I had never heard "fuckstick" or "cumfuckers" used in a complete sentence before! It was quite common for cops to withstand a tongue-lashing while completing a legal function like a search warrant service. We normally handled it in a calm, professional manner, as evidenced by the response from our fearless leader, Sergeant Chuck Stiles.

"Shut the fuck up, lady. For Christ's sake, sit down. I mean it: *sit down!* Either sit down or we're gonna handcuff you and put you down, *understand?"*

No, she didn't understand 'cause her blaring mouth filth drowned the man out!

"Get the fuck away from my babies, you buttfuckin' dicklickers!" As these poetic vocals cascaded out of the Fitch matriarch's pursed lips, she made the mistake of advancing angrily in my general direction. She was suddenly yanked back, airlifted, and her ass dumped dramatically back onto her threadbare couch. Biff Corbett (also known as Detective Sunshine) had definitely gained the lady's attention. She glared back at too-tall Biff, silently for a change, as he slapped a set of bracelets on her wrists. She squirmed in the seat, her hands pinned behind her.

"Motherfucker! *That hurts*, you asswipe!"

Trust me, no one would have sexual intercourse with Mother Fitch! She continued spewing her periodic verbal vomit over the next hour and a half as Stiles stood by her side. We went about our duties of serving the warrant. The house was a treasure trove! Three of the bedrooms were obviously occupied by our suspects. We found indicia for James Gaylord, Brenda Fitch, and one Dennis Ray Fitch inside them. Family photos depicting the smiling trio, some in cracked frames, dotted the living room. A small plaque affixed to James Gaylord's room read *"Chunk's Room."*

Boy, this Chunk guy was a packrat. He kept everything, including evidence placing him at the scene of many of our burglaries: restaurant receipts, drill bit purchases, all dated and timed to correspond with several of the safe jobs. Bank deposit receipts showing he had deposited hundreds of dollars' worth of quarters a day or so after a safe was drained of the very same coins. Chunk even made sure his Honda was serviced every four thousand miles! The boy had driven that Accord thousands of miles, too, up and down California, going as far as taking it to Jiffy Lubes in our towns just before or immediately after many of the jobs. God bless him! As I continued rummaging through Chunk's junk, I found a dinner receipt from the Olive Garden on Carmel Mountain Road in San Diego. Somehow the date and time of the two meals bothered me. I grabbed my case notebook. Thumbing through important dates and times, it smacked me right in the face.

I excitedly called Stiles into the bedroom. All he could say was "Holy shit, let's hope they keep their video!"

The receipt noted the following: *February, 6, 2000, 7:22 p.m. Cash Sale. $36.55, Olive Garden #203, San Diego, California.*

One hour after Dennis Fitch and James Gaylord had eaten their grilled chicken piadina and classic calamari dinners, Frank Gilroy was murdered by the Driller inside the San Diego DMV. Mr. Gilroy had bled to death less than four blocks from where the brothers had stuffed their faces! We intended on stuffing this evidence right down their throats!

Brenda Fitch's purse contained a realistic-appearing California identification card with her picture on it, in the name of Brenda Starnes. Down at the bottom of the sack, among shredded cigarettes; loose, sticky Life Savers; and an open lipstick cylinder was a crumpled receipt. Unwrapping it, I saw a month's personal mailbox paid receipt for "Home Away from Home" in Forest Grove. It was signed "H. J. Stimson." Homer's girlfriend had kept a memento of their torrid love affair—ahhh!

Biff went through our main crook's room. Dennis Fitch was a neatnik. His was the only clean room in the whole place. A plastic stand holding a black safe lock dial, with the locking mechanism behind it—a prop used by legitimate safe technicians to practice dial manipulation—sat proudly on his dresser. It was his toy—his Rubik's Cube! A set of hand weights and numerous boating magazines sat stacked in one corner; they were all addressed to him at the Seal Beach address. Corbett found no drugs or other obvious physical evidence in the room. At the tail end of the search, Buford went through his underwear drawer (yeah, we have to). On the bottom, under pairs of size-thirty-two tighty-whities, were two neatly folded receipts.

One, under the letterhead for Oceanside Harbor, was a current three-month payment for Slip R-12 in the name Todd Starnes.

The second was a handwritten bill of sale, signed by Mike Reardon. It read:

> *To whom it may concern, on this date (March 1, 2000) I have sold my 1997 twenty-one-foot Sea Ray (Sundancer model), CF #F321457, to TODD STARNES for the sum of $14,500.00.*
>
> *The sale includes two sixty-horsepower Mercury outboard motors. Sale is as-is.*

As our sheriff's deputy sat parked down the street, keeping a watchful eye out for a dark-colored Mazda Miata, we were finishing up our mission. The last place we perused was a screened-in porch room, just off the sliding glass door to the living room. The place was what we later called Dennis Fitch's training room. A four-foot-tall, ancient-appearing Major brand standing safe sat in one corner of the room. Broken drill bits littered the floor in front of the door, which sat ajar. A paper template was stuck to the door, surrounding the spindle. More than one hole had been drilled into the steel door. It looked like he was hunting for just the right sweet spot, learning how to perfect his craft. An older power drill was discarded nearby on the floor; it smelled like burned electrical wiring.

Most of the floor was littered with tiny silver-colored curly metal shavings—these being the drill-bit castoffs, the result of hot bits grinding into the cold steel door. We took a dozen pictures of the layout, packaging up the loose pieces of evidence and taking the dead drill. We later called the SO for a floor jack and dolly to haul off the behemoth safe, its steel mouth standing agape, as if objecting to its discovery.

We began gathering our evidence, putting our gear away, and checking off items on our mental checklists. When you leave a place you're authorized to search, there's no going back—not without another warrant, that is—so this was our last stab at nailing shut the Fitch/Gaylord family coffin. As I walked by a large glass-front antique display case in the corner of the living room, I stood staring at the ten eerie baby dolls displayed inside on the shelves. All the infants were clothed differently, festooned with frilly, ornate dresses, their eyes staring coldly back at me. They gave me the willies, and as I stood there eyeing them, the harpy on the couch surged back to life.

"Fucking *get away from my dolls*! You touch my babies, and I'll sue your ass, you fuckin' *bastard*! Leave my babies alone—they're fucking mine!"

Well, being that I was a duly authorized law-enforcement officer, armed with a state of California search warrant, authorized by a magistrate of Orange County, I pulled open the bubble glass door to the case. As the bitch screamed, gyrating and jumping, I picked up one of dem dere babies. The epithets and screaming came faster and louder as I started examining the little doll's clothing, turning the little things around, looking inside the opening at the back.

"Oh my, Brenda, what do we have here?"

The little sundress had a Velcro closure holding the clothing together at the back, and when I pulled the garment open I saw that a hollowed-out area in the center of the doll had a wad of greenbacks folded neatly inside the space. Pulling the stash out, counting the bills, I found ten Ben Franklins. My goodness!

Fitch was no longer cussing; she was wailing. I'd defiled her baby! As she looked on, I proceeded to fondle the other nine. When the dust cleared, and the ten plastic infants sat naked on the floor before me, I had recovered ten thousand bucks! Every dollar of it was seized as evidence of her son's ill-gotten gains. By the time we called for the deputy to come over and transport Momma Fitch to the

Orange County jail, Brenda was like a whipped puppy—an old, short, fugly-looking puppy!

While my partners and I ripped apart the Fitch homestead, Detective Tim Larson and two other guys from the task force drove up to the Carl's Jr. on Pacific Coast Highway in Dana Point. Parked in the back, they spied James Gaylord's red Honda, so they decided that one of them would go in and make sure ol' Chunk was really working. Ron Williams volunteered. It was now about nine thirty, and those doughnuts from the 5:00 a.m. briefing were wearing off. Figuring they might as well grab a bite before arresting the culprit, they placed their orders with Williams and sent him inside to do some scouting and shopping. James Gaylord was working the front counter, wearing a brown Carl's Jr. apron, with that big-ass smiling gold star emblazoned across his expansive chest. He wore one of those cute paper hats, too! His nametag said "James G." Williams walked up to Gaylord and made a positive ID.

"Welcome to Carl's Jr., sir. May I take your order?"

"Yeah, sure…I want two English muffins with sausage, one biscuit with cheese and bacon, and three coffees—to go."

"Cash or credit?"

Williams handed him his Visa card, and Gaylord rang it up. A few minutes later, the order came, and the detective walked back out to his partners. The trio choked down the food quickly and slurped down the lukewarm coffee.

Now sated, the cops figured they had dillydallied long enough. The three sauntered into the store, and Larson walked through the spring-loaded door to the kitchen, with Williams trailing. Standing in the doorway, the female manager immediately approached the pair.

"Excuse me, you can't come back here." A shield and star stopped her cold in her tracks.

"We need to speak to your employee, James Gaylord." They pointed in his direction.

Gaylord turned toward them in time to see the displayed shields, and the blood drained from his face. Not one to run or fight, Chunk merely shuffled over to the duo, turned around, and put his hands together behind his back. Tim Larson obliged him by snugly affixing cuffs to his chubby paws.

After a quick pat-down, they got Gaylord's belongings from the manager and walked him outside without a word being said. It was one of the easiest arrests any of the three had ever made! As they reached their unmarked, Gaylord turned to Ron Williams and said, "Look, I'm sorry, mister. I only did it a couple of times."

The three investigators tossed interested glances back and forth, and Williams, sensing a spontaneous declaration, said, "Did what only a couple of times?"

"Just take it. It's in my pocket," he said, glancing down to his left. "I never used your number or any of them in it now. I'm sorry."

Reaching into Gaylord's left pants pocket, Tim Larson retrieved a small black rectangular plastic device with a slit down the middle: a credit-card skimmer. The white label on the underside read "Alibaba Inc. Made in China."

Larson looked at Chunk, chuckled, and said, "You think this is why we busted you? Don't know how to tell ya this, Mr. Gaylord, but you're under arrest for murder, attempted murder, conspiracy, and burglary. Does that clear things up for ya? Oh, and by the way, we're towing your car. Here's a copy of the search warrant for it."

James Gaylord just went silent as the detective laid the copy in his lap. Chunk knew his life was over, all thanks to Big D.

As Chuck Stiles, Ditch, Biff, and I left the house in Seal Beach, we heard Larson and the guys report that they had one in custody from the Carl's Jr. We knew we were only batting seven-fifty; two out of three were bagged, but the biggest fish was still swimming around out there. Dennis Fitch, our Driller, was in the wind. His mother screamed, *"Fuck off!"* when Stiles dared to ask her the whereabouts of her son. We called Larson, and he asked Gaylord the same question. Chunk just started bawling, refusing to answer. We had one more lead to follow—that boat slip in Oceanside.

As we drove away from Rhapsody, I placed a call to someone we all wanted to hear from.

"Hi, Will. How ya doing, partner?"

"Well, I'm OK...beat, but OK. I'm here with the Orange County crime guys, and I've been told not to talk to anyone now. I hear Susan's OK, but I want to see her, and they won't even let me do that before they talk to both of us. I'm a little pissed."

"William, take it from someone who's been there. You'll be fine. Just give them what they want, but make them take care of it now. Don't drag this shit out for days like they did last time with me. Is our admin team there?"

"Yeah, Sergeants Thomas and Maxwell are."

"Just a heads-up. They'll sit in with the criminal detectives, then take over after they're gone. Don't let that bother you; they want an administrative statement to find out if you did everything right according to the almighty general orders!"

"Right...well, I gotta go, Kev. It's show time. They're ready for me."

"Hang in there, buddy. We're thinking of ya!"

Ending the call to Phillips, I couldn't help but feel his pain. Regular folks have no idea what a cop goes through when he or she shoots someone on the job. They think nothing much happens to them. Hell, on *NCIS* they're shooting someone else before the hour is up! Citizens protest for justice, but little do many know (or care) that even when things are done by the book, cops are subjected to administrative "justice." They can even be fired if policy isn't followed. All their t's must be crossed and all the i's dotted. The process can drag on for months, and all the while the officer wonders what's going to happen. Will they lose their job? Lose security for their family? Many cops suffer from the nightmares of PTSD. They relive the shooting, sometimes night after night, for months. I know this because I'd been there. Will's journey down the rabbit hole had just begun.

Chapter 20
SINK OR SWIM

It took about thirty-five minutes to drive down the coast. Oceanside harbor wasn't a small place, so it took another twenty minutes of slow cruising through the parking lots before we hit pay dirt. There it was: the '97 black Mazda Miata, parked outside a row of docks marked by a big *R* on the column. Standing next to the ramp, we got our plan together. Ed and Biff would stake out the car while the sarge and I would check out the slip Fitch was paying for. Deputy Gingras, our sheriff's deputy, would stay out of sight up at the top of the ramp to take the Driller off our hands, if and when we hooked him. It was a solid plan—especially since we had no idea if the punk was even here!

Stiles and I walked down the ramp wearing our civvies, no sheriff insignias anywhere. Just a couple of fisher guys out for a stroll on the docks. Halfway down the walkway, checking numbers, our fears were realized when slip R-12 was vacant. Shit! I just knew the asshole had taken a six-hour cruise south toward Ensenada. He was probably down there sipping margaritas on the Malaecon in Ensenada right now, chowin' down on fish tacos! Chuck and I just stood there, looking at the water as it rippled through the open space of the boat slip. Like sand through the hourglass…

We were walking back to the parking lot when an old fellow sipping a Coors, lounging in a chair on the deck of a weathered sailboat, spoke up.

"You guys lookin' for Big D?"

Surprised at the question, Stiles nonchalantly said we were, and that the guy was an "old fishin' buddy" of ours. Chuck said we just wanted to catch up with ol' Dennis and maybe plan a fishing trip.

"Well, you two, in your fancy pants and dress shoes, don't much look like you know how ta bait a hook, but, regardless, the guy's been gone since six. He's been staying on the boat. Told me he was goin' out for stripers when he passed by this mornin'. I betcha he'll be back within the hour, though. Those buggers stop biting 'round noon mostly…"

I asked, "Was he alone or with someone?"

"Nah, goes out by himself mostly…saw him go out with a fat guy once but not lately."

"Do ya happen to have Big D's cell phone number?" I just wanted to know if this guy would burn us.

"Nope, he's not one of my favorite people—sort of an a-hole, if ya know what I mean."

We thanked him, and as we turned to walk back up the ramp toward the parking lot, the old fart said, "Have a nice day, *officers*."

Regrouping, we called Oceanside Harbor Patrol and gave them the model and CF number of the Sea Ray. Our plan was to stake out the slip and hope the Driller wasn't spooked. We were counting on the fact that the old man of the sea really didn't care for him much and wouldn't drop a dime on Fitch to tell him his "ol' fishing buddies" were waiting for him! The black-and-white backed off, and we parked next to the sidewalk, nearest the water. We had a bird's-eye view of his slip. We waited, *and we waited*.

I mused to the others, "Noon, huh? I wonder if that guy was just fuckin' with us. Maybe Fitch got a call and he's heading south. Think we should call the coast guard?"

Chuck Stiles was far more patient. "Take a chill pill, Rhino; it's not even four o'clock yet. Lots of guys stay out fishing till almost dark. Just sit tight."

The sergeant was wise. Right about 4:15 p.m., we got a call from the harbor patrol boat. "Your boy just passed us, coming past the breakwater now."

I was excited. "You sure? Did you verify the CF number?"

"Got most of it. Numbers matched, and it's him all right. He's got huevos. The name on the stern is *Safe Harbor*. He's probably about five or ten out from the R dock."

Back to plan A. Ed and Biff stood by in the parking lot. Chuck knew I wanted to be there when he was hooked, so he and I walked back out on the wooden planks of the dock. The uniformed deputy hid up near the bathroom, at the top of the ramp. He'd come down after dickhead was in custody, to take him away. I was a little nervous, considering I wasn't supposed to be get involved in the arrest. I hadn't bothered telling Stiles as such, because, well...*you know*.

As Chuck walked past the old-timer, the salty dog just laughed. I stayed about four slips back from R-12, looking busy, and Stiles hopped on a Boston whaler, which was moored about fifteen feet from the other side of Big D's slip. It didn't take long before the good-looking Sea Ray slowly motored around the corner and down the side of R dock.

As it approached, I heard the engine rev slightly; the gears shifted into reverse, then into drive, propelling the vessel gracefully toward its mooring. All twenty-one feet of the Ray pivoted perfectly, and it eased into the waiting space. I've been around boats most of my life, and this was a frigging textbook docking! Too bad this bastard hadn't become a ship's captain instead of drilling and killing for a living!

The Sea Ray hadn't even touched the rubber bumper at the nose end of the dock when the Driller jumped out holding the bowline. It was Dennis Fitch, all right—a bit heavier than in his pictures and sporting collar-length hair now and a goatee. Despite the physical changes, I recognized him right off. I could see Chuck shooting looks my way as we mentally formed our plan to swoop him.

Fitch was methodical about tying his boat up: first bow, then stern, after putting the bumpers out to protect it from dock damage. He spent about fifteen minutes putting stuff away inside: covering the windshield, wiping it down, and so on. He had no idea what was coming. I started wondering if it would be Orange or Santa Barbara County that would seize the Sea Ray. I was glad he was taking care of our boat. It was all over but the shouting.

After he'd finished buttoning up the vessel, he picked up a large Styrofoam cooler off the deck containing two striped bass, each looking to weigh about twelve pounds. Their bony tails hung way over the sides of the container. Nice catch! He held two fishing poles in one hand, too, as he stepped from the boat and carried it all toward the bow on the ramp. Chuck Stiles had nonchalantly hopped off the whaler and was slowly walked up behind him.

I began walking toward him but stopped short about twenty feet away when I saw Fitch snap his head back as Stiles ordered him at gunpoint: "Dennis Fitch. Sheriff's Office, *freeze*—you're under arrest!"

Big D stopped cold. He slowly placed the white cooler down and the poles next to it. Following commands, he put his two hands on the back of his head; he was going peacefully. I kept my gun out but down at my side. The scars on my chest ached in anticipation, but I began to relax. It was over. *So I got cocky.*

"Hey, Fitch, do you remember me?"

Stiles was in the process of handcuffing Fitch, who stood about three inches taller than the sergeant. Chuck had a cuff on his left hand when Big D said, "You're from Santa Barbara…right?"

I smiled and nodded. "Yeah, asshole. It's me!"

Suddenly, after hearing the familiar click of a cuff snapping shut, Fitch rapidly pivoted his body to the left and punched Chuck straight on in the face with his free hand. I saw the sarge stumble back and fall off the dock. I later figured he was out cold 'cause he belly flopped, falling out flat, parallel to the surface.

After disposing of the sergeant, Fitch raised his two hands up, one sporting the loose manacle, and started closing the gap between us—he made a growling sound as he came at me. My Glock .40 came up right after Stiles hit the water, and I took a bead, center mass, on his advancing frame. I began to squeeze one off; the entire time my brain was blasting, "Shit, *oh fuck. Yours to lose, yours to lose!*"

Just shy of the point where my pistol's hammer reached its fully cocked position—preparing to drop, sending Fitch straight to hell—I discerned a flash of yellow on my right side, and I heard a familiar pop followed by a buzzing sound. Deputy Ralph Gingras, on a full run, had come up beside me and nailed the bastard with his Taser. The barbs stuck firmly into Fitch's chest. *Thank you, Jesus!*

The Driller was now doing the funky chicken, shaking and gyrating around on the narrow dock, slick with seawater and fish scales. The Styrofoam cooler, containing his prize catch, was kicked into the drink, along with the two fishing poles. As I watched, Big D kept fighting the stun gun's effects. He didn't want to go down. Didn't want to lose. But fifty thousand volts had a different idea.

Suddenly the hulk stiffened and fell to his right, doing an almost perfect headfirst swan dive into the murky drink! He nailed the Styrofoam box, dead on, and pulled the Taser away and out of the deputy's grasp. White fragments of ice chest exploded everywhere. Gingras ran to check on Stiles, and I ran over to see where the hell our driller-diver was. The yellow plastic electric gun floated above nothing but foamy bubbles surrounded by white flecks of what remained of the cooler. The Driller was nowhere to be seen, tiny bubbles rising from his watery grave—nothing but busted-up Styrofoam and a couple of floating fish. I just knew that asshole was backstroking off to Mexico!

"Control, Santa Barbara David Ten requesting assistance, Code 3! Suspect Dennis Fitch is in the water, Dock R, Oceanside Harbor. Notify the harbor patrol, we need 'em to respond. Sam One is also injured; send paramedics."

I could hear the patrol boat's siren as they rapidly motored toward us. Frantically running back and forth on the dock, side to side, I kept looking for our soggy suspect. I couldn't believe we had him, and now...

"Control, David Ten. Have the responding deputies take up positions on docks P through U. The suspect's in the water somewhere between these docks. Ed and Biff come on over and watch from the sidewalk up there."

The patrol boat arrived and began cruising up and down, motoring back and forth, checking the docks. About ten deputies positioned themselves to establish a tight perimeter, and Corbett and McCormick watched from above. The sarge was fine: soggy, dazed, and embarrassed but OK. My side felt like fire. I was pissed, though, so the pain was an afterthought. How the hell could we have let this fucker get away? He'd eluded us so many times. I figured this was one more disappointment in the case. I regretted being there.

By ten o'clock that night, we wrapped up at the harbor. OCSD would keep the dock secure because we needed to make sure the doofus wasn't hiding out somewhere under the dock or, for that matter, lying with Charlie Tuna on the mud at the bottom.

The next morning, as I rose in my hotel room after a restless night, I got a call from Chuck Stiles before my first cup. My eyes looked like two piss holes in the snow, and my head throbbed with an emotional hangover.

"Guess what? The Dive Team found him…yup, flat on the bottom, right where he fell in. He sank like dead weight, passed on to the big DA in the sky! That's the good news. On the other hand, the homicide dicks want to talk to us. See you downtown in thirty minutes."

I spent all that day following in Will Phillips's footsteps from the day before. I fielded hundreds of questions from sheriff homicide and from my own administrators. I got the impression Orange County SO would have preferred that I'd shot the bastard! Now, the press was all over the fact that he'd died after getting Tasered. I pitied poor Ralph Gingras! He did the right thing; he saved my bacon. Had I put a hole in that asshole, I would've been in very deep poo-poo. I wasn't even supposed to get involved in an arrest, being puny and all! I owed that Gingras guy a steak dinner. Regardless, I still caught plenty of shit later from Ron Casey.

"Rhinehardt! What was it about me telling you not to get involved in arrests that you didn't understand? Holy crap, the chief is all over my shit like white on rice! He thought you didn't even have a gun, for Christ's sake. I had to tell him I told you to carry. He's threatening to block your promotion for not following his orders—what a prick!"

The Orange County investigators did a good job. It seems that Brenda Fitch reluctantly admitted that her oldest offspring didn't even know how to swim. He was piloting a boat on the open ocean, but couldn't even dog paddle! I suppose he spent too much time perfecting his thieving to learn the side stroke. He shoulda worn some floaties! A month later the coroner confirmed that Big D had died as a result of accidental drowning, not heart failure or anything relating to the effect of the Taser. That old man of the sea, who sat watching about thirty feet away when Dennis did his chicken dance, corroborated all our statements.

"I figure that Big D was lookin' like he wanted a piece of that other feller's ass after he knocked the guy into the drink. I was waiting for that cop to shoot him, too; he probably should have. That young deputy sheriff did a good job...wasn't anyone's fault the shithead fell in the water other than his own. He should've just given up!"

I managed to stay in the mix, so along with other members of the task force, we served the search warrant on the red Honda owned by Chunk Gaylord. Bingo! In the truck, inside a black Samsonite carry-on bag, we found the Driller's equipment: drill, lever bar, chain, carbide bits, templates, vice grips, channel lock pliers, bolt cutters, radios, and much, much more. There was even a damn grappling hook in there! It took months, but the Department of Justice managed to positively match the tool marks left at several of the crime scenes to the tools found in the Driller's bag of tricks. It was like the whipped cream and cherry, piled high on the prosecution sundae we planned to serve our family of crooks in court. It would have been a one-two knockout punch for Dennis Fitch, but alas he had taken the easy way out.

A couple of weeks later, the dust was clearing for Will and me, but the party wasn't over. The OC district attorney determined that all the shootings were justified, but the investigation over at Dragon Cleaners revealed more than any of our agencies had hoped for. It seems that the guy my partner shot, Jesus Santiago, kept detailed records of all the operations done at the Shop. When Olegario Zapeda did his fiery dance before Hernandez had snuffed him out, he didn't manage to burn all the records, just himself mostly.

Most of the important paperwork stayed intact, including Santiago's business ledger. Dates, times, and transactions were all recorded there, including his dealings with Dennis Fitch. He kept names and numbers for the Santanas and Lopers working for him, too. He even kept gang rosters, with addresses of the gang's shot callers and lieutenants. Chuy even had a journal of the altered checks that had been passed: their amounts, by whom, and where they were peddled. Santiago must have held a master's in gangland management! He was one organized El Gerente.

A separate spreadsheet documented just under a thousand stolen credit-card numbers and their providers. Besides Big D, and several others, it looked as if brother James Gaylord had recently sold several numbers to Santiago as well. Seems that Chunk filled the gap after his older brother "went fishing." The Shop appeared to be selling all their hot numbers to just one buyer: Vladimir Kuznetsov.

The FBI was now networking with Interpol. Solntsevskaya Bratva (the Soviet Mafia) was at the root of the credit-card and identity-theft syndicate over there, based out of Yakuza, Russia. Kuznetsov ran one of its brigades, specializing in cybercrime. The Russian IPA, the *politsiya* (their federal police) were now preparing a large-scale crackdown, armed with the information provided by the Driller task force. Chances are they wouldn't be reading those crooks their rights.

Within a one-month period following the takedown at Dragon Cleaners, members of the Orange and Los Angeles county gang task forces raided thirty-three STS/Santanas and Lopers residences and clubhouses in Orange and southern LA counties. Fifty-five arrests were made, and $375,000 was seized in the raids, along with hundreds of false California ID cards and piles of stolen checks. Six assault rifles and forty handguns were also seized.

Three other gangbangers met their maker while resisting arrest during these mutual aid operations, and two deputies received minor injuries along the way. Street gang members have lots of guns, but they can't shoot worth a shit. The good guys run the biggest gangs in the United States, and they practice what they preach! The heat focused on gangsters in Southern California during this period burned so intensely that street violence was down to its lowest level in ten years! In one strange respect, our Driller did more to end gang violence than any crook in recent history. It was little consolation to the widow of Frank Gilroy, though. May he finally rest in peace.

James Gaylord never had it in him to fight. He pled straight up to all charges. He wouldn't see daylight for at least forty years. I thought the judge went easy on him because, let's face it, he's Chunk, for God's sake. Lovely Mother Brenda pled guilty to PC thirty-two on the advice of her attorney: accessory after the fact to homicide, attempted homicide, and burglary. She's cooling her heels for twelve years in Chowchilla State Prison. She can rest easy in her eight-by-ten-foot cell, secure in the knowledge that she raised her two boys right.

Oh yeah, I almost forgot to mention, she sued all of us for the wrongful death of her bottom-dwelling son, Dennis. She used one of her free phone calls, a day after his death, to contact the LA law firm of Steven P. Blaelach. Blaelach was well known by the legal staff of law-enforcement agencies throughout California. He usually showed up after the guns stopped smoking or when a prisoner was prechecked at a hospital with an owie before being booked. He showed up whenever ambulance chasers like him could smell blood in the water, as long as that blood bled green cash.

Turns out Blaelach was the only one who really made out after Big D flunked his swimming lesson in Oceanside harbor. I was perturbed to learn that both Santa Barbara and Orange counties settled with the grieving mother for twenty-five thousand apiece! When I spoke to our County Counsel lawyer, she told me that we would have prevailed in court, but it was well worth it to settle for that amount since it may have cost us more just to defend ourselves. Blaelach was well known for his delaying tactics. It could have dragged on for years! Settling a case for cash, with a no-fault indemnity clause, was far too common nowadays. Since her barrister negotiated just under 50 percent of the award, Brenda Fitch got a pittance to put on her jail books.

The criminal court judge sitting on her case agreed that since our harpy had no visible means of support at the time of her and her son's arrests, and evidence indicated Dennis Fitch had paid all her bills for quite some time, the cash I found keistered inside her ten babies was proceeds of the Driller's crime spree. It was subsequently split between the two primary agencies, and the Sea Ray was auctioned off after a similar decision was reached. So, in reality, between the lawsuit and the seizures, it was about a monetary wash for both counties.

I later got a note from a correctional officer buddy of mine saying that the esteemed Mr. Blaelach had filed another writ, and Brenda Fitch was allowed to keep a couple of her zombie dolls in her cell "for emotional support." *Give me a friggin' break!*

You may ask what happened to the girl, that undocumented Latina whose disclosures almost singlehandedly took down the whole Southern California criminal enterprise? Well, some stories are destined for unhappy endings.

As promised, the Orange County DA offered Yolanda Tafoya a reduced sentence for her statements. Twelve years, out in six, with mandatory deportation. She'd committed multiple felonies, so her exit out of the United States was nonnegotiable. Luis Ocampo had taken a shining to the girl, so he followed her case and told her he would make sure her name would be changed and that he'd work personally to ensure, to the best of his ability, that she could start a fresh life in Mexico, away from murderous cartel eyes.

Then, during follow-up interviews, before any trials began, the OC gang task force found out she was much more valuable than they'd imagined. She was offered a sweeter deal. Six years, out in three (or less), for testimony in just one priority trial. Luis caught wind of the offer and called up Randy Moore. He wanted to speak to Yoli, to tell her that she might regret it if she agreed to it. Sometimes it was far better to hunt the two birds in the bush, because if you take the one in your hand, it just might crap all over you! Randy Moore admonished Ocampo. "Leave it alone, Louie. Let fate take its own path."

Several months passed, and a very pregnant Tafoya pointed a trembling finger at the orange-clad defendant sitting at the defense table in OC Superior Court number two. She identified Manual Quiroga, the powerful Loper shot caller, as the man she had witnessed speaking to her lover, El Gerente/Jesus Santiago, on multiple occasions. One such occasion was at Dragon Cleaners, where the pair walked inside, into the legendary Shop.

Two weeks later, Yolanda gave birth to a bright-eyed, black- and curly-haired baby boy in the infirmary of Chowchilla State Prison. They took the infant from the prisoner soon after birth—she'd agreed to allow its adoption. After all, the little guy only reminded her of Chuy, and despite all of it, they had truly loved each other. She couldn't imagine raising the child without him. As the baby left her grasp, and the lights of the cell were extinguished, she cried herself to sleep.

One week after "Martillo" Quiroga was sentenced to forty-five years to life for his misdeeds, he put out word he needed a *calaca*. That snitch, Yolanda Tafoya, had to die. The insidious cancer of the Mexican Mafia had infected not only most of the cities in California; it had a death grip on our prison system. It was just a matter of time before another *vata*, probably her cellie or a good friend, would sink a honed shank into that young heart and fulfill his command. Word around the hood was that several Lopers were placing bets she wouldn't last six months.

EPILOGUE

The day after he nailed Chuy Santiago to the cross in the middle of that Santa Ana intersection, Will Phillips was allowed to visit Sue Wilcox in the hospital. Gangsters, besides being violent, were cheap. Thank God. The creep shot her with a lead, round-nosed nine-millimeter round. They cost less than the deadlier semijacketed bullets. The projectile wasn't designed to disintegrate, and since that caliber traveled faster than most, the bullet tore through and through, between Sue's clavicle and scapula. She'd endured ligament damage and some nerve damage but was expected to make a full recovery. Her weightlifting days would be put on hold for a while, though.

As Will chatted with her, just after lunch, another visitor entered the room: LASD sergeant Randy Moore. After a perfunctory "Hi, how ya doin', Will?" Moore slid up to the side rail of Wilcox's hospital bed. Leaning over, he laid a kiss on the muscular female detective. Full on the lips! It wasn't one of those gotta-kiss-your-grandma smooches or a peck from Aunt Mae; it was a full-on, hard-pressing, betcha-their-tongues-are-doin'-the-hoochie-coochie kind of osculation. Will swore he saw Moore slip a little titty-grabbin' action in, too!

My young partner's bottom jaw must have bounced off the linoleum of the hospital-room floor because the observant patient caught the expression and queried her stupefied visitor.

"What's up with you, Phillips? You look like you just saw the Pope smoke dope. Give it up; what's your problem?"

"Ah, well, nothing I guess...I just thought...Well, you said something a couple weeks ago, made me think you didn't have a boyfriend." Moore shot him a "say what?" look.

"What you talking about? I told you I had a partner. Randy and I keep it on the down low at work, but we live together. We're talking marriage. You need to pay closer attention to details, *detective!*"

Well, shut Will's mouth, and call him stupid! Later that week when Phillips came home to the waiting Rachael Storm in Buellton, he laughed off his earlier deduction that partner Susan was a lesbian. He mused that the love-making at the Wilcox/Moore residence probably included a trampoline and a weight machine!

I made it home after my ten-day assignment in the bowels of Orange County greeted with balloons and a computer-generated banner that read *Welcome Home, Pop!* Honestly, I was beat, but the sight of Tommy standing with his walker, Jim beaming from ear to ear, and my lovely Julie made the ordeal over the last couple of months bearable.

I learned that Tom had been considering reupping in the army because the VA had assured him that after rehab, they were somewhat confident he would be certified for active duty. He admitted that his shoulder wound was his biggest concern, not to mention the limp he couldn't seem to shake. He had to be fit enough to perform physical training—pushups and pull-ups. He had more than a few doubts about his future abilities in those areas. He told me he'd enrolled at Alan Hancock College and was considering a career as a nurse or physical therapist. I was doing the happy dance inside over the news!

Jimmy was in his last semester of high school and was pulling in a 3.8 GPA. The boy (I had to quit calling him that) had just finished taking the SAT and felt confident he'd scored high. He proudly showed me the applications he was filling out for UCLA and Cal State Northridge. His counselors had told Julie that with good SAT scores, he was a shoo-in at either school.

Shit, where the hell had I been? Seems like all this had just blown right by me while I was concentrating on work. It seemed like just yesterday I was screaming at my immature kid over speeding tickets, and overnight he'd become a man. Right in front of me he'd matured; I had missed it all. It was like I had been a spectator standing outside, a nonparticipant in the lives of the ones I cared for the most. As the evening wore on, I felt depression wrapping its dark, clammy arms around me. I finished out the night lying on a chaise lounge on the back porch, just staring up at the night sky. The scars on my chest were screaming hello.

"Penny for your thoughts, my love?"

Looking up, I saw Julie standing beside me with a cup of hot decaf. God, she looked gorgeous in the moonlight! How the hell did this woman end up with me?

"Jus' thinkin'. Tom's doing great. Jim's a scholar and actually talks to his father now. Hell, he'll be leaving soon, too. I miss taking him to those ballgames, playing catch out front with him…just hanging out with my boys. Where did the time go, Jule? How did all this happen so fast I can't even remember being a part of it? I'm a lousy dad. I've fucked up by the numbers, I guess."

"Knock off the pity party—you're a great dad! Who made sure Jim got a job back when he was like a rudderless boat? Who was there when Tom got his first wrestling trophy? Or when he graduated from boot camp? How 'bout when he came off that plane on a gurney? You—it was you crying next to me. You go out there every day and show them both how to lead, not to follow. You're their role model, Kev. I'm just their cheerleader. I'm your biggest fan, and you know it. You're our hero, baby!"

The tears just welled up and exploded out of me as my wife curled up with me on that lounge out back—we were two people celebrating our lives together under a blanket of God's stars. We laughed and cried together as we rejoiced, remembering the mosaic of our lives. And they were great lives, too, not depressing memories. I realized that our family, our love for each other, was the shining light in my existence. It was never just my job—not my accomplishments or what I was. We just laid there in each other's arms, rejoicing in what the important things in life really were...then the damn chaise broke, and we fell flat on our asses on the cold concrete of the porch!

A month after the Driller met his watery grave, Chief Sam Walters sat in the Sheriff's office, and the conversation was tense.

"Todd, you can't do this. Hell, I ordered the guy not to carry his piece. Casey told me he told him not to make any arrests, either. Shit, he almost shot that asshole down in Oceanside! No way, I won't back you on this. I probably should've given him time off, for Christ's sake!"

"I don't know how to tell you this, Sam, but the guy's looked up to around here. He was the fellow who solved the Redbone murder. The press loved us 'cause of him! Hell, he got those crooks sent to prison, forever. Then, working this case he almost gets killed trying to catch this asshole. Do you have any idea how much crime was solved by us and Orange County because Rhinehardt and the others put so much effort into working that case? Well, the press and I do! He deserves it, damn it, and that's final."

"I disagree."

"Sam, shut your piehole! For just once in your life, keep your friggin' mouth shut! I know why the damn commanders hate your ass. Do me a big favor: *get the hell out of my office!*"

I was sitting in my cubicle later that same day when I got the phone call. "Kevin, how are you doing this morning?"

"Um, fine, Sheriff...What can I do for you?"

"Come on up to my office; we need to talk."

The lawsuit had just been settled. I knew they gave that bitch money because of how we (I) had "resolved" the case. I'd been back to full duty for six weeks now. Casey had expressed his dissatisfaction about my involvement in Fitch's arrest, but I thought things had calmed down. Was I wrong? Deputy Janet Billister was Sergeant Billister now. Yeah, they gave her the sergeant's promotion over me. No surprise, I suppose. I was hoping for forgiveness way down the road.

I was checking all of this off in my pea brain, figuring my shirt wasn't so white at the moment. So, as I walked into the oval office at the end of the administrative area, my stomach was doing barrel rolls. Shirley, the sheriff's secretary, smiled and waved me in. I entered the expansive room to find Ron Casey sitting across from Todd Billingsly. The big boss man sat behind a beautiful oak desk. An antique .45-caliber Thompson submachine gun, a gift from the FBI, sat in a trophy cabinet behind the sheriff, mounted on the wall. The sight of that historic Tommy gun temporarily eased my anxiety around the anticipation of the unknown.

"Kevin, are you aware that Bob Roberts has filed his retirement papers? He leaves at the end of the month."

"Roberts? No, really? I thought Bob was a lifer, that he'd die behind his desk someday." A nervous chuckle passed among the three of us.

"Well, he's soon to be history, and congratulations; you're getting his badge."

I was stunned—not because I wasn't qualified for it but because I hadn't seen it coming. "*Thank you!* I was hoping for the last promotion, but all things considered…I appreciate it."

Ron Casey spoke up. "Kevin, I've been speaking with the commander, and we intend on reconfiguring CID. Our idea is to get back to the idea of using specialists for people crimes, distinct from property cases. When we just reach into the barrel and pull out a name to work a homicide, robbery, or sex case, we don't always get the cream of the crop with the expertise we need. Working murder, like burglary, takes experience. You've proven you have that experience when it comes to solving the hard ones. Your peers look up to you. You're a leader here. That's why we'd like you to stay in investigations as the sergeant of our new major crimes unit here in Santa Barbara."

From exhilaration to terror in less than two minutes! I must have looked like Bambi in the headlights because Casey frowned a bit and told me, "Take some time to think it over if you need to. Just get back to me by tomorrow, OK?"

I almost turned to Billingsly and asked, "If I say no, do I still get the sergeant's badge?" I held my tongue. As I walked out of the office, I didn't know whether to celebrate or barf my guts up.

Julie was thrilled. What an honor, what an opportunity. All I kept thinking was…what the fuck! I'd been working investigations for going on thirteen years, between the narcotics and criminal sides. I was looking forward to time off the pager, if you know what I mean, to the comforting knowledge that most of the time I'd get to come home on time, spend actual full, uninterrupted weekends with my family. No callouts and no late nights or weeks away from home looked very inviting. The unknown of a new job in a high-stress unit scared the bejesus out of me. If I did good, I might would make lieutenant in a couple of years. If I screwed up, or I fumbled a political football, this would be the result: "Twenty-yard penalty for technical foul. Go directly to graveyards for the next ten years!" I didn't sleep that night.

The next morning, amid running the congratulatory gauntlet around the bureau, I cautiously made my way to Lieutenant Casey's office.

"Well, are you my new sergeant?"

"I'll do it, under one condition."

"Condition? You have a condition?"

"Respectfully, I'd like discretionary input into who works for me. I know these guys, maybe better than anyone. If I'm getting the tough cases, I want tough, talented guys to solve them. I think that's reasonable, Ron. I get to call you Ron now, right?"

Smiling, Casey said, "I suppose you have a point. I'll run it by the commander, but you know that he and I have final say. I take it then I can have your office nametag made up, Kevin?"

"Yes, God help us all!"

———

No doubt about it, my life was changing. Tom Rhinehardt was now a nursing student, well on his way to a medical career. He walked with a slight limp, moved out to his own place, and was seeing a young Latino gal. She cooked a mean tamale! A month after leaving the military, he got a call from his commanding officer. Our son, our hero, was to receive the Silver Star for bravery under fire. I couldn't wait to tell him how proud I was to be his father.

Jim Rhinehardt graduated high school and was set to start Cal State Northridge in the fall. We were happy to gift him his first car. All he needed to do was pay the insurance!

Will and Rachael were completely out of the relationship closet now. They moved into a home in Solvang together, and word was Willimena was contemplating popping a certain question. I knew all this because I had a new bestie, who now worked for me in the Major Crimes unit.

Julie decided to go back to college herself. She began satellite classes with Phoenix University. My sweetie was looking at a psych major. After living our crazy life together for the last twenty-four years, they could have just handed her the diploma!

As for me, I got called out eight times the first weekend I sat behind that desk in the big office down the hallway in CID. The sign on the door read, "Kevin Rhinehardt: Sergeant, Major Crimes." Life was good—*well, most of the time!*

ABOUT THE AUTHOR

K. C. Reinstadler served for thirty-two years as a criminal investigator in Southern California, working his way up to lieutenant. He has based the plots and many of his characters of his novels on real  events and people he encountered during his years on the force.

Reinstadler enjoys travel, scuba diving, and riding his Harley Davidson. He is retired and still resides in California with his wife, Jill.

Made in the USA
San Bernardino, CA
05 April 2017